It Happens for a Reason

Celebrating
30 Years of Publishing
in India

Also by Preeti Shenoy

The Secret Wish List
The One You Cannot Have
It's All in the Planets
The Rule Breakers
Why We Love the Way We Do
A Hundred Little Flames
The Magic Mindset
A Place Called Home

It Happens for a Reason

PREETI SHENOY

HarperCollins *Publishers* India

First published in 2014

This edition published in India by HarperCollins *Publishers* in 2023
4th Floor, Tower A, Building No. 10, Phase II, DLF Cyber City,
Gurugram, Haryana – 122002
www.harpercollins.co.in

4 6 8 10 9 7 5 3

P-ISBN: 978-93-5629-272-7
E-ISBN: 978-93-5629-280-2

Typeset by Ram Das Lal

Printed and bound at
Replika Press Pvt. Ltd.

FSC
www.fsc.org
MIX
Paper from
responsible sources
FSC® C016779

This book is produced from independently certified FSC® paper to ensure responsible forest management.

For Satish, Atul and Purvi, without whom
I am only one-fourth, not whole
And for Anukul who makes me think

Love is like the wild rose-briar,
Friendship like the holly-tree
The holly is dark when the rose-briar blooms
But which will bloom most constantly?

– Emily Brontë

Your absence has gone through me
Like thread through a needle.
Everything I do is stitched with its colour.

– W.S. Merwin

Prologue

There are many ways in which your life changes. Sometimes, these changes happen slowly. Like a sapling growing. You notice that a seed has sprouted but you don't pay much attention to it. Suddenly, before you realise it, it is a little plant, firmly rooted, with leaves, stems, buds, and it grows, slowly but steadily, changing every single day, with small, seemingly imperceptible changes, which later all measure up, add and contribute to it.

Sometimes it happens overnight. Like a phone call, after which you can never go back to what was before.

But it is rare that both these changes happen together. In my case, they haven't exactly occurred at the same time, but they have happened one after the other. I usually do not think much about it, and I am not one to philosophise, but for the past day and a half, lying in this hospital bed, I have had plenty of time to think.

The hospital is as unfriendly a place as can be, with its stark rooms, antiseptic smell and the Spartan pieces of functional furniture—just what is essential and nothing more—do not help. Dr Shylaja, a spinster at sixty-four, attired in starched cotton sarees as stiff as her unsympathetic heart, runs the hospital with the precision of a military sergeant. She is extremely good at her job, and one of the best in the country. Which is why my parents thought it would be a good idea to get me admitted under her care. Whatever it is, I am here now. And it feels like a nightmare.

Except, it is no dream. The IV drip is real. So is the little rubber tube that goes into my right nostril.

'It is for the oxygen, so that the oxygen levels do not fall. It might be a little uncomfortable but you will be okay soon,' a smiling nurse says in her heavily-accented English that screams she is from Kerala, as she adjusts the tube in my nose.

The intravenous drip attached to my left arm hurts a bit, but when the nurse asks if it's too painful, I shake my head. I have been admitted here since last morning. Dr Shylaja has visited twice. There are nurses walking in and out, writing down all sorts of things and every now and then checking if I have 'dilated enough'. They also keep checking my temperature, my blood pressure and assure me that I am 'doing fine'.

How can my life have changed so drastically in less than a year? Yet it has, and it is a choice that I made. Ten months ago, I was on the cover of *Glamour*, which is no mean achievement. And even though my parents never approved of my modelling career, I know my mother boasts about it to the ladies in her circle. Privately they have ticked me off, castigated me, tried to knock some sense into me (in their words) and tried to make me use my intelligence, instead of my body. But I don't see anything wrong in what I did. My mother has never been around for me. Nor has my dad.

Agreed, they have given me every single thing that money can buy. There is nothing I have lacked, including an expensive boarding school education. But I don't think my parents care for me. The only time I got a chance to see them was during the two months of summer vacation, which I hated. Dad was always travelling, and for my mother, I was just a minor inconvenience that got in the way of her very hectic social life. Once, when I was seven, I had walked into my parents' bedroom and climbed into the bed between them. My mother had woken up and screamed at me and told me to go back to my own room. I had pretended to, but I was just outside the door when I heard hushed whispers, and the male voice was not my dad's.

'Damn—do you think she realised?' he had asked.

'I don't think so, but I think you better leave,' said my mom.

A few months after that, I was sent to a boarding school which was where I celebrated my eighth birthday.

Being popular in school, I was always invited by one friend or the other to spend the summer holidays with them. It was always Suchi's house I chose. Somehow I never wanted to spend time at home and it suited my mother just fine.

Suchi, with her loving, large family of three older brothers, a mother who was affectionate, and most importantly, parents who loved each other, and had time for their children—it was everything that I craved for but didn't have.

I wish she were here with me now, instead of in the US, where she is doing her Bachelor's. While in school, the grand plan was that we would both study together. But life has a way of foiling promises made when you are twelve, no matter how sincerely and earnestly they were made.

Had Suchi been here, she would have understood. Unlike my parents who never could figure out why I needed to have a career in modelling when they could give me all the money in the world. There is something that is unexplainable, which no amount of money can buy. It is a feeling, a bond, a deep connection with something larger than oneself—heck, I can't even begin to explain all this to my parents. Besides, I don't think they will have the time, even if I want to try.

Now, lying in the hospital bed, I think that never in my life have I felt this helpless, this out of control, this dependent, this *scared*. I wonder what the hell I have let myself in for. But I can't turn back the clock now. This is my decision and I am sticking to it, no matter what.

Dr Shylaja walks in again and asks the nurse to get the CTG machine. She does not bother to explain to me what it is, or why she is using it. She never says a single word more than is necessary to a patient. Any question is met with a frown or a nod of the head. The nurse applies a gel to my tummy and then places an elastic belt around it. It has two round plates, about the size of a tennis ball, and it feels cold as it makes contact with my skin. I wince. To distract myself I turn to the machine and try not to look at Dr Shylaja's face. The machine starts printing out what I presume to be heartbeats on something that looks like graph paper, the kind we used in math class, but this one is way longer and smoother.

Dr Shylaja studies it, and then tells the nurse, 'She will need prostaglandin. Start it. Call me when dilation is six.' Then she walks out without a word to me. As though I don't exist. Most of the time I don't care, but this time I want to yell at her, ask her if she has a heart. Can't she see I am worried, scared, but trying to put up a brave front?

I wish I had *someone* here with me, to reassure me that things are going to be okay. Now I wish I had told Manav to come. I know he would have, had I asked him. But I didn't want to.

The nurse performs a vaginal examination. I hate it.

'Hurting?' she asks kindly.

It doesn't hurt. But it kind of humiliates. I don't think she will understand that though.

'I will be putting catheter. This is for gel,' she says, and then I can feel something being inserted into my vagina, and that is when I start crying.

Soundlessly.

I don't think the nurse realises though. She leaves the catheter there and assures me that everything is going to be okay.

I am so exhausted that I don't care anymore. I lie on the hard, steel bed, in the hospital gown, my legs spread out, with a tube down there going inside my body, a tube inside my nose and an IV drip in my arm. More than the pain, it is how helpless I feel in the situation I am in, which gets to me. I just want this to be over as quickly as possible.

And after about six hours of this, it starts. The tearing pains. I am barely aware of what is happening anymore. This pain is nothing like I have ever experienced before. I feel like I am going to die. It comes in waves. Barely does one wave of pain subside, than a fresh one hits me.

I try not to scream, but it is hard. I can vaguely hear the nurses running, asking for Dr Shylaja.

She arrives. By now I am sweating profusely. It comes again and I scrunch my face in agony and dig my fingernails into my palm.

'You have to push. Push hard or else I will have to cut you up,' she says.

That does it. After all of this, I cannot bear the thought of going under a knife.

I push strenuously with all my might, and then abruptly, it is over.

I lie back in relief, exhausted, and out of the corner of my eye, I can see the doctor holding up my baby. And even before the doctor says anything, I know it is a boy.

My son. He is beautiful. Covered in blood. Scrunched up. Wrinkled. Tiny. And then he cries.

I am too stunned to do anything but stare in a daze.

I have just given birth to a baby boy. I cannot believe it. I am no longer a girl now. I am a mother.

This is my very own baby.

I weep, half in relief, half in joy.

The baby is placed on my chest and amazingly starts to suckle. I am shocked at how instinctively and naturally the baby is doing this, and how comfortable I feel.

They take him away to be cleaned, and after I am cleaned up as well, I am told to lie down with my legs close together, one on top of the other. After spending the last many hours with my legs wide apart, this feels odd. I am told that the hospital has a policy of bringing the baby to the mother only during feed times, so that she gets complete rest and time to recover.

The nurse asks me to call her if I need anything.

I nod. Out of sheer exhaustion, I fall asleep.

After I sleep a while, I want to see my baby, and so I call for the nurse. A new nurse walks in, a middle-aged one, whom I have not seen before.

'Can you please bring him to me?' I ask.

She smiles and says she will.

She brings him wrapped in a blue towel, and there is a little tag around his wrist. His hand is so small, it is tinier than my forefinger. I cannot help marvelling at him, as the nurse places him on the bed beside me.

'Are you alone? Nobody staying with you? ' she asks.

'No—I'm on my own,' I say.

'Oh,' she says. She is silent for a minute.

'Do you want me to stay for a while? I am on night duty today.'

Somehow I am glad for her offer. It is as if I want to share this magical moment with somebody. Anybody, really. And this nurse seems so motherly and protective. I find myself warming up to her instantly.

'Yes, please, thank you,' I say, and she smiles and settles down on the attendant's cot.

'He is very sweet. Does not trouble at all,' she says as she gazes at my son, who has begun stirring in his sleep.

She shows me how to hold him, sit on a chair and then feed him. I learn quickly.

I ask her how often she has night duty, and she says she prefers it, as she is all alone in her house. She lost her husband many years ago, and she has only one daughter, who lives abroad. Most of the other nurses have families and young children, and she is happy to be on the night shift instead of them, she informs me.

'So are you working?' she asks.

'I used to. Now I am not,' I say.

'Oh—what does your husband do?' she asks.

How do I answer that? That the child's father does not even know that I have given birth? That my parents wanted me to give up this baby for this very reason. That I went against their wishes, and decided to throw away my career, my studies and everything that I had, just to have this baby.

'Ummm, I don't know,' I say, and she nods.

I think she understands.

'Not so easy to raise a child alone. I was nineteen when I had my daughter, and her father passed away when she was four months old. Bike accident,' she says, and there is a faraway look in her eyes.

I nod. I am simply too delirious that I have my own baby.

And what I do not tell her is that I am nineteen too.

CHAPTER 1

There are two ways to deal with bad grades. If they are yours, you study. But if they are your child's, if you are anything like me, you yell at them. Or you try to understand them, even when you think you know all the answers, because that's what all the parenting guides tell you to do. The latter usually helps and throws up win-win solutions. The former results in them turning into a wall. Trial and error has taught me that the latter, though a harder route, is always a better option.

'Do you want to explain these?' I ask my son, trying not to grit my teeth and trying harder to keep my voice sweet and calm, like the parenting manuals advice.

Don't yell. Whatever you do, do not yell. Stay calm.

'No,' he says, as he blows a lock of hair away from his forehead with a practised upward puff of nonchalance, both hands stuck in the pockets of his jeans, indicating the end of any further discussion from his side.

He is almost as tall as me, and he now looks me in the eye with the classic I-can-defy-you-and-there-is-nothing-you-can-do-about-it pose that most teens adopt once they reach a certain height.

Of course, I don't let go so easily. I am not his mother for nothing.

'That is not an acceptable answer and you know it.' I try to sound calm but my voice betrays me.

'So?'

'What do you mean "so"? How many times have I told you that nothing less than an A will do? Do you want to end up like me, working two jobs, struggling like a donkey? Or do you want to have an awesome career?'

'You didn't end up like this because of your grades. Be reasonable. You walked out on your parents because you wanted to have me and you refuse to take their money,' he says calmly.

My anger at his reply spikes to an all-time high. Most of the time, I am reasonable and unruffled. I discuss things with him and treat him like an adult. But now, I am so mad I could punch him.

But that is not going to help. The rage, the sheer helplessness at his cool demeanour, plus the facts that he has so calmly and clearly stated act as catalysts, and I explode, giving vent to the fury that has been swelling inside me and that I have been trying to contain. I fling his report card across the bedroom and his answer papers neatly stacked inside it go flying and scatter all across the room.

'You … you fool. I struggle so much to raise you well and now this…' I am unable to complete the sentence.

He calmly picks up the report card and stacks all the answer sheets neatly inside. Then he hands me a bottle of water.

I breathe in and out deeply and glug some down.

He is fifteen going on twenty-five.

'Ma, I have told you so many times,' his voice is gentle, as though he is the parent, explaining something patiently to an errant child.

'What?'

With my outburst, our roles are reversed now. I feel like an unreasonable teen throwing a tantrum, instead of the other way around.

'That these are just the mock exams. They do it on purpose—give everyone bad grades. They are strict with correction. They want to shake you up so that you work harder for the boards,' he says. He has now done a complete turnaround and changed from the sullen defiant teen to the understanding son that he usually is.

'So what, Aryan? Why can't you study harder, make your answers perfect, and get marks even in mocks?' I demand.

I have never compromised on academics and the one thing that I insist on is good grades, even though I am a relaxed and indulgent parent in most other things.

'It is impossible, Ma.'

'Why is it impossible? Has everyone in your class got only Cs and Ds? Isn't there anyone who has got an A or an A star?'

'Yes, a couple of them did.'

'Who?'

'Nitin and Monika.'

'Then? It isn't impossible, right? It is not like they are smarter than you. It is probably because they work three times the amount that you do.'

I try to be as patient as I can. It is so darn important to get a good education, and that can happen only if your grades are good. Had I got a proper education, I wouldn't be struggling like this, working two jobs, living in this decrepit old mansion that is charity from Neelanjana aunty, who no doubt means well.

Deep down I long for a place of my own. I don't think that will happen anytime soon though.

For one, my unusual choice of career as a dog-sitter requires a place like this, which has a large compound, so that the dogs have enough space. And two, I am perpetually broke, my salary from the gym just about lasts till the end of the month. I don't have much of a choice here. This is what makes me so angry when my son gets bad grades, due to lack of effort. I work my butt off, and the least he can do is put in that much application in his academics.

It isn't anything that I haven't told him a million times before. But I cannot help myself, and so I repeat it even though I am aware that I am beginning to sound like a broken record.

'I don't want to be like them. They are nerds. They don't have a life. All they do is study, study and study. Come on, Mom!'

'Listen, if you continue getting grades like this, Nitin and Monika will be the ones who will be employing you in the future, and you will be washing their cars, and saying "yes sir" and "yes ma'am" to them.'

'Hell, no. That ain't gonna happen. I will help you take Paw-Factor to a whole new level, Mother,' he says, adopting an American accent and speaking like a gangster. 'And please don't do the parent thing on me. It doesn't suit you, you know.'

Before I can answer him, our doorbell rings. Twice.

I know who it is even before I have answered it.

'Oh no—not again,' I groan. As it is I am angry with Aryan, and to now have that obnoxious irritant Damodar Shinde ringing my doorbell—it's the last thing I need today.

I answer it with my fists clenched, because I know what is coming.

'Yes?' I say as I open the door, barely concealing my anger, almost barking at him.

The dogs start whining and I glance at my watch. It is

nearly six-thirty in the evening. It is amazing how animals never need a clock. Damodar couldn't have chosen a more inconvenient time today for his usual rant.

'The dogs—this noise has to stop. You cannot create such a racket. My mother lives with me and she is a heart patient. You have no consideration at all,' his words tumble out in quick succession, grating on my already frayed nerves.

'It is their feed time, and they will stop as soon as they have their food, which will be done immediately if you let me,' I reply, bristling with anger.

'Do you want to help me feed them?' Aryan asks as he steps forward, between Damodar and me. Aryan is so protective of me. My anger at his bad grades fades.

'Hmmph. Bloody dogs, bloody bitch,' Damodar mutters as he stomps off.

'He is referring to his mom. Nutcase. Doesn't he have any other work?' says Aryan.

'I guess he doesn't. Just forget it, Aryan. He is retired and cranky,' I reply.

'Yeah—and single and living with his mother. His wife must have abandoned him and run away. Such a prick.'

'Language, son,' I say, even though Aryan is right. He *is* a jerk.

Jamu kaka, who lives in the outhouse on the property grounds, walks in with the food for the dogs. He has been with me ever since Aryan was two-and-a-half, and he is unfailing in his duties. He helps with the dogs, keeps an eye on them and is the general caretaker when I am away, working at the gym. He also tends to the rather large garden the bungalow boasts of. It adds to the ambience, and the whole place is full of trees and garden vegetables fondly tended to by him.

He cooks the dogs' food in the outer kitchen, a mixture of

vegetables, meat and rice, which they love. As he carries it in, in a large vessel, the dogs are all excited and prance around him, following him to their bowls. He looks like the Pied Piper, but instead of rats, there are dogs. I oversee their feeding.

After they are fed, some of them go about doing their business, and then they are put into their crates, where they sleep. The crates are all in four large bedrooms inside the house. They are decorated with polka-dotted curtains, and have individual little mattresses that most dog owners are delighted with and can't help exclaiming over when they first come to check out Paw-Factor to board their dogs.

Most days the dogs are very tired, as they have been rollicking about the whole day, and they fall instantly asleep. But there have been times when I have sat up stroking a particular whiny dog that has separation anxiety. Once I didn't sleep the entire night, and as a consequence was late for my gym shift the next day, and got ticked off by Mahesh, the chief instructor. This lot that we are currently housing are all well-behaved and sweet though, and not much trouble at all.

I mentally do a headcount, to see that they are all there. There is Jojo the German shepherd; Salt and Peppa, the two Labradors; Shiro, a pampered beagle; Manga, who is a cross between a German shepherd and an Indian dog; Zoobi, a rescued Lhasa Apso; Calvin, a boxer; Duke, a mixture between a terrier and a cocker spaniel; Mini, another beagle; Sheri, a Dalmatian; and Angel, an Indian dog.

The Paw-Factor nets me a good profit most months, especially so during the holiday season when we are full up. There is always a demand for a good boarding house for dogs. When the care is top-notch, people don't mind shelling out any amount of money. They only want to ensure that their beloved dogs are well cared for.

Shiro has finished his meal and has come for a cuddle, and Aryan strokes him.

'You are so good with the dogs, Aryan,' I tell him.

'Naturally, Mom, I grew up with them,' he smiles as some more dogs come to him, now that they realise free hugs are being given by Aryan. He patiently pets each one of them.

After the dogs are settled, Jamu kaka goes back to the outhouse, which he has transformed into a cheerful living space. This is an old mansion—at least a hundred years old—built in the British era, and hence has an outhouse, which was the norm those days. He returns at five in the morning to let out the dogs. Sometimes I think that half my success in this field I owe to Jamu kaka—I could never have managed without him.

'What's for dinner? Have you made anything?' Aryan asks as we proceed indoors. He is constantly hungry.

'I know, you're a growing boy and you need your food,' I say, mimicking him.

'Which means it's Maggi for dinner, yaay,' he retorts.

'No it isn't. It's paneer paratha,' I reply.

'Double yaay then,' he says.

I roll out the parathas, fill them with the stuffing, and they sizzle on the griddle. I serve it to him piping hot with a dollop of butter, and a bowl of thick curd and store-bought red chilli pickle. He takes a bite and exclaims that I am the best cook in the world.

'Ma, these are so tasty, you should start a restaurant,' he says between mouthfuls.

'You know I don't enjoy cooking much, and besides, who wants to cook for fifty people. No, thank you, I would rather look after our doggie-babies,' I reply.

'That too is a point,' he says.

I join him and we finish our meal together. I have cut some watermelon and Aryan is happy as it is his favourite fruit.

Dinnertime is one part of the day that I look forward to. It is when the hustle and bustle of the day is over, the dogs are settled, and I get to spend some uninterrupted time with my son.

I sometimes wonder what it's like for other mothers. Are they as close as I am to my son? Or is it because of my unique circumstances that I feel this way? There is nothing in the world that I don't discuss with Aryan. He chats with me freely on all subjects. Even about sex. When he was younger I used to wonder what I would tell him about his father when he started asking the normal questions that a child asks. He first asked me when he was four. I told him that his father did not live with us anymore, that he lived in a different place. When he had asked why, I said that he worked there. That had satisfied his curiosity.

I sometimes wonder if he misses his father. I don't think he does. Maybe because he has never known what it is to grow up with a father, he seems to have quietly accepted the fact that this is how things are.

Besides, Prakash and Suchi have always been around. They have stood by me like pillars of rock. Prakash has spent hours and hours with Aryan, taking him out, teaching him how to ride a bike, flying kites with him, making clay models with him, and generally doing almost all the things a father does with his children. Sometimes the thought does creep in that I am fortunate that they are childless, but then I immediately chastise myself, because it is not out of choice. They have tried to conceive for years and years. Prakash is happy to adopt a child, but Suchi is unsure.

'How do I know I can love another's child as unconditionally,

Vee?' she has told me many times. In a strange way, I understand.

'Ma,' says Aryan, having finished his dinner now and rinsing his plate in the sink. He always clears up after a meal.

'Hmmm,' I respond automatically.

'I forgot to tell you that I answered your mobile when you were in the shower. Suchi aunty called.'

'Oh, what did she say?'

'That she wants us to join them for dinner tomorrow, and apparently there is someone she wants you to meet.'

'Oh no, not again,' I groan.

Suchi has been trying her best to fix me up with 'nice guys' for many years now. I haven't liked any so far. There have been a few who I went out with on a second or third date. Then, somehow the interest fizzled out. Suchi feels I am very hard to please, and that it would be impossible for any man to fulfil all the conditions I have inside my head. My standard reply to her is that I have no conditions, no matter what she thinks, and if a good guy comes along, and things fall into place, I am always game.

I do want to share the rest of my life with someone, but only if he is the right guy. I definitely don't want a guy just for the sake of it. I have enough on my hands already, without adding the complication of a man in my life. If I decide to do so, he has to be completely worth it.

I have to say, Suchi has been quite consistent in her determination to try and fix me up with a guy. Finding a match for a thirty-four-year-old woman who lives with dogs, has a day job as well as a teenage son to boot, isn't exactly the easiest thing in the world. But she hasn't given up on me yet.

Every single person who hasn't yet found 'The One' will agree that there are times when you do not know the reasons for that aching emptiness that envelops you, leaving you with a longing so intense, for someone special to share your life with. I am no different. Aryan will leave for college in a couple of years and the fact is that I will then be completely alone. Even though I was always aware of it, it is slowly beginning to seem more and more real.

Which is why I agree to meet all of Suchi's set-up dates, even though I groan outwardly. Perhaps deep down, without even realising it, I am hoping that the next one may turn out to be 'The One'.

'Why not, Ma? Are you afraid you will meet your Prince Charming after meeting so many toads?' Aryan smiles.

No, I met my Prince Charming, your father, seventeen years back. Except that he dumped me and ran away, leaving me straddled with raising you.

'Maybe, maybe not,' I reply.

I guess there are some things, you can't discuss with your child after all, no matter how close you are.

Chapter 2

'So have you decided what you are going to wear tonight?' Suchi asks, as usual optimistic that this one is going to be Mr Right.

I, on the other hand, after years of experience of being let down by men, the moment they hear I have a child, am not so enthusiastic to dress up for the occasion. Anyway, if it is to happen, it will even if I am in my shorts and dirty t-shirt, with dog hair all over me. This is what I keep telling Suchi. She doesn't subscribe to my theory though. She comes from the school of thought that instructs women on how-to-dress-right-to-hook-a-man. If I gave her a chance she would pick out my clothes and my shoes, and then organise my entire wardrobe in a colour co-ordinated manner with whatever is the latest trend arranged prominently, much like a posh dress shop that displays clothes far beyond the means of ordinary folks like me, who have to work hard to make both ends meet. She has been like this ever since our school days and hasn't changed in this matter at all. Back then, she would tell me the latest trends and what the look of that season was, and I would barely stifle a yawn as I pretended to listen.

She sometimes reminds me of my mother, with whom I

didn't exactly have a friendly relationship. But I haven't ever told Suchi that. She would be horrified if she knew that I consider her pushy in the sartorial department. She likes to mother me and I let her as long as she doesn't interfere in things that matter. Also, she has been around so long that she is almost like a sibling.

'I thought I would turn up in shorts and vest, just after we have fed the dogs,' I tease her.

'Yes, that would be very good, but if you turned up in just your bra and thongs, it would be even better,' she chuckles.

'I am not looking for a one-night stand, my dear,' I clarify in mock anger.

'Who said anything about a one night stand? We were just discussing clothes,' she counters, and I smile.

I have thrown her off the subject of my clothes, which was what I intended in the first place.

'So who is this mystery man that you are trying to set me up with?' I ask.

'Hey, I just thought it would be a change for you. He isn't looking for a date or anything. He lives in the UK, and happens to be in India, on work. He is Prakash's friend. Since he is coming over, we just thought it would be nice if you and Aryan joined us,' she replies.

Most people would have believed Suchi, as she says this without even a moment's hesitation. But when you have known her as long as I have, you would know that she never does anything unplanned or without a motive. Suchi and I are as different from each other as can be. I can be a little reckless, impulsive even, and I do not much care for dainty dresses and outfits. I think it is more important to have a body that is supremely fit and I am very proud of my day job as a gym instructor. Suchi, on the other hand, is slightly overweight, very conscious of what she wears, and at any given point of time, her hands and feet look like she has just stepped out of a beauty salon with a perfect manicure and pedicure. Her home is as impeccable as mine is messy. I know her so well by now I can easily deduce without a doubt that if she has invited me for dinner, with a friend, there has to be an agenda.

'This guy doesn't by some chance happen to be single, right?' I probe with a smile, knowing what is coming.

'Oh, now that you mention it, he is recently divorced, so I guess that does make him single,' she says, and we both guffaw.

'Oh you are incorrigible, Suchi. When will you quit trying to set me up?'

'When you start living like a normal thirty-four-year-old, not some crazy old ding-bat who lives with hundreds of dogs, none of whom you even own,' she says.

'Come on, I make a living out of it. Paw-Factor is my business. I won't give it up for a guy.'

'Okay, okay. Nobody asked you to. Now wear something pretty when you come this evening, okay?' she cajoles.

'I'll think about it,' I reply, and when I hang up the phone I am still smiling at our little exchange.

The dinner will probably turn out to be better than I expect. That is the thing about these set-up dates. You keep your expectations low and even the smallest positive that happens seems great. I think about this when we're in the car. Suchi has texted me to make sure that I haven't forgotten, and I text back that we are on our way.

When Aryan and I arrive at Suchi's place, in our second

hand i10, we find a BMW parked in the driveway. Aryan checks it out and gives a little whistle.

'Wow, 7 series,' he exclaims. I know exactly what he is thinking. But a second hand i10 is the best I can do at the moment. It takes me back to a time in my life when I had four cars at my disposal. Each morning when I left for school, it was a little game for me. There was a fleet of top-end luxury cars at home, and I would pick which would ferry me to school. Of course, this was before my mother decided to send me off to boarding school in Kodaikanal.

But that seems like eons ago and another lifetime. I have created a huge wall between 'life before Aryan' and 'life after Aryan'. I am now on this side of the wall. The reality now is that I am perpetually short of money, but I am proud because every single rupee that I spend is what I have earned.

'Ma, come on. It's fine. So what if we only have an i10? I bet the guy who has this doesn't have a son as nice as me,' says Aryan. It is almost as though he can read my thoughts.

'Hey Veeee,' Suchi greets me with a hug and it is impossible not to catch her signature perfume, Autograph from M&S, which she is so fond of. She is dressed in a white loose flowing top that shows off her shoulders, black trousers, open-toed heels, golden loops in her ears, and a matching bracelet. She sure looks dressed for a party. I, on the other hand, look like I have hardly made an effort, considering that I already knew it was a set-up date. I have worn an old, well-fitted black top, jeans and no jewellery. I have brushed my hair loose, instead of the usual ponytail that I wear it in.

Suchi holds me at arm's length and surveys my outfit.

'Couldn't you have dressed up a bit?' she hisses under her breath.

'At least I took a bath after feeding the dogs,' I laugh.

She ushers us in, and the gentleman she wants me to meet stands up to greet me. Mentally I give him two points. He has got the opening right.

'Nimish,' he says as he extends his hand for me to shake. Open grey jacket, no tie, white formal shirt and well-polished formal shoes. Also he is tall, clean-shaven and his voice is deep. Tick marks in all departments.

'Vipasha,' I say as I shake his hand.

He looks at me like he has seen me before and I know what is coming. It has happened so many times that I am no longer surprised when it does.

'Hey, your face is so familiar,' he says as he knits his eyebrows, concentrating, trying to remember.

Any second now ... eight ... seven ... six ... five... four ... I mentally count, which is what I do when this happens. Here it comes.

'Aren't you Vipasha Mishra of Double Bubblegum fame?'

I debate whether I should deny it, tell him that a lot of people have asked me that question as I resemble her, or just tell him the truth. It takes me only a second to decide. I nod and he smiles.

'I knew it! God I used to watch that ad each time it aired,' he says with obvious joy on his face.

Of all the advertisements that I modelled in, he has picked the bubblegum one. Please don't let him start humming the tune, I think.

He starts humming the jingle and I cringe inside.

'*Double the bubble, double the fun*! God, I remember it all. You were fabulous!' he exclaims.

'Were, has-been, was ... yes, go on, I am used to it,' I say, only half joking.

'God, no, I didn't mean it like that. Half the boys in my school had a crush on you,' he says.

Then he turns to Suchi, who is clearly enjoying all of this.

'You could have at least warned me that I would be meeting a hot model tonight, I would have made more of an effort,' he says.

I smile. Five points for that response.

'Meet Aryan, my son,' I say as Aryan shakes his hand.

I can see he is surprised. Suchi hasn't told him about Aryan either. Most men at this point cannot help saying that nobody would guess that I have a son who is this old, and that I look more like his older sister than his mom. I expect that comment from him too, but he surprises me.

'So, what do you do, Aryan?' he asks. He hasn't addressed Aryan as 'young man', and has paid attention and remembered his name. Two more points. The rate at which he is gathering points, he is soon going to be submerged in them.

'I'm in the tenth grade, at the International Academy,' replies Aryan. He is proud of his school, which is ranked among the top institutes in India. The fees are exorbitant, a fact that I never fail to remind him of. What he does not know, however, is that I pay only one-fourth of it. His school has a bursary system, through which deserving students, whose parents cannot afford the full fees, are funded by the school. About thirty percent of the students in his class are bursary students, but there is no distinction made whatsoever, and nobody other than the parent and the school ever knows if a student is a bursary child or not. It is the parent's choice whether or not to disclose the information to the child. I have chosen not to. I don't see any reason why Aryan needs to know how the fees are paid. He got into the school in grade five, by taking an entrance exam like every other child who aspires to get into the school. Aryan had topped the exam. At that time he was too small to be told about the financial arrangements, and later, as he grew up, there was no need to. For Aryan, it is always a matter of pride to say that he goes to the International Academy. Everyone has heard of it, and it has a list of distinguished alumni too, which includes sports stars, television anchors, authors, diplomats and ministers among others.

'That's nice. So, do you like your school? Is it as good as they make it out to be?' asks Nimish.

'No, it is better,' grins Aryan.

Then Aryan tells Suchi that there is a PowerPoint presentation that he has to make and submit in school the next day. He had actually wanted to work on it at home, but I had dragged him here for dinner. He asks if he can use her computer or her laptop.

She tells him to use the desktop upstairs, and Aryan scoots off.

Suchi serves the drinks. She does not even ask me what I will have, instead automatically pouring me a glass of my favourite Rose Shiraz. I love it that she makes the effort to stock up on that wine just for me. Nimish surprises me when he says he will not have alcohol. I would have expected him to be a whiskey guy.

'So, have you always been a teetotaller?' I cannot contain my curiosity.

'Oh no, no. I love my whiskey. But I am on an abstinence challenge. I want to see if I can resist for a hundred days.'

'And who challenged you? And why a hundred days? It sounds like the banner of a Bollywood super hit movie.'

He chuckles. 'Oh, nobody challenged me. It is just a test of my willpower,' he says.

'Oh, you don't have to test that. That is something you have plenty of,' says Suchi. 'You know, he ran the Boston Marathon last year,' she adds, turning towards me.

'Oh wow, that is terrific!'

'Thanks. I intend doing it this year too.'

'It must be killing to train for it, right?' asks Prakash.

'It is. But you do it over a period of many months, and you keep punishing your body till it becomes stronger and stronger.'

He is now talking my language. This is what I keep telling people at the gym when I am training them.

Suchi serves us a lovely meal. There is Caprese salad, bruschetta, sautéed mushrooms lightly tossed in garlic, a spicy roasted vegetables platter and two kinds of pastas. It is a welcome change from the usual dal-rotis that we have almost every single day at home. I can make out that Aryan is pleased with the food, too. Suchi is always a perfect hostess. She takes such care in planning menus, setting the table, getting the right linen, flower arrangements and everything needed to make her guests feel pampered.

'Ummm ... this is delicious,' I say, as we tuck in.

My mobile rings and I am surprised to see it is Jamu kaka. The last time he called me on my mobile was seven years back, when he had a fall and had to go the hospital. Then too he had turned up for work after a day, with a bandage around his head.

I excuse myself from the table and answer it.

His voice is garbled due to a bad connection. I catch bits and pieces and my hands go cold. I am so shocked, I can barely breathe. I hope to God that maybe he has made a mistake. But a tiny voice inside me dismisses that possibility. Jamu kaka is an experienced hand. He doesn't make such mistakes easily.

Suchi has caught on and figured out that there is something wrong. She is at my side now.

'Is everything okay, Vee? What happened?' she asks.

I feel so sick, I want to throw up.

'No Suchi.... It is an emergency. I have to … I have to get back immediately. So sorry—I will call you,' I say. I cannot bring myself to say the awful thing that has happened, because I am hoping against all evidence that it may not be true.

I excuse myself and tell Aryan that we have to go and we leave without even proper goodbyes.

Chapter 3

On the way back home, Aryan asks me what has happened. All I am able to tell him is that something has gone terribly wrong with the dogs and Jamu kaka wants us to come back immediately.

'Why aren't you telling me what has happened?' he persists.

'Just let me concentrate on the driving, Aryan. I want to get there safe,' I reply, trying to make my voice sound as normal as possible. I try hard to focus. My mind is anywhere but on the road. I am unable to think clearly. A panic has gripped my throat with iron hands and refuses to ease its grip. I have had just one glass of wine, and even though I know I can handle it and it isn't potent enough to impair my driving, I want to take no chances and I hope that there are no police testing for drunk driving. I zoom through the Outer Ring Road, which is now desolate as it is nearly eleven-thirty. I am in luck and nobody stops us.

As soon as I pull into my driveway, I know instinctively that this is so much worse than what Jamu kaka said on the phone. As soon as I park the car, Aryan is out in a bound, rushing towards the house. Nothing prepares us for the sight that greets us.

There is green bile everywhere. The floor is covered with puddles of blood, in little patches. Five of the eleven dogs that we are boarding are lying deathly still on their sides, with their limbs stretched out straight. Jojo the German shepherd and Salt and Peppa, the two Labradors, appear to be breathing, but in a laboured way, and all three are hyper salivating. I don't have to even take a second glance at Shiro and Zoobi to know that they are dead. The others are in their crates. They are whining piteously. It is as if they have sensed that something is terribly wrong.

'What happened? Have you called Dr Saurabh?' I ask Jamu kaka.

He nods as he cradles Jojo's head in his arms, and he looks as though he will cry any minute. I have never seen him this distraught, this shattered.

Aryan is speechless. He runs and gets the dogs' bowls and we try to make them drink some water. They are unable to even lift their heads. None of us knows what to do. I hear the rev of an engine then. I have never been this glad to see Dr Saurabh in my life.

He comes over and takes out his stethoscope and examines Jojo, Salt and Peppa. Then he whips out his mobile and dials a number.

'Yes, it is an emergency. Please rush an ambulance,' he says and he gives them directions to reach the Paw-Factor. He then examines Shiro and Zoobi and confirms what I suspect.

'They are no more,' he says, and Aryan cannot hold back his tears. I have not seen Aryan cry since he was eleven.

I have gone into freeze mode. The outer me is calm, composed and clear-headed. The inner me is screaming in agony, my brain reeling with questions. How? Why? What happened? I want to know the answers. But I can see that

Jamu kaka is in no state to answer anything that I may have to ask. So I keep silent and concentrate on the next steps to be taken.

'What have they eaten? It is a clear case of poisoning, but just to rule out all the possibilities, we should do a necropsy,' says Dr Saurabh.

It is only then that the thought hits me: I have to tell the owners of these dogs. Shiro's owners are on vacation in Leh, and Zoobi's owners, a childless couple, are on a social service assignment in Cambodia.

'I don't know what they possibly could have eaten, but I will need to contact the owners,' I say. The pain I feel is as though a boulder has crushed my insides.

'I would suggest you do that as fast as possible,' nods Dr Saurabh.

Jamu kaka has stood up now and is bent over. He slowly walks to the side of the house and leans against a pillar. 'Didi, I am sorry, very sorry. Maybe it is the food I cooked for the dogs. Maybe a lizard fell into it,' he says. I can see that guilt and regret are eating him up.

Dr Saurabh says, 'Well, if that were the case, all the dogs should have succumbed to it. Haven't they all been given the same food?'

'Yes, all were given the same food,' I confirm.

'It is clear that the dogs have ingested something deadly, and if it is poison, it is usually life-threatening. Common symptoms are convulsions and frothing at the mouth before they succumb to it,' he says.

He shows not a trace of emotion. How can he be so clinical and composed? I want to scream. But then, I guess, for him, it is just a job. For me, it is my life. I have no idea how I am going to face the owners.

Sorry, but I killed your dog because of carelessness and negligence.

Except, I wasn't careless or negligent. I truly wasn't. I love those dogs and I play with them. I do care. This isn't just a business venture for me. I wish there were something I could do to undo the happenings of the last few hours.

In all the years that I have run Paw-Factor, there has never been anything like this. The worst incident that ever happened was, many years ago, a large dog had bitten a smaller one, but it was not serious and we had immediately informed the pet owners, who had been very understanding about it. Another time, there was a dog that developed severe diarrhoea and we had called Dr Gopal, who we used to consult back then, before Dr Saurabh came into the picture. He had prescribed medicines, and the dog had recovered. There were also the usual cases of dogs getting fever, not eating, missing their owners too much—all of which I could easily deal with. But a disaster of this magnitude, on this scale, has never struck me. This is the worst nightmare I have been through.

The only difference is that nightmares end and reality is welcoming. Here the nightmare is the reality.

The ambulance from the veterinary hospital that Dr Saurabh is associated with arrives within twenty minutes and all the dogs are carried in, one by one. I am in a total state of shock and yet am able to operate calmly. It is like I have split into two people—one has taken complete control and the other has collapsed in grief.

I tell Jamu kaka and Aryan to stay back at home. Dr Saurabh says that if I am not up to driving, I can hitch a ride in his car. I gratefully accept.

My phone rings just as we head off behind the ambulance. It is Suchi.

'Hey—what's happened? Are you okay?' she asks.

No, I am not. I have two dead dogs and three who may not survive. And there is nothing I can do. I want to burst into tears.

'Suchi—something's happened to the dogs. Two are dead and three are critical. I'm rushing to the hospital with Dr Saurabh.'

'Oh dear,' she says. But I don't think she understands. This is not an 'oh-dear' situation. But then, Suchi has never been fond of animals. She can never understand why people call them 'babies' and treat them like children. She has never petted a dog, and for her, Paw-Factor is just something that helps me earn my bread and butter. She would never get the magnitude of a disaster of this nature.

'Look, I'll call you later,' I say.

'Okay, Vee. Take care, it's going to be fine,' she says.

Fine? How is it going to be fine? I want to yell. Nothing is going to bring back Shiro and Zoobi. I don't have the mental strength to talk to her anymore.

'Bye, Suchi. I will get back to you, as soon as I can, okay?' I say and hang up.

I glance at my watch. It is past one-thirty in the morning. There is no point calling the Mehras, Shiro's owners. They would be fast asleep. I debate on whether to text them or not and decide that it is best to speak to them. Then I think about Mary-Elise and Benjamin, Zoobi's owners. I wonder what the time difference between India and Cambodia is. In the end I decide to wait till morning to call. The priority is to try and save the lives of the three who are still breathing.

Dr Saurabh tells me that there is an Emergency Service and Intensive Care Unit at the veterinary hospital for advanced trauma or emergency patients, akin to their counterparts in human hospitals. He also tells me that theirs is one of the best hospitals in Bangalore, and they have state-of-the art facilities and expertise. They function 24x7, all 365 days of the year, and the unit is staffed by trained technicians. Maybe it is his way of reassuring me, seeing how distraught I am, but none of it makes an impact on me as he cannot promise me one thing that I need to hear—that the dogs are going to be fine.

As soon as we reach the hospital building, Dr Saurabh is out of the car in a jiffy, and runs up the stairs. The other doctor has been alerted and he greets Dr Saurabh and then directs the staff.

Dr Saurabh seems to be in total control as the dogs are rushed inside.

I wait outside on one of the steel chairs, feeling so alone for the first time since I started Paw-Factor. I wish I believed in the power of prayers, like I did back in school, when faith was unquestionable and when St. Antony answered all our prayers. Right now I am just numb with disbelief.

After what seems like eternity, Dr Saurabh emerges and says that the worst is over, and they have managed to pump out the poison. However, the dogs have now been hooked to intravenous fluids as they are terribly weak.

'Will they be okay, Dr Saurabh?' I ask.

'We are only doctors. We cannot promise miracles. They need to be kept in the hospital for a day at least. So there is no point in you staying on here,' he says.

I peep through the tiny glass window of the ICU room and it is heart-wrenching to see these helpless, mute animals, hooked on to scary-looking equipment, with tubes coming out of their bodies. Their chests are rising and falling. And I guess that is a good thing. But I cannot bear to continue looking, and so I tell Dr Saurabh that I will take a cab home.

'At this time of the night? I would certainly not recommend that option,' he says.

I have never talked to Dr Saurabh outside the required treatments that he has done for the dogs at Paw-Factor. In the past he has just zoomed in, done his work and vanished just as fast. This is the first time I am spending this much time with him, and now I find his manner of being so formal in speech a little peculiar. I have never heard anyone speak such fully-formed, grammatically-correct sentences, as though he has rehearsed it from a dialogue written for a play.

'Well, I have to get home and I don't have a car,' I point out.

'May I have the pleasure of dropping you home?' he asks.

Under normal circumstances, this would have elicited a chuckle from me and I would have had a witty comeback as well.

But today I just say a simple 'yes'. The words have dried up. There is a lump in my throat and a terrible sinking feeling of having fucked up big time. I completely recognise this feeling.

The last time I had this feeling was sixteen years ago, when I was eighteen, pregnant, and had to tell my parents about it. My life had taken an irrevocable turn then. The sick feeling in the pit of my stomach tells me that it is about to take another turn now.

And the thought that haunts me most, as Dr Saurabh drives me back, is that my world as I know it is about to be turned upside down, when I call the owners of the dogs in the morning, to deliver the news that their beloved pet is no more.

What I have no idea about, is that it is going to hit me with the force of a hundred gale-winds.

Chapter 4

I haven't slept a wink the whole night, even though Dr Saurabh has assured me that the dogs are in good hands. He has reasonably pointed out that everything that can possibly be done has been done. What has also kept me up is the thought of what I am going to tell the owners of the dogs that have died.

I wait until seven o'clock. Jamu kaka has refused to go back to his outhouse and watches over the rest of the dogs like a hawk, feeds them, lets them out and plays with them. But his shoulders are slumped in defeat. The other dogs too seem to sense that something is amiss and are strangely subdued. One of them comes closer and licks his face, as though to tell him that everything is okay, and I can see Jamu kaka fighting back his tears. He hugs the dog and breaks down silently. I can't bear to watch anymore. The sick feeling in the pit of my stomach has spread all over now and I feel like I am about to throw up.

Being a Monday, Aryan has to go to school, but seeing the state I am in, he says he does not want to attend and would rather stay around with me, till he is certain that I am okay. He has become extra-protective of me, of late. But I don't want him to miss his classes. So I tell him I will be fine, and give him some money to buy lunch from the school canteen. I pace up and down the corridor, and as soon as he leaves I go into the toilet and throw up violently.

My hands are trembling and my heart is pounding in my ears when I make that call to the Mehras. It is Mrs Mehra who picks up.

'Haan Vipasha, good morning. What happened? All okay with Shiro?' she asks.

She has boarded Shiro with us since he was a four-month-old puppy. They must have boarded him at least twelve times, and never once have I called her. This is a first.

'Mrs Mehra. I am so terribly sorry. There has been an accident,' I say and I cannot speak beyond that.

'What accident? Is Shiro okay?' There is panic in her voice now.

'He … he … he is no more. I am so sorry, Mrs Mehra.' I cannot recognise my own voice as I force the words out of my mouth.

'What the hell are you saying? What happened? Hello?' she yells and I am unable to control the tears now.

Mr Mehra comes on the line and calmly asks what happened.

His voice seems controlled, measured. I find myself explaining it all to him. That it was a terrible accident and three dogs are fighting for their lives, and two have passed away. That we do not know what caused it yet, but whatever best we can do under the circumstances, we are doing. The dogs got the finest medical care.

Of course that doesn't make any difference to him. I guess when you are suddenly told that your pet is no more, the medical care that they got is of little comfort.

'What kind of a boarding place is this? We pay a bomb because we are assured of quality services. How can you be so careless? Falling sick is still forgivable. But you are telling me he is *dead*? Do you know that Shiro was like a son to my wife?' he now thunders.

'I am so sorry, Mr Mehra. I am so terribly sorry. I feel miserable about this,' I say.

'Wait till we get there. Then you will know what terrible is. We are coming by the next available flight. You will be damn sorry then,' he says and hangs up before I have a chance to let him know that I've had to make the decision to bury Shiro. There is no facility in the city to keep the bodies of dead animals. Dr Saurabh has told me that his hospital has modern incinerators to dispose of the bodies, or if the owners want a burial with a spot, then a private organisation has land for the same. For a certain amount you can buy a final resting spot for your dog, and visit the grave whenever you choose. Since a decision had to be taken, I opted for the latter. A dead animal decays very quickly, and Shiro has been buried, as has Zoobi. Opting for a place in a pet cemetery is an expensive affair, but it is the least I can do. If I were a dog owner, that is what I would have opted for. But how can a grave stone be a consolation for a life taken?

I have a cup of coffee to calm my nerves. I need to make that call to Marie-Elise and Benjamin. I've found out that the time difference between India and Cambodia is about one-and-a-half hours, which means that it must be about nine o'clock in Cambodia. My mobile does not have international dialling, and so I make a Viber call to them and it is Benjamin who answers the phone even though I have dialled Mary's number.

'I am terribly sorry Benjamin, but Zoobi is no more,' I say.

'Sorry?' he asks. He does not understand.

'There has been a horrible accident, and Zoobi died last night.'

Each word feels like a blow to me. Each word stings, hurts as I say it.

There is a stunned silence at the other end. I wait for the volley of words, the verbal abuses, the accusations.

'Hold on,' he says and I hold my breath.

He comes back on the line in about two minutes.

'What happened? How did it happen?' he asks, and I find myself explaining the whole story once again.

'Well, it is okay, I am certain you did your best. It is probably—what do you say—destiny? Zoobi was a rescue and maybe she is in a better place now, *oui*?' he asks.

I am so surprised at how calmly they have taken it. He explains that their assignment in Cambodia was extended by a year and they had been wondering what to do with Zoobi. As much as they wanted to take her along, having her would have made it very hard, as they were involved with an organisation that was building a hospital for the poorest sections of society there. Their work was difficult and time-consuming, and they wouldn't have been able to look after Zoobi. They had been considering putting her up for adoption.

After he hangs up, I sob incessantly for Zoobi. I am unable to control it. How dispensable is the life of a canine companion who has given them nothing but love? How can they not be affected like me? Is it because I care too much? Or is it because this has come as a shock, and I have just seen the dogs frothing at the mouth, fighting for their lives? I don't know. But I am terribly sad that Benjamin and Mary-Elise do not seem to care.

Dr Saurabh calls and I pick up the phone immediately. I

don't realise how tense I am and that I have been holding my breath till he says, 'Vipasha? I have some good tidings for you.'

I find myself exhaling and asking, 'Are they fine doctor?'

'Yes, I am happy to inform you that all three have made it and are out of danger. You may take them home after three o'clock this afternoon. Or, if you so desire, we have a drop-off facility too, for a charge, of course,' he says, in his usual formal manner.

I could have hugged him, kissed him, fallen at his feet and told him that he is God for rescuing all three. The relief is so great that for a few seconds I am unable to speak.

'Hello, are you there or is this line disconnected?' he asks.

'Oh, yes—thank you so very much, Dr Saurabh. Thanks a lot,' I say.

I tell him that I will come across immediately to check on them and he says that won't be necessary. He has personally examined them and they are doing fine. He says he will send them back in the hospital van, and they will arrive safely at Paw-Factor at around half past five. He says he gets off duty at seven o'clock, and if I want, he can come across after that just to check on them.

'That would be terrific,' I say. I am so grateful to this man.

'I shall arrive after half past nine, and no later than a quarter to ten,' he says.

I still find his way of speaking strange. He speaks properly framed sentences, as though he has carefully rehearsed what he is going to say. Yet he is fluent and spontaneous.

'Thank you, so I will see you tonight then,' I say and just as I hang up, the phone rings again. It is Suchi.

'Hey Vee—what's the latest? You okay?' she asks.

What can I tell her? That I am fine? Or that my heart feels so heavy that I wish I could just tear out the darn thing and throw it away? Or that I feel like I need a drink real bad, but it is still early morning and I have a whole day to endure? Or that I wish I could rewind time and go back to when everything was fine? How can I explain the sense of loss, misery and shame that I feel at losing Zoobi and Shiro? How can I explain that, though I did not own these dogs, they were entrusted in my care, and now they are dead. How can I make someone who does not even like animals understand that, for most pet owners, their pets are as dear to them as their own children?

'No, Suchi. I am not okay. I wish I could somehow undo this,' I finally say.

'Awww.... Do you want me to come over?'

'No, that's okay.... Just give me some time. I am still in shock. I need to sort out a few things,' I say.

'Okay. Tell me when you are up to it and we'll be over in a jiffy with a bottle of wine and hey guess what Nimish wanted to connect with you. He wanted your number. Shall I give it?' she says.

I am in no frame of mind to feel even a remote sense of joy. In fact, I had forgotten all about Nimish, after this development. It is only now, when Suchi mentions it, that I even remember him. Of course I can make out that Suchi is happy that he wants to connect with me. And knowing her, she would have passed on my number already.

'As though you haven't given it to him. Whom are you trying to kid, Suchi?' I say.

'Ha ha, yes I have. And he said he would call you. Don't let all this affect you too much. Pick up his call, okay?' she says.

Don't let all this affect you? How can I not?! Paw-Factor has been something that I have been so proud of. Nearly thirteen years and never once has there been anything like this. In fact, one of the things that we are so proud of is our track record of perfect care. The dogs are happy to come here. Everyone in Bangalore knows that you have to book months in advance in order to board at Paw-Factor, because of the quality of care that we give. We take care of them, as though they are our own, and I am so darn fond of these dogs. I don't know if Suchi understands all this or whether this is her way of trying to distract me because she knows how down I am.

So I just tell her I will. She says she has to go for a meeting with a corporate client who is opening a new branch in UB City, one of the poshest commercial establishments in Bangalore. Suchi does gardens and landscaping and has some high-end clients. She says she will call again soon to check on me. To be honest, I just want to be left alone. I am in no mood to be 'cheered up', even though she means well.

I decide that I won't go to the gym today. I text Mahesh that I am unwell, and will not be coming in. I have two personal training sessions booked, so I text my clients saying that I am ill, but Mahesh can take their sessions, if they wish. One of them cancels, and the other decides to attend. I inform Mahesh that it is the chest, triceps and shoulder day, and tell him the routine that the client has to follow. I also tell him to stick to just ten minutes of cardio. Mahesh can easily handle it.

My job at the gym is something I look forward to usually. The treadmills, the weights, the dumbbells, the exercise mats, the machines, the music—the whole atmosphere instantly makes me happy; plus I love helping people get fit. The money I make from the job at the gym is less than one-fourth of what I make from Paw-Factor, but the happiness I derive from it is just as much as what I get from taking care of the dogs who board with us. I hate cancelling on a client, because I know how much it means to them, but today I have no energy left for anything.

I slump into the armchair on the veranda, and when Jamu kaka asks if he can get me some tea, I nod gratefully.

Aryan has football practice today which means he will be home only at six o'clock. I now wish I had asked him to stay around. It would have helped me feel better. I can't help worrying about how the dogs are faring even though Dr Saurabh has assured me that they will be fine. I try to read a book, but am hardly able to concentrate, and I now wish I had gone to the gym. It would have helped me take my mind off the dogs.

Dr Saurabh calls and tells me that the dogs are on the way. And when they arrive, they show no signs at all of having been through a life-threatening trauma. They bound up joyfully and are greeted by excited yelps from the other dogs. I slump back in relief and I can see that Jamu kaka is overjoyed too.

When Aryan arrives from school, the first thing he does is rush towards the dogs. He too is delighted that they are fine.

'How could it have happened, Mama?' he asks, as he hungrily wolfs down the sandwich that I have prepared.

'Dr Saurabh said it is poisoning. The necropsy reports will come in today, and then we will know for sure. He is coming over later, just to check in on the dogs, and we can ask him then,' I say.

Aryan has a group project to complete and he asks me whether I'll be okay if he goes over to a friend's place, as a group of guys are meeting there and working together on it, and it will probably be late. He wants to know if I can pick him up later when he's done, and I tell him I will.

'Thanks Ma, you're the best,' he says as he heads off for a shower and then leaves for his friend's place.

Dr Saurabh arrives on the dot and I am very glad to see him. He greets me and immediately goes to the kennels. He examines all the dogs, not just the three that have been with him, and he says they are all fine. After all that I have been through in the last twenty-four hours, this comes as welcome news, and my gratitude for this guy goes up a few more notches. It is a huge relief to have him around.

I invite Dr Saurabh inside and ask him if he would like to have a drink. He says that would be nice. It is the first time that he has stepped into the house. After the trauma of last night, and after all the efforts that this man has taken, I feel it is the least I can do.

'Call me Saurabh,' he says. 'Dr Saurabh sounds very formal.'

I smile as he misses the irony that, when he speaks, he does sound formal, proper and reserved.

I ask him what he will have and he opts for vodka. I pour myself a large gin and tonic. After all the excitement of last night, I need this.

'This is a beautiful place and you have done it up well. It is a visual treat,' he says as he settles into the cane wicker armchair by the standing lamp. The lamp lights up his face and I realise it is the first time I have actually looked at him properly. He *is* good-looking, with a strong jaw line, clear skin, straight hair cut short and he's clean-shaven. He is wearing a broad striped formal shirt and dark blue trousers. Funny, how I have never noticed his clothes or his looks until today.

'Thank you, I love this place too,' I say.

'I am afraid the dogs have been poisoned. The necropsy reports show ingested poison consisting of difethialone and zinc phosphide, administered through raw meat. These are ingredients commonly found in rat poison too,' he says as he calmly sips his drink.

I nearly choke on mine, at the very matter-of-fact manner in which he states it.

'Raw meat?' I am puzzled. 'We never feed our dogs raw meat. Jamu kaka takes utmost care in the preparation of their food.'

'Yes, all five had ingested raw meat. The beagle and the Lhasa Apso had ingested it in more quantities than the other three. That is the reason they succumbed and the others survived.'

I am stunned. How did the dogs get raw meat? Where did it come from? I think for a few minutes and a chill runs down my spine. I can hardly believe it.

'God—excuse me, Saurabh. I just have to speak to Jamu kaka,' I say as I walk towards the outhouse.

'May I accompany you?' asks Saurabh and he follows me.

I go out to the veranda and call out to Jamu kaka. He is out almost immediately.

I tell him what Dr Saurabh has just said, and his face goes pale. We walk towards the east end of the compound, the one that shares a wall with Damodar Shinde's house. And even before I go near the fence, I know what has just occurred to me is true.

Jamu kaka walks closer to the wall and on top of the shrubs that form a border, entangled in the foliage, he discovers pieces of raw meat.

'Oh god, the fucking bastard,' I say.

Jamu kaka is too shocked to speak.

Saurabh looks at me for an explanation.

'The dogs have been poisoned. It is my neighbour, Damodar. The bastard hates the dogs,' I say.

'Madam, we have to go to the police station,' says Jamu kaka. 'He cannot get away with this.'

My blood boils at the unfairness. My instinct is to go across and knock on his door and punch out the bastard's teeth. It is a mixture of deep sorrow, anger and helplessness that I feel.

'That I will, but let me speak to him first,' I say and I march across to his compound and ring his bell along with Jamu kaka and Saurabh who are right behind me.

He opens the door after what seems like an eternity.

'You ... you bloody bastard ... you poisoned the dogs! What kind of a monster are you?' I am dimly aware that my voice sounds like a screech even though it is with great effort that I am able to get the words out.

'I have no idea what you're talking about. Why are you shouting?' he says as he smirks.

'Don't pretend you don't know. The necropsy reports have just come in and the dogs have died from poison.' My voice has an edge to it now. I am ready to hit him.

'In that case I suggest you take more care when you cook their food. Or you better check what they have eaten when you are not watching. You are hardly at home to supervise them, and you have the gall to accuse me. Good night,' he says and he bangs the door shut on my face.

I don't even realise I am breathing hard and that I have clenched my fists. I wish now I had hit him. Hard. Anger and outrage blinds me. The words aren't coming out.

In the end, it is Saurabh's calm manner and the way he is so practical that come to my aid.

'We have no proof. Anyway the dogs are already dead, and there is nothing we can do to revive them. The others are okay. I would suggest we go home,' says Saurabh.

We walk back and my head is reeling with what has just happened. I could see it on his face—his smirk, that gleam in his eye, that look which said 'You-deserve-it-bitch'. After this encounter, I am a hundred percent certain that it is he who is behind the poisoning.

And just as we reach the gate, we see a black Honda City pull up. Behind it, is a cavalcade of a few more vehicles. I instinctively put my hands to my face to shield my eyes from the glare of the headlights. I wonder what is going on. Why have so many vehicles made a beeline for the Paw-Factor?

Then my hands go cold as my eyes adjust to the sudden light and I see the people in the vehicles getting out.

It is the Mehras.

And behind them are television crews with their cameras and they are all getting out and walking towards me.

Chapter 5

It is Mr Mehra who is leading them.

'Oh, here she is. The owner of Paw-Factor,' he says as he nods towards me.

Mrs Mehra is just behind him and she is now screaming, 'She killed my baby. It is her. I trusted them and this is what happens,' and she dramatically points a finger at me and wails. The television cameras promptly focus on her.

Bloody hell—this means the cameras have been running ever since they arrived. Mrs Mehra seems to be playing up to them, and while I know her grief is deep and genuine, her histrionics shock me.

Suddenly I find a spotlight shining on my face, and a few microphones are pointed towards me.

'What do you have to say about the deaths of the dogs that were entrusted in your care? Isn't it gross negligence on your part?' asks a bespectacled girl.

'Animal rights organisations have stated that an FIR for negligence should be filed against you. What are your comments about that?' asks another young chap who is tall and lean.

'How can you not supervise the dogs? We know that you are not around most of the time,' says a third girl.

What the hell? Where have they been digging up information like that about me?

They all speak very fast and there is urgency to their voices, almost as if this is a matter of national emergency. They are drumming up the drama.

I am paralysed and the TV cameras zoom in on me. I feel like a prey being hunted by vultures. The whole thing feels surreal—like something that is being enacted on television. Or a bad soap opera. Except that I am the star here. Or rather, the villain. The star is obviously Mrs Mehra.

'It ... it was an accident. The dogs were most likely poisoned,' I manage to stammer.

It is a mistake to have even opened my mouth. The reporters are waiting for me to say anything at all and they now pounce on my words.

'How can you say "most likely"? Does that mean you are not sure? How can you not be responsible?' screams Mrs Mehra. 'Do you know that Shiro was my son?' she bawls even more loudly than she did earlier and the television cameras soak it up hungrily. This is the kind of footage they want. This is what will drive their TRPs up.

Saurabh steps in and tells them that he is the vet who treated the dogs and the necropsy reports have proved that the dogs were poisoned with raw meat. This is a new twist to the tale and the reporters now surround him, happy to have got new bait and fresh meat to add to their breaking story.

'At no point ever, in the history of Paw-Factor, have the dogs been fed with raw meat. It is clearly a case of outside poisoning and this needs further investigation. I would appreciate it if you left us alone. This has been an extremely traumatic and stressful time,' he says as he puts his arm around me and leads me home. I tell Jamu kaka to go back to his outhouse and to not open the doors. The television cameras capture every bit.

Once we are inside, Saurabh and I watch from the windows. We can see Mrs Mehra still wailing and I note that the volume of her cries goes up several notches when the cameras focus on her. They seem to be interviewing her now. Once that is done, they shoot footage of the house and the surroundings, and then they leave in about twenty minutes.

The longest twenty minutes of my life.

I want to go and explain to the Mehras, but having been a witness to how Mrs Mehra has behaved so far, I feel it is best that I leave them alone.

We go back to our drink and Aryan calls. He wants to know if he can stay over at his friend's place as there seems to be a lot more work to be done. He asks if I can pick him up the next day, so that he can change and leave for school. It takes a supreme effort to not tell him that television crews were here and that I am badly shaken. I do not want to worry him unnecessarily. I make my voice sound as normal as I can and tell him that it is fine. In a way I am glad that I don't have to drive over and pick him up. After the attack of the television crew, I am craving for another drink.

'Thanks Saurabh. I don't know how I would have got through this ordeal without you. Why don't you stay for dinner? It's just pizza and it won't take long to make,' I say.

'Thank you. That is kind of you,' he says.

I am glad for his company and he has handled the situation so well.

He perches on a breakfast stool as I grate the cheese for the pizza.

'I don't get too many dinner invitations. This is nice,' he says as he sips his drink.

I am surprised at his candidness and the direct manner in which he states this, without even a trace of emotion in his voice. I don't know what to say to the declaration that he doesn't get any social invites. Most people would not flaunt that fact.

'Hmm.... Maybe it is because people don't get to know you well enough,' I offer a reason. That is the only thing that I can think of saying.

'Yes, you are right. I have mild Asperger's and it is difficult for people to connect with me. But I have no problem with that,' he says and laughs.

I have no idea whether he is joking or not and anyway I have never heard of the term Asperger's.

'Are you joking? And what in the world is Asperger's?' I ask.

'Oh no. I am not joking. It is a condition. Mine is only very mild though. It was diagnosed only in my twenties and it doesn't affect me as I have learnt to deal with it. Only that the dinner invitations come rarely. Most of the living beings I interact with have four legs and a tail and their dietary habits differ a little from mine,' he says with a deadpan face, and I smile.

I am actually beginning to like this guy! He is so honest, matter-of-fact, and feels no pity for himself. He isn't even apologetic. Just accepting. I decide that I will read up about Asperger's the first opportunity that I get.

I pop the pizza in the oven and set the timer. I ask him if he will have another drink as he has finished his and he says that he has to drive back, and so, while he would have loved to, he has to say no.

I pour myself another drink though. I just want to forget the day's happenings.

As we wait for the pizza to bake, we talk. I learn that he has studied veterinary medicine at no less than Cornell. He says the college offers a very small number of merit-based scholarships that are awarded on the basis of outstanding academic performance, and there was just one scholarship for an Indian student, instituted by a family of Indian origin, which he had won. Once he completed his course, he worked in one of the best animal hospitals in Brooklyn. He returned to India a couple of years ago and is one of the founder members of the hospital that he currently runs.

'Wow—no wonder it is this good. You are personally involved in everything,' I say.

'Yes, when you are passionate about something, it shows. There is no point doing something that does not make you feel happy just to earn money. If you hate what you are doing, you are then just wasting your life,' he says and I nod. I can completely relate to that. I made lots of money when my modelling career was at its peak, but I don't think I enjoyed it at any point of time. I am a far happier person now. Or at least I was happy till this fiasco happened.

'Yes, I agree completely. Very few people do what they love. Most are stuck in a rut and drag themselves to work. I guess we are among the few lucky ones for whom their work is a passion. My other job is as a fitness instructor, and when I go to the gym, I forget everything. It doesn't pay as much as Paw-Factor but it does make me very happy.' The alcohol is beginning to take effect now and I feel nice and relaxed.

Talking to Saurabh is actually helping me feel better. I take another sip, tuck in my legs, and settle in comfortably on the sofa.

'So how did you start Paw-Factor? Have you always been interested in dogs?'

'Oh, it's a long story and I am not sure you want to hear it all,' I say as I look into his eyes. How can I tell someone who went to Cornell on a scholarship that I dropped out of college?

'Oh it would be of utmost interest to me, I assure you. I am deeply curious and would be honoured if you share your story. Did you grow up with dogs? You seem to have a way with them, from what I have observed of your interaction with them on past occasions,' he says as he looks back unflinchingly, and I smile at his choice of words.

'Actually I haven't ever owned a dog. Most of my childhood was spent in a boarding school. But our school had four dogs, and I used to spend a lot of time with them. We weren't allowed to, of course, but that never stopped me,' I say and he smiles.

I recall how the dogs in the school campus used to follow me around. I would save some choice morsels from the school cafeteria for them, and also spend a part of my allowance on a certain brand of biscuits that the dogs loved. Whenever I spent my summer vacations with Suchi, at her home in Kerala, I would spend a lot of time with her two dogs. Theirs was a very large property, and dogs were more a necessity than a luxury. During the day, the dogs mostly slept in their kennels, and in the night, they were let out. They would patrol the huge compound, guarding it against foxes and intruders. Suchi's house was in the middle of a rubber estate, and there was always the possibility of petty thefts. Besides, it used to be pitch-dark after sunset, and there were no other houses for miles around. The dogs kept vigil throughout the night. One summer, they had alerted the whole house by their incessant barking. It was I who had roused Suchi and we had both woken up her parents. It turned out there was a thief and the dogs had chased him. We found him perched atop a guava tree, with a pouch full of rubber milk on his back. Suchi's dad had alerted the cops and they had taken him away and given him a sound thrashing.

'Dogs have always been a part of my childhood, and I am so comfortable around them. In fact, I find them calming. They are so faithful, loyal, and will give up their lives for their owners,' I say.

'I know exactly what you mean. But many people do not empathise with this,' he says.

I nod.

'So you started Paw-Factor after college? And what is your background? Where did you attend college?' he probes.

'Oh, no. Actually, Paw-Factor came about entirely by chance,' I say.

'How?' he asks.

I am not sure how much information is too much. Where do I start and what do I tell him? And how much does he want to know?

I am aware that I have had a little more to drink than usual.

'Hmmm.... See, I will have to tell you my whole story,' I say.

'That is exactly what I want to hear,' he persists.

'Okay then. Here goes,' I say and draw in a breath.

He looks at me expectantly, like a child settling down before a favourite cartoon show. I can't help being amused at his interest and enthusiasm.

Saurabh is so darn different from all the men I have met so far. And he seems really sincere. He has been very supportive, too. So, I decide to tell him the whole story. It is something that I have never shared with anyone. Only the people who have been in my life for a very long time know.

'It goes back to my college days. Do you remember the "Face of the Year" contest where the winner appeared on the cover of *Glamour* magazine, which used to exist in those days?' I ask him.

He furrows his brows. Slow recognition dawns on his face.

'Vipasha Mishra.... Oh yes. You are the model. No wonder I felt I have seen you before. I indeed have!' he exclaims.

'Yes, that's me. Well, I retired at the peak of my career. I dropped out of college to have my baby,' I say.

He doesn't look shocked. He just nods encouragingly. He doesn't even ask about the baby's father. He listens intently. I am aware that I am talking a lot. The alcohol and the day's events have completely hit me now. After I finish, he says that he will check on me the next day, and that he thinks I should rest. I vaguely remember him helping me out of the sofa, and then saying bye and leaving, closing the door gently behind him.

I wonder if I said too much. But then it was he who wanted to know. And somehow, when he asked, he sent me hurtling down memory lane. I haven't even thought about all this for so many years, but now that he has put it in motion, all the memories that I have suppressed come flooding out.

I can recall every single detail like it happened just yesterday, instead of seventeen years back.

Chapter 6

When I look back, the most prominent thing I can remember about my growing-up years is the hurt and confusion. Maybe that was why I decided to keep the baby when I discovered I was pregnant. It was as though the baby was one stable thing that was exclusively mine—something that nobody could take away from me, something of my very own, where I was in charge. Something to cherish, to love and to adore.

Those days I often wondered why in the world my parents stayed married. They led separate lives anyway. In the end, I concluded that my father probably stayed in the marriage because of some kind of obligation he felt towards my mother's family. He had taken over the family garment factory when he married my mother, an only child. My grandfather was too ill to manage it. After he passed away, it was my father who developed it into the business empire it became, with his sharp acumen, go-getting nature and shrewd, calculating, risk-taking abilities. My father was a natural entrepreneur. But somewhere along the way, he also turned into a workaholic. It was as though he knew no other way to exist. Even the sports that he played for relaxation were because they would advance his business. He decided to learn how to play golf, as he figured out that many business deals were made on golf courses.

With me, my father's policy had always been non-interference. He left everything to my mother. It was she who decided shortly before I turned eight, that it was an appropriate time to enrol me in a boarding school in Kodaikanal. We flew first to Bangalore, where we stayed with Neelanjana aunty in her large rambling mansion, which I was told was the ancestral home. I fell in love with the house immediately, and asked my father why we couldn't stay there all the time. He laughed and said that most of his work was in Mumbai. I heard the house would soon be locked up, as Neelanjana aunty was leaving for the US where she had been offered a place for her research programme in the University of Ithaca.

Neelanjana aunty was many years older than my dad, and it was she who had raised him after their parents passed away. Their father had passed away when my own father was only two, and two years later, their mother had died too. I guess Neelanjana aunty wanted to escape from the memories that this house held, or perhaps she sought a better life in the US. But I was too young to understand it then. I couldn't fathom why in the world anyone would not want to live in such a beautiful house. I was too young to notice the damp patches, the peeling plaster and the hundred other things that needed fixing. I made a wish that day that I would come and live in that house. Little did I realise that my wish would come true, but not in the way that I imagined.

We drove up the Western Ghats in a white wheezy Ambassador car and I remember sliding from one end of the seat to the other as the car turned on the hairpin bends. My mother frowned at me and I giggled. Then I stuck my head out and breathed in the fresh, unpolluted mountain air.

Having been raised in Mumbai till then, I had never seen that much greenery before, and I fell in love with it instantly.

I took to the school easily and never felt homesick. Home, to me, was a lonely place. But here I had so many things to do, so much to look forward to. I was introduced to the staff and taken to the playground and later when I came back I was told that my parents had left. My mother never was one for emotional farewells, and I think she must have left in relief, that I was no longer her responsibility. I remember feeling angry and a little bitter at the time, but those feelings soon vanished, when I discovered all the activities that the school offered. The school matron was a kind-faced large Irish woman named Mrs Horlicks. She fussed over my food, my hair and generally kept an eye on me. It was more attention than my mother had ever given me, and I found myself settling very easily and comfortably into the boarding school life.

It was here that I first met Suchi. She was in the bed next to mine and I heard her muffled sobs under the pillow. And though we were forbidden to talk once lights were off, we exchanged our stories in hushed whispers. She was in awe of me when I told her that I didn't miss home at all and that I liked it here. I was fascinated with the tales of her house and her large family. Her home was in a village near Kottayam in Kerala, and she said the schools near her place weren't as good as this one. Her parents wanted her to have a well-rounded cosmopolitan education, which was why they had sent her here.

Over the several years that we spent at St. Hilda's convent, we discovered many things together, and from friends, we became sisters. Suchi was indeed the sibling I never had.

The first thing we learnt in boarding school was that our life was governed by bells. There was a bell to wake up, a bell to go for meals, a bell when it was time to shower, a bell for study time, and of course school bells that rang throughout the day which took us from one lesson to the next, from one activity to the next. We learnt to make our beds as soon as we woke up. There was no one to come back and nag you to wake up, and if you did not make your bed, or if you missed breakfast, there was of course punishment. We also learnt to run to the showers as soon as the bell rang to grab the ones where the hot water would last a little longer than the others.

We learnt to keep our stuff tidy, as there were surprise inspections by the matron. If we were messy, we got a demerit or a red mark. Once you notched up three red marks, your privileges were taken away. We would not be allowed to leave the dorm for anything other than classes and the worst was when the Saturday outing to the local market was banned. We did not have to wash our clothes, but we did have to be responsible for them. This meant that if we needed clean clothes for the following week, we had to remember to send it for wash this week. We had to make lists of the items given to the dhobi and we had to count and check them when they came back.

We learnt how to study by ourselves, and we also learnt to light candles and pray desperately, in the chapel, just before exams. Suchi told me that if we prayed hard to St. Antony, we would get great marks. So we did. It was only a couple of years later that we both discovered that St. Antony was actually the patron saint for lost items. Suchi had laughed and said that, as a special case, he would grant good marks to just the two of us, as it is our marks that are lost, and we had continued praying to him before exams.

We also learnt to manage our money, as the allowance permitted was a very strict, tiny amount, about seventy-five rupees a month. This was the same for everybody, and parents were not permitted to give their child anything above this amount. We learnt to manage our money well, as we learnt quickly that if we spent it all in the first week itself, the rest of the month we could only watch empty-handed while our friends, who had spent judiciously, got treats for themselves. We also learnt the tricks of surviving boarding school food. If there was anything good, we wolfed it down fast and went for a second helping before it ran out. We also learnt to 'save for each other'. If there was something that Suchi did not like but I wanted (rosogullas, for instance), she took her share and saved it for me. I did the same, when it was gulab jamuns. We learnt not to be fussy about food, and we learnt to survive on just about anything.

Little did I suspect how much the things learnt in school would stand me in good stead later in life. It would teach me to survive, manage with very little and would ensure that the discipline that I had inculcated inadvertently would come to my rescue.

It was during the summer vacation of class eight that Suchi and I discovered boys. Till then, anyway, we'd never had much chance to mingle with them. Being in an all-girls' boarding environment, our interaction with members of the opposite sex was limited to our Saturday outings. Even then, it was the harmless crush that a few odd girls had, mostly on shop-keepers. I remember Asha, one of our classmates, developed a major crush on a guy who owned a bakery. She had, much against our advice, written him a note and passed it to him. The scoundrel had read it, smiled and said it was sweet. Asha was ecstatic and waited for a reply, which she was sure she would get the following Saturday. The next day he had turned up in school and given it to the principal Sr. Therese, who had summoned Asha to her room. Poor Asha had come back sobbing, and for months afterwards had not stepped out for the Saturday outings.

Of course Suchi and I did no such thing as passing notes to guys. We were too cool to fall in love and things like that. At least, that is what we told ourselves. But the summer after class eleven, at Kottayam, Suchi broke our pact. She said she was in love with one of her distant cousins, Sujith, who was staying in her home while he worked on his summer project. I had gasped and asked her how she knew she was in love.

'It is easy to tell, Vee, your heart just sings. Everything looks beautiful and you just long to be with him,' she said.

Sujith was doing a course in film-making from the Pune Film and Television Institute, and he had chosen to make a documentary in Kerala for his summer project. It was because of him that I met Ankush. That was when I realised that all that Suchi had told me about being in love was true.

It is strange how the smallest and most innocuous of things, done on an impulse, can actually change the entire course of your life. Had I decided not to accompany Suchi and Sujith to Kottayam city for ice cream that day, many years ago, my life would perhaps have taken a different turn, and I would not have ended up as a single mother at nineteen.

'Come with us. The weather is blistering hot. What will you do sitting here all by yourself anyway?' Suchi had said. Her parents were visiting relatives in Chennai, and it was one of those occasions when Sujith, Suchi and I had the entire house to ourselves for two days. By then, all of Suchi's brothers were in the US.

Sujith, three years older than us, had just turned twenty and had got his driving licence only recently. He was dying to show off his driving skills, take us around Kottayam. Feeling all adult was such a high.

It was about an hour's drive from Suchi's home to the Whoop Scoop Ice Cream Parlour, which was the best parlour in Kottayam those days. 'You have to try their butterscotch sundaes. They are to die for,' Suchi said. Sujith maintained that it was the 'choco-vanilla shake topped with extra cream' that was unbeatable.

The drive in the open jeep had been fabulous. It felt exactly like what one sees in the movies. I had never been in such a vehicle before. I remember how my hair was flying in the wind as we whizzed past the greenery on both sides of the road. It was a beautiful drive. Sujith was a careful driver, and Suchi sat next to him in the front, while I took the back seat. He switched on the music and John Denver's voice came on. *Take me home, country roads...* he crooned. It was the perfect song.

'Wooo-hoooo! Go faster, Sujith!' Suchi urged.

'No way. One has to be careful on these roads,' Sujith was quick to respond.

'You are so scared, Sujith. What is the point of you having a driving licence? Here, let me drive the jeep,' she teased him.

'My dear little cousin, you can wait till you are eighteen. Then you can apply for a *learner's licence*. Once you have waited for about six months, you can *try* to pass the driving test. Yeah, with your skills, maybe in about ten attempts you *might* clear it. It will of course be a few years by then. So for now, please be content sitting in the passenger seat, and taking a ride with me at the wheel, okay?' he retorted in an exaggeratedly slow tone, and she scowled.

Then he turned up the volume so high that none of us could hear anything. Sujith and I sang along and laughed. Suchi scowled some more.

It is funny how the smallest of details stick in one's memory, even after so many years. Perhaps it was fated that my life would take a different turn. Maybe there are many gods above for whom we humans are mere toys. Like a video game. 'Here—let me make this human and that one meet and see what will happen', or 'Let me kill off this human and see what chain of reactions it sets off', or 'Let me make these two friends fight and see if they have the sense to sort it out and get their friendship back'. I cannot think of any other explanation for the events that occurred that day.

Sujith stopped the vehicle in front of the parlour and told us to go in. He said he would park it in a proper spot and then join us. We walked into the ice cream parlour and both Suchi's and my eyes were instantly drawn to the tall figure who had his back towards us. Hands stuck in the pocket of his jeans, he was staring at the flavours on offer, which were hand-written on a blackboard next to the counter. Both of us sidled up next to him, pretending to read the menu while stealing glances at him. Suchi looked at me, raised an approving eyebrow and smiled. I had to stifle a giggle and turn away.

His looks were striking, with his broad, muscular shoulders, longish straight black hair, and a mouth that made you want to kiss him instantly. His stubble only added to his charm.

'One double scoop watermelon please,' he said, and almost instantly Suchi said, 'Oh, no, no—I wouldn't take that if I were you. It tastes terrible over here.'

'Oh is that so?' he said and turned to look at us properly. I drew in a sharp breath and I am sure Suchi did too. He was so good looking, it seemed as though he had leapt out of an advertisement in a men's magazine—one of those that showed gorgeous-looking hunks with perfect muscles. He had a fine nose, full lips and sharp cheekbones. I never knew guys like him existed in real life. And in Kottayam, of all places, which was just a small town in Kerala.

'Yeah—try the coconut cream instead, it's terrific,' said Suchi.

'All right, coconut cream it is. Make that a double scoop,' he said to the guy behind the counter.

'And which flavour for you both, madam?' another server asked Suchi and me.

'Chocolate for me, please,' I said.

'You don't even try any of the other flavours. Try the sitaphal. It's very good,' Suchi said.

'No thanks—I will stick to chocolate,' I said.

Suchi went for the sitaphal and out of the corner of our eyes, both of us could see that he had taken the seat facing the door, and had settled down to have his ice cream, when Sujith walked in.

Sujith too went for sitaphal, as Suchi almost bulldozed him into trying it, and when we got our respective ice creams and turned to get a seat, we heard the guy exclaim, 'Good lord—Sujith! What in the world are you doing here?'

Sujith looked up, surprised. He hadn't noticed him till then and now his eyes lit up.

'Oh my god! I could ask you the same, Ankush Bhargav!' Sujith exclaimed.

Then they hugged each other—a man hug, barely touching each other, and finishing it off quickly with a double pat on each other's shoulders.

'Meet Suchi, my cousin, and this is her friend, Vee. And Suchi, Vee, meet Ankush, my classmate at FTII,' he said.

'Hi,' both Suchi and I smiled, and I tried not to stare at him. But it was impossible not to. And it seemed like he was one of those guys who knew the effect he had on women.

'So how come you're here, bro? I thought your folks lived in Mumbai? Or was it somewhere abroad?' Sujith asked.

'Mumbai—but my aunt lives in Aluva, and she insisted that I visit my other aunt in Kottayam. Where do you live?' he asked.

'About fifty kilometres from here, in a small village whose name you won't be able to pronounce,' smiled Sujith.

'Yeah man—these Mallu names are tongue-twisters. They are beyond me. Come let's sit down,' he said as he pulled a chair to a table that already had three chairs, and we all sat down.

I was aware that Suchi hadn't taken her eyes off him. Neither had I. It was like both of us were hypnotised by this guy's charm, looks and manners.

'So, Vee—is that a short form, or did your parents name you after they took a ride on a rollercoaster?' he said and smiled.

Everybody laughed and with that the ice was broken.

But I was not one to let go of a dig at my name so easily.

'Yeah, thank the lord they didn't name me after visiting a house of horrors, or else I would be named "Aaaah",' I quipped back and they all laughed again. Especially him. He was even more irresistible when he did so, with his perfect teeth and deep-throated laugh.

'Vipasha is my full name. But friends call me Vee,' I said when the laughter subsided.

'So what do I call you?' he asked, his eyes twinkling in amusement.

'It depends on what you want to be,' I replied. Flirting with him was coming so naturally to me and I was enjoying it.

'Ah—you have a point there. A tiny inconsequential one perhaps, but a point nevertheless,' he said smoothly.

'Not inconsequential at all, as it is my name in question,' I said.

'How does it matter, just call her Vee,' Suchi interrupted, breaking the monopoly he seemed to have asserted over the conversation with me.

It was almost as if she *wanted* to butt in. Like she did not much approve of all the attention that he had been giving me, and she wanted a share of it.

'Okay, so Veeeeeee it is,' he said, and his eyes did not leave my face. I was beginning to feel a little uncomfortable, when Sujith's phone rang and he excused himself to answer it.

'Yes... Oh, okay... No, no problem. I will go... Yes, she is with me. I will take her along... Yes, don't worry…' were all we could hear of his side of the conversation.

By the grim look on his face, we immediately knew that something was wrong.

It turned out that their great grand-aunt, who was based in Ernakulam, had passed away. She was ninety-eight. The funeral was in a few hours, as they didn't want to keep the body for long. The call had been from Suchi's parents, who wanted Sujith and Suchi to attend the funeral at Ernakulam, as they wouldn't be able to make it back in time for the funeral.

Neither Suchi nor Sujith were close to this aunt. In fact, I had never heard Suchi mention her even once. But Suchi's parents felt that it was important that they attend, as otherwise, there would be nobody attending the funeral from their side of the family. Sujith said it would take about an hour-and-a-half to reach Ernakulam.

I did not want to attend the funeral since it would predominantly be a family affair and it wouldn't really be appropriate.

'But if I drop you back home, we would easily lose more

than an hour. Which means that by the time we reach Ernakulam, the body would already have been taken away for cremation,' said Sujith.

'No point in reaching after that,' Suchi agreed.

So I told them that I would take a bus back to Suchi's home.

'But you don't even know where the bus station is. And you can't read or speak Malayalam. How will you manage?' Suchi said.

'Hey listen, I can drop her to your house. It's not a problem at all,' said Ankush.

'Do you know the way back?' Sujith asked and I nodded. They would take about four to five hours, and by the time they got back home, it would be at least eight o'clock. Suchi asked if I was okay with that, and I said I would manage. She handed me the key to the house and told me to feed the dogs, and let them out.

And that was how it had all begun. It was as though the universe had conspired for us to be together that day. When you are seventeen, four hours with a charming, attractive guy who makes you feel beautiful and acts as though you are the only woman on earth that matters, seems like a slice of heaven. Even though I wasn't happy about the circumstances under which the opportunity had come, I was still delighted at the chance to get to know Ankush better.

My heart hummed a happy tune as I got into the car with Ankush and directed him towards Suchi's home.

Of course, I had no idea about the strange games that the gods were playing that day. I had no idea of what was to come in the future and how it would twist the course of my life, switch tracks on me and throw me on a path I would never have imagined treading even in my wildest dreams.

Sometimes things happen for a reason, though they are not obvious at that moment, and there is nothing you can do to control them.

CHAPTER 7

Kerala is such a beautiful place, and as Ankush took the wheel, it felt like we were driving straight into a picture postcard. He was driving a gorgeous red convertible with a left hand drive and I was impressed. Even though I didn't know what make it was, I knew it wasn't a common one just by looking at it. Ankush noticed my reaction because I raised an eyebrow, although I hadn't meant to.

'Hey it's my uncle's. He is crazy about automobiles and this is an imported one. A Ford Mustang 92. He has a fleet of about eight vehicles and he allowed me to take this one.'

I nodded, feeling wonderful about getting a chance to go on a drive with him. There is something so darn exciting about a car ride with an attractive guy.

It's not like I can drive this on Mumbai roads,' he shrugged as we got in.

'I know. The crazy Mumbai traffic. Like yours, my parents live there,' I replied. I don't know why I felt the desperate need to establish some kind of common connection with Ankush.

'Oh, is that so? Then how come you are here and not in Mumbai?' he asked.

'The same way that you are in Kerala,' I replied and he smiled.

'Yes, this is a lovely place. I have to admit that. Although my mother had to literally arm-twist me into spending my vacation here. Her sister, my aunt, has been insisting I visit ever since they moved to Aluva about four years back. It is only now that I made it.'

'I spend every vacation in these parts. I hate going home,' I said.

'Oh, so you don't live with your parents?'

'Oh no—I study in a boarding school. St. Hilda's in Kodai. You might have heard of it.'

'Of course! Who hasn't? So cool—I am with a Hilda's babe! I can boast to all my friends,' he said, and his eyes twinkled again. I wasn't sure if he was making fun of me or not so I decided to change the topic and ask him about himself. He was easy to talk to, charming, attentive, and to top it all, he seemed to like me. He made it easy for me to converse with him.

'So how did you decide to go to FTII? You must be twenty, if you are Sujith's classmate, right?' I asked.

'Actually I just turned twenty-one last month. I come from a filmi background. Have you heard of Bhargav Productions? The one that makes these awful commercial Bollywood horror movies?' he asked.

I had no idea what he was talking about. I'd never watched a Hindi movie. It wasn't allowed in our school, and during summer vacations, Suchi and I were always too busy having fun to bother watching movies—Hindi ones at that.

'No—I don't know much about Hindi movies,' I confessed.

'Oh, you haven't missed much. They are horrid. The only reason Dad makes them is that we make our money from them. Anyway, Dad insisted that I do the course. Not that I like it much.'

'Oh, so what do you want to do then?'

'Hmmm.... What will you give me if I tell you?' he said and he was smiling again.

'Could you tell me what is so amusing?' I demanded and he laughed.

'Just that you seem to get hassled if I so much as tease you even a little bit,' he replied.

How could I have told him that I had never met a guy as attractive as him, and I had no idea if he was joking or not. Also that I was a bit in awe of him—he was older, and so self-assured. He was not treating me like a kid, which is what most guys would do with girls who were four years younger than them.

'I don't get hassled easily,' I said, after a bit of awkward silence.

'Okay, if you say so,' he replied.

When we reached Suchi's home, he was fascinated.

'Oh this is fabulous. It is right in the middle of a plantation. It's lovely!' His joy was obvious and it made him look even more radiant. Even though it wasn't my home, I was happy that he was impressed.

'Yes, it is,' I admitted.

Having spent every summer vacation here, I had forgotten how much of a delight all the greenery actually was, and how stunned I had been when I first set eyes on the ancient ancestral home, with its cobbled driveway lined with multi-coloured hibiscus flowers that were in bloom throughout the year. The main door, which was a heavy antique one, was impressive too, as were the hundreds of orchids that bloomed in pots that flanked the car porch. Suchi's parents had indeed furnished the place tastefully. But I had got used to it. Now I was looking at it anew through Ankush's eyes, and the beauty and charm of the place struck me again.

As we walked in, I remembered what Suchi had said about the dogs.

'Hey, are you afraid of dogs? I have to feed them and let them out.'

'Well, as long as they don't bite, I'm fine.'

We went into the kitchen, and the caretaker had already prepared the food for the dogs. I took it outside and Ankush followed me. I placed the food bowls on the kennels and let the dogs free. They were beautiful Dalmatians named Spotty and Dotty. Suchi always joked that they were very imaginatively named. I petted them as I spoke to them, and then I placed the food bowls on the ground, and they began eagerly lapping up their dinner.

Ankush watched me with interest.

'You love animals, don't you?' he asked.

'Yes. I love dogs. I also like cats and turtles and most other pets. Except snakes,' I replied.

'I have never had any pets at all, though I could keep one if I wanted to. And by the way, I am a boarding school product too,' he said.

'Oh! Is that so? Where did you study?' This was a real surprise to me.

'Bergner International, Mussoorie,' he said, and I was even more impressed, if that were possible. It was one of the finest schools for boys in the country. No wonder he was so polished, so suave.

'Our school has a reciprocal agreement with the Grammar School in Australia, and each year two students get to swap schools for an entire semester. I got that chance, and that was the only fun part of the school. Otherwise, it was pretty much the usual stuff,' he said casually. Like studying in Bergner was no big deal.

'What? Are you kidding me? You have the privilege to go to the finest institution in the country and you are saying it was just okay?'

He looked surprised. I don't think he expected someone like me to actually be grateful for being able to study in a particular institution.

'Oh. I never thought of it like that. I mean, I didn't have a say in the matter—it's a family tradition to study there. What about you? Do you like your school?'

'Oh I love it! I would have hated it had I studied in cramped, crowded Mumbai.'

'That is true. Nothing like the pure, unpolluted air we get to breathe in these mountains, and nothing like being away from cities.'

I then led him to the drawing room. I asked him if he would like some tea, and he said he preferred coffee. I went into the kitchen and made two large mugs for both of us, and when I turned around I saw that he was right there, propping his shoulder against the door.

I handed him his mug and we walked into the drawing room and sat on the large wooden antique swing that hung from the ceiling.

'I ought to be getting back,' he said and he sounded like he did not mean it at all. It was an I-am-saying-this-because-I-have-to tone.

'Stay for a while, at least till they come back,' the words were out even before I could think. I so wanted some more time with this guy.

He didn't seem to need much convincing. 'Hmm … all

right, I will just have to make a phone call and tell my aunt then,' he said.

He called her and told her that he had met some friends of his and he was spending time with them, and that he would be a bit late.

'Just so she doesn't get worried,' he said to me as he hung up.

I could have done a little dance to show him how pleased I was; instead I nodded like it was no big deal.

'So what are your plans after you finish twelfth? You finish after a year, right?'

'Yes, and I have no idea. I know people are supposed to have figured out what they want to do by this time and all that. In fact, Suchi has already got a seat in the college of her choice in the US. I wish I was as sure as she is,' I said miserably.

This question of what I would do had been plaguing me forever now and I was still unable to make up my mind. Having taken arts, all that I could think of was a BA in history or literature or some such, but I wasn't keen on anything in particular.

'Well, look on the bright side, at least you have a choice. My decisions were already made for me,' said Ankush.

Sometimes we long for things we don't have. To me, Ankush's situation seemed great. His parents had already decided his school, his college and his career. Mine didn't seem to be bothered. Whatever I did was okay by them. Not once in all the summer vacations that I'd spent with Suchi had my mother even asked me to come home or spend some time with her. She seemed to be fine as long as I spent the mandatory ten or fifteen days with her, and then I would tell her that I wanted to spend the rest of my holidays with Suchi and she would readily agree. Ammu aunty, Suchi's mother, looked forward to having me over, as did Suchi. My mother would briefly speak on the phone with Ammu aunty, who would assure her that it wasn't a trouble at all. My mother would then be okay, and I too couldn't wait to escape to magnificent Kerala, from dreary, crowded Mumbai, even though we had a sea-facing apartment in Worli, which was a huge luxury as per Mumbai standards. The routine did not vary at all, and that is how, each year, I found myself growing closer to Suchi's mother than my own.

I don't know why I found myself sharing that with Ankush though. I had just met the guy. Funnily though, he seemed to understand.

'Hey, it's okay. None of us gets it all. At least you have great friends,' he said, and put his arm around me.

'Yes, true. Thanks for listening, and sorry, I said more than I intended to.'

'Don't be silly. It's perfectly okay,' he smiled. There was a comfortable silence for a few seconds before he spoke up again. 'I'll be back in Mumbai when my course finishes. By then you too will finish your course, right?' he said.

'Yes, and after that Suchi will be off to the US while I will be figuring out what I ought to do next.'

'You know what you should do? You should try your hand at modelling. My uncle, my dad's brother, is associated with this modelling agency. You have the looks and the height for it. I strongly suggest that you give it a shot,' Ankush said.

I laughed. I had not even considered that as a career option and I thought that he was teasing me again.

'Hey—don't just dismiss it. I'm dead serious. In fact, that is what occurred to me the moment I saw you. But I didn't want to just say it, in case you thought I was hitting on you or something.'

'And how do I know now that you aren't?' I was grinning like a Cheshire cat now.

'For one, it is you who said that you don't know what to do after your twelfth, and how lost you'll be after Suchi leaves and all that. Two, I don't do relationships.'

'What do you mean you don't do relationships? That is absurd! What if you fall in love with someone?'

'Love is temporary. It doesn't last. I have seen far too many relationships break up. My own parents don't live together anymore. My mom is off to Machu-Pichu right now, holidaying with the current guy in her life, and that is why she couldn't have me over. Dad is at a shoot and I didn't want to spend time on the sets. That is the real reason why I am with my aunt right now.'

'Well, maybe you have seen only the bad ones. Maybe there exist some great ones. My folks too aren't very happy in their marriage. My dad travels most of the time,' I tell him.

I cannot bring myself to tell him about that terrible memory when I discovered mom with another man, shortly after which I was sent to boarding school.

'How many happy marriages do you know, Vee?' he asks.

'Take Suchi's parents. They have been married about twenty-eight years now and they have four kids. They're still together.'

'But being together doesn't mean that they are happy,' he said.

And I did not know what to say to that. Deep down, I *wanted* to believe that Suchi's parents were happy. I didn't want to dwell too deeply on their relationship, in case that too turned out to be a farce—like my own parents' marriage, or that of Ankush's parents. If that happened, then my faith that happy marriages existed would have been shattered forever. So I said nothing.

By now, Ankush and I had talked so much and shared such a lot that the natural thing was to exchange phone numbers and e-mail ids. And by the time Suchi and Sujith returned, it felt like I had known Ankush all my life.

'So you two managed fine, I can see,' said Suchi as she entered and flopped down on the sofa.

'Yes... You have a beautiful home—and a beautiful friend,' said Ankush.

Suchi raised her eyebrows and cleared her throat in an exaggerated way. Sujith laughed and I blushed.

'So I should get going then. It is pretty late already,' said Ankush. This time he stood up and all of us thanked him.

'Oh it was a real pleasure, I had a great time. Honest,' he said as he looked at me and I blushed once again. I just couldn't control the colour rising to my cheeks.

It was probably at that exact moment that I fell in love with him.

After Ankush left, Suchi told me that the funeral was quick and a lot of members from all the related families had turned up. I had a difficult time concentrating on what she was saying. Ammu aunty called to check if they had returned home safely, and Suchi began narrating all the details to her mother.

'So what kind of a guy is Ankush?' I asked Sujith, after Suchi hung up. I just had to ask him. I was missing him already, although I did not know how that was possible as I had just met him a few hours ago. All I knew was that I wanted to know more about him.

'What do you mean, what kind?'

'Well, he is your classmate, you would know things about him.'

'I think you would know more than me by now. I have hardly interacted with him. He is in the same batch, but he is doing a different course. We worked together on an event once, and I think he is cool.'

'So much interest in him, Vee. I can see you are already crazy about him,' said Suchi.

'Like half the girls in FTII,' remarked Sujith.

'Of course not, I am not crazy about him. I was just asking because I found him quite interesting. Did you know his father is a Bollywood film producer?' I said, quickly denying what they suggested. I wasn't ready to admit it to them yet, though deep down I knew there was some substance to what Suchi had just said.

'Yes, they make those stupid movies,' Sujith said.

'That's what he said too. That shows he is so grounded and down-to-earth, isn't it?'

'That he is,' agreed Sujith.

Later that night, I found that I just couldn't stop my thoughts. All I could think of was Ankush. I relived every moment with him in my head.

And for the first time in my life, I knew clearly what I wanted.

I wanted to see him again.

Chapter 8

Ankush and I met twice more in Kerala. The first time, he asked Sujith and Suchi along too. Suchi's parents readily agreed as long as Sujith accompanied us. Somehow Suchi's parents believed that Sujith was responsible, older and would take good care of us. Only Suchi and I knew how much of a myth that was—but we played along. 'Whatever eases their worries works for me, as long as they let us go out,' Suchi often said.

All of us went for a boat cruise along the Vembanad Lake, through the banks of the Kavanar River and then to Kumarakom Bird Sanctuary. There were mangroves along the path and I closed my eyes just to savour the moment. It was serene and felt like paradise. We spotted many birds, including herons and bitterns. I wished I knew the name of some of the beautiful birds we saw. Sujith video-recorded all of it. He said he planned to use the footage in his documentary. The trip was memorable, and by now Suchi seemed to have got used to the fact that, when Ankush was around, he would have eyes only for me. I found it hard to contain my joy and excitement. I had never been on trips like these before, and it made me feel so adult, to be able to do this.

The second time we met, it was a proper date. Ankush called and asked if he could take me out. Strangely I felt I had to ask Suchi's parents' permission. After all, I was staying with them, in their place. Ammu aunty agreed without too much of a fuss. All she said was to keep a cell-phone with me and to not stay out too late. Those were the days of the bulky cell-phone—when mobile phones had just come into India. I did not have a phone of my own, but there was a common one in Suchi's home, which was used by whoever was going out. I felt touched that Ammu aunty cared enough to tell me to keep the phone. I doubted if my mother would have ever done it. She probably would have just been glad that I was out of her way.

'See—I knew he had the hots for you. And you are so in love with him,' Suchi said.

'Come on, Suchi. It isn't like that at all.'

'Of course it is. Now do you have something decent to wear or no?'

'Hey, listen, I don't want to dress up or anything. This isn't like a romantic date or whatever.'

I felt that by allowing Suchi to give it too much importance, I would perhaps make it an even bigger deal than it was to me. Maybe deep down, I had a premonition that it was too good to be true. Ankush was so much more than I deserved. And it was as though I just couldn't believe my luck that someone in his league was taking interest in me and asking me out.

'Don't be silly. Of course it is! Come now, let me help you choose what to wear,' Suchi said as she led me to her collection of clothes.

I did not have the heart to refuse. She seemed so eager, so keen. I would have been happy in my usual jeans and a tee, but she insisted on a denim skirt and a dressy top. And I obliged. I refused to wear her high heels though, and ended up wearing sneakers which she said did not go well with my outfit. Skirts are always worn with heels, she proclaimed.

'Please! It's not like he is going to take me to a five star hotel where I have to be all posh and polished,' I said.

He had taken me to a waterfall instead. It was a spot ideal for shooting movies, he said, and I saw that he was right. It was beautiful—a real feast for the eyes. The water roared as it cascaded down the rocks from a height of about a hundred feet. The scene was framed in foliage so dense that it was almost impossible to see the sun. It felt like we had been transported to a different world—a magical one like we'd read about as children, in fairytales. For a few moments, we were both speechless, stunned at the natural beauty that lay before us.

'Gosh, you're right about it being perfect for shooting movies, this is such an amazing place,' I said.

'Although, you can be sure my father will have some monster coming out of the water to gobble up the skimpily-clad heroine,' he laughed.

Then he pulled out a rug, a thermos flask, a box of packed sandwiches and another box of cut fruits. He even had plates and cutlery.

'Wow—you came prepared!' I was delighted.

'Actually it was my aunt who organised all this when I told her I was taking you out,' he sheepishly admitted.

'How did you find the route to this place? This is your first time in Kerala, isn't it?'

'Ever heard of something called maps?' he smiled as he pulled out a paper from his pocket on which his aunt had drawn the directions to this place.

'You have some pretty awesome relatives.'

By then the air between us was so charged with the attraction we were feeling for each other. It was hard to ignore.

'Not as awesome as you,' he replied, and it was then that we kissed for the first time. It felt like the most natural thing on earth. I wasn't shy nor did I feel awkward, and he tasted so good.

Of course I wanted to go further. I knew he wanted it too. I could tell by the bulge in his pants. He was stroking my thigh and I willed him to go higher.

But he stopped.

'Not in a public place, Vee,' he said, and we had to be content with just holding each other and kissing again and again. It was as though I couldn't have enough of him.

We didn't get a chance to meet again in Kerala, and I soon went back to St. Hilda's with Suchi, while he went back to Pune, to finish his course.

We kept in touch throughout though, on e-mail.

We were allowed to check our mails and use the Internet for about half an hour every day, and I never missed my chance. Those were the days of dial-up connections. St. Hilda's prided itself on being one of the first schools in the country to have Internet, and encouraged students to write to their parents. Sometimes it took forever to connect, and on some days it wouldn't connect at all. Earlier, I wouldn't bother to check—I hardly got any mails. But now I logged in eagerly every single day, hoping to have heard from Ankush.

Sometimes there wouldn't be a mail for many days and I would be disappointed. And then he would write. I would want to reply immediately, but I didn't want him to think that I was overly keen or desperate. So I would force myself to wait for four or five days before writing back.

His mails were always brief, to the point—more like updates of what he had been up to, and mostly to say that he had been terribly busy. Ankush wasn't much of a writer.

I, on the other hand, used to write long emails full of details, describing the school building, the dorm, activities we'd had that day, the surroundings, the forthcoming tests and all other happenings. Then I realised that his replies were short and succinct. I started modifying my mails to suit his style and I tried to make them brief, just like his.

If he noticed, he never mentioned it. Nor did he ask me about why my mails had become shorter.

He remembered all the dates for my board exams though. Before each exam there would be a mail wishing me luck. He would also remember to wish Suchi. So, along with praying to St. Antony (which we still did), both of us also started waiting for Ankush's mails.

Once the exams got over, Suchi did something unexpected. She said she wanted to see Mumbai before she took off to the US. She had been accepted into Arizona State University for a degree in landscape design, and she was leaving in four months.

'I have never been to your home, Vee. Don't you think it will be nice? We have four whole months. Maybe we can spend two in Mumbai and two in Kerala. What do you say? And this way we will be together when the results come in too. So we can console each other if we do too badly,' she said.

I could hardly refuse. After all, I had spent every summer with her for years. It had never even occurred to me that she would actually want to come to my place in Mumbai. I had told her about my home and about Mumbai, and I hadn't painted a very rosy picture. That was the way I saw it, and now she wanted to be a part of it. I was touched, but I was apprehensive too.

When I asked my mother, she actually sounded happy about having Suchi over, which surprised me.

'It will be nice to have your friend over. Her family has been extremely kind and we would be more than happy to host her,' my mother said.

When Suchi came over, my mother was the epitome of a great host. I don't know if she was doing it because she felt she had to return the favour, or if she was genuinely happy to meet my friend. But it was the first time that my mother was greeting me at the airport. Usually it was the chauffeur, who had been with us for ages, who would pick me up. Once or twice, when I had arrived home for my vacation, my mother wasn't even around. So when I saw her at the airport waiting for us, it was a shock for me.

She hugged me warmly and then she hugged Suchi too.

'Gosh, your mom is more stylish than in the pictures you have shown me, and she looks more like your older sis,' Suchi had whispered.

It was only then that I realised what a stark contrast my mother was from Ammu aunty. My mom had dressed in a Louis Vuitton skirt that ended just above her knees and a lace white blouse. She wore Gucci glasses and held a Jimmy Choo handbag. She had a single solitaire as a pendant and a matching ring and earrings. Her nails were perfectly manicured, her short hair was stylishly set and her heels made a clickety-clack sound as we left the arrivals gate to wait for the chauffeur to bring the car. Ammu aunty wore only sarees, and a large bindi. Her hair was always carelessly tied back in a knotted bun, and she rarely bothered about matching handbags, heels or any such thing. The two couldn't have been more different. I hadn't even thought of comparing them till now, but Suchi was clearly in awe.

Once we were home, my mother actually made time to stay with us for a meal. She chatted with Suchi and asked her all about her course in Arizona, about her home in Kerala, about her three older brothers (who were all working in different parts of the US) and a lot more. They were chatting like old friends and I was beginning to feel irritated and left out.

When the meal was over, I dragged Suchi to my room and told my mother to carry on with her plans, and that Suchi and I would be busy. My mother looked disappointed and said that she had planned to spend the day taking us shopping, but that was okay.

'Oh—no problem at all, Aunty. Just give us about half an hour and we will all go,' Suchi replied on my behalf and I gave her a murderous glare.

Once we were in the safety of my room, Suchi shut the door and turned towards me angrily.

'You know what Vee, you are behaving like a spoilt brat. Your mother is making an effort and she is so sweet and kind. I think you are horribly biased against her.'

'Ha—what do you know? You have known her only for the last two hours. I have known her all my life. I can see that she has already bought you over with her money.'

'Shut up. You are being obnoxious. How dare you say things like that? You should know better.'

I did, but I was too jealous and too enraged that my friend, my soul sister, who had always been on my side, was now taking up for my mother. I guess it was easy for Suchi. She had a loving family, three older siblings, parents who cared, admission in a great college—her life was going so smooth.

Couldn't she see that I had only her?

But all of it was about to change.

Only, I did not know it then.

Chapter 9

The day after we landed in Mumbai, Ankush called. He said he was coming down to Mumbai from Pune for the weekend, and asked if we wanted to meet. I, of course, wanted to. I told him Suchi was with me and that she was signalling furiously in the background asking me to go ahead and meet Ankush and that she would be fine. I laughed as I mentioned it on the phone and Suchi pulled a face at me.

Ankush invited her too and said he would bring a friend, a guy he grew up with and who he had wanted to catch up with. He said we could all go out somewhere and it would be fun.

That was how we met Manav. Manav was the exact opposite of Ankush, physically. He was stocky and, at about five foot eight, only very slightly taller than me. He wasn't exactly handsome in the conventional sense, but there was something about him that would cause women to take a second look. Maybe it was the mischief in his eyes, or maybe it was because he was so full of energy that he couldn't sit still but bounced about like a basketball. Also, he talked a lot.

Manav was one of the few students from Bergner who had opted to do their graduation in India. He had completed his

Bachelor's in mathematics from St. Xavier's in Mumbai and was now doing his MMS from one of the best management institutes in the city. He had been a year senior to Ankush in school, but the two got along well. Ankush said that he was one of those lucky bastards who was naturally brilliant, and that he had prepared for the entrance test for just two months, and then cleared it easily.

But that did not strike a chord with either Suchi or me, even though we knew how hard it was to get into a top-ranked management college. What struck us was this was the first time that we had come across a guy who loved to talk. Manav had a story for each occasion, each one funnier than the last, and we were all soon roaring with laughter as he narrated each with exaggerated dramatic gestures. Some of the stories were from their school days, and they involved Ankush as well. At one point Ankush was laughing so hard he had to hold his sides and stop walking.

'Is whatever he is narrating true?' I asked Ankush between fits of laughter.

'More or less, but it was never that funny when it happened in school,' he said.

'That is because all these sound tracks and music effects that Manav is providing were absent,' said Suchi and we chuckled helplessly again.

We went to Essel World, which was one of the best amusement parks those days, and had a crazy time trying out all the rides. I sat with Ankush for some of the rides and with Suchi for a few others. Suchi wasn't too keen on sitting with Manav.

'I don't want him to get the wrong idea that I am his date or something. Sorry I am spoiling your fun with Ankush,' she whispered when the boys had gone to get us drinks.

'Ankush and I are not an item or anything. At the most it is a one-sided crush,' I replied.

'I don't know if it is love or lust, but he sure is attracted to you,' Suchi said.

Later, as we were all heading home, Ankush said that he had spoken to his uncle about me, and that he wanted me to give modelling a try. He said he had arranged for a photo shoot and also a few short screen tests to take place the following Tuesday, to see how I looked on camera. He asked me to come to his uncle's studios then.

'What? I never even agreed! Why in the world did you do that?' I almost yelled.

'Because, that's the only way to go about it. Or else we would only be speaking about it and not doing anything. I do think you will be fabulous.'

Later that day, when we said bye to the boys, Manav asked for both our numbers and e-mail ids. He said his course was very hectic and demanding, but he'd managed take the day off as he badly wanted to meet Ankush. He said we were the first set of seventeen-year-olds he had met who were not silly or giggly.

'Well, I am eighteen and Vee will soon be too,' Suchi reminded him, which sent us into a discussion of how old we were when we started school. Suchi had always been a year older for the class, as there was a cut-off date for admission into each class at St. Hilda's, and Suchi's date of birth had ensured that she missed it by ten days. There were girls who had missed it by a single day too. St. Hilda's was that strict about admission and age criteria. Being a boarding school, they did not mind if the child was a couple of months older. But a younger child was a no-no. Manav understood and spoke about how this very rule had ensured that he was always the youngest in the class. Then we had discussed zodiac signs and laughed at each of our traits, as Manav enacted them. This was the first time we had come across a guy who knew the zodiac so well. Ankush said that Manav was a closet geek and he had read at least a million books, and in his free time, his hobby was reading the dictionary. That sent us into laughter-land again.

When we were back in my room, Suchi said she completely agreed with Ankush about modelling and that it was a great idea. She said, 'If I had even half your looks or your figure, I would definitely give it a try, that too when it is literally falling in your lap. What do you have to lose? I will come with you to the studios.'

I had expected the studio to be big and intimidating. But it turned out to be an apartment in the suburbs. Ankush had come along with us, and his uncle was friendly, jolly and fat. He wore a silk kurta and pyjamas and had shoulder-length thin hair which looked dishevelled, as though he had just tumbled out of bed. He wore a thick gold chain and several rings on his fingers. But any apprehensions I had from his looks, he soon put at ease. He wanted to know where I was from and how we had met Ankush. He also mentioned how highly his nephew had spoken of me. He said Ankush's sense of judgement for casting was always right. I had never even thought of terms like casting and I could now see the professional side of Ankush. He chatted amiably and asked if the lemonades he ordered were fine. He assured me not to worry and then he took us through the process. He said all I would have to do was pose for the pictures. Once we were comfortable, he called out to a guy and asked him to get someone to do the make-up for me.

I was nervous. I didn't even want to be here in the first place, but Suchi found it all very exciting.

The designer had laid out several costumes on a clothes rack. Stylish, wonderful clothes. There were all kinds of lights and umbrellas. It was a busy place, and there were two other shoots happening simultaneously.

When the make-up artist finished with my face, arms and legs, I barely recognised myself.

'Good lord—I look like someone else,' I told Suchi.

'Stunning you look,' she replied.

'See these are very bright lights, and this is the kind of make-up that will look good in these lights. Don't worry, these guys are some of the best in the industry, they know what they are doing,' said Ankush.

So I just did what I was told. I was asked to pose on a chair, where they took at least a hundred shots, some of me smiling, some gazing away, some looking up, some looking straight into the camera, some unsmiling. Then I had to change into another costume and do it all over again. I posed in dresses, in denim shorts, in jeans, in an evening gown, and they even dressed me up in a saree. There were two women to assist me and they hovered around me in the privacy of the changing room, holding out the clothes, helping me with the fasteners and hooks and pins—all of which was new to me.

I was surprised at how quickly I got used to the routine.

'God, she is good,' said Ankush, hovering around proudly. That encouraged me and I gave it my best.

After we were done, I washed the make-up off my face in the restroom, and changed back into my own clothes, and we headed back home, giggling and laughing all the way. Suchi was going on and on about how novel it was, how awesome that I'd got an opportunity like this and it was an experience to cherish and so on. I asked her to shut up, though secretly I felt it *had* been fun, and I did feel good trying out all those clothes and being treated like a princess. But in a couple of days, the excitement wore off and we forgot all about it.

My mother was involved in several social organisations those days, but she was making an effort to spend time with Suchi and me at meal times. I was happy that, at last, she seemed to be interested in my life. My father, I hardly saw. He was always someone I would only fleetingly get a glimpse of. Sometimes, though rarely, he would be there at the dinner table, and he would ask me how everything was going, and I would answer that it was all good. Our conversations never progressed beyond that.

Ankush and I never went on an exclusive date in Mumbai. He never asked me out, which puzzled me a little bit. After that kiss in Kerala, I thought we had something between us, but the way Ankush was with me now, it seemed like he just wanted to be a friend and nothing more. I didn't know what to do about it. It wasn't like I could say, 'Hey Ankush—why did you kiss me if there is nothing between us?' I did want to. But of course I did no such thing.

I was happy though that every weekend he would come from Pune, call me up and then all three of us—Suchi, he and I—would hang out together and do something fun. Manav couldn't make it as he always had something or the other going on with his course. But he had added me on Yahoo Messenger, which everyone used those days, and we would chat almost every day. I would sit up long after Suchi had slept and chat with Manav on the desktop in my room.

Funnily, my friendship with Manav now seemed to be developing well, through online chats. Initially I chatted with him mainly because he had known Ankush for so long and I loved to hear him talk about his friend. But, gradually, the topics of our conversation changed and we started chatting about each and everything under the sun. I began enjoying the chats with him as he was funny and witty. Besides, he typed with lightning speed. He confessed that he could type with his eyes closed as he had done a basic typing course. I don't know how much truth there was in that claim, but I must admit the guy was very quick with his responses—almost like a machine. Even while I would be typing out a response to something he asked, a volley of paragraphs would come my way and I enjoyed all that he had to say.

Once I mentioned my chats with Manav to Ankush. 'Oh yes, he is just something else,' agreed Ankush, and he seemed pleased that I was getting along well with Manav.

Ankush told us that he had applied for a Master's in film studies at the University of New South Wales as well as in Sydney. If accepted into either, he would be going there soon. 'But I will also be doing a lot of DJing. Music is my first love. There is so much more happening on the music scene in Australia, than in India,' he said. Though the thought of Ankush leaving filled me with a strange kind of dread, yet I was happy that he was doing what he was interested in.

I never asked about the photo shoot that he had arranged, and neither did he mention it. In fact, I had forgotten all about it when, about twenty-five days later, I got a call.

'Good morning madam, I am calling from the office of Bhargav Entertainment, am I speaking with Vipasha?' said an official-sounding voice. It took me a few seconds to figure out that it was Ankush's uncle's office.

Now this official-sounding voice on the phone was telling me that my portfolio had been accepted by a modelling agency and asked when I could make it to the office to sign the contract.

I couldn't believe it. I ran to tell Suchi and she gave a delighted whoop and hugged me.

'Don't you know that is one of India's top modelling agencies? And do you even realise how many of their models have made it big in Paris?' she said as she held my hands and danced around the room, reeling off the names of international models who were from India.

I had only vaguely read about them, and now here was the agency which was representing them, offering *me* a contract. It was all like a fairytale coming true and I was the star.

When I told my mother about it, though, she was not happy at all.

'No Vipasha, I don't think it is a good idea. I will discuss it with your father,' she said.

'But why?' I asked.

'Because I would rather you did a corporate job. With your intelligence, you are capable of so much more than just posing dumbly for photos. Also, looks will fade, Vipasha. It is education that will stand you in good stead.'

But I was in no mood to listen.

'Well, this is only temporary. And I am being represented by Glitz Model House, no less. Do you know many of their models walk the ramp in Paris?' I said.

That did not impress my mother much.

'It is a horrible world and a lousy industry to be in. I have heard what goes on in those circles. I would rather you stay away,' my mother said.

That only made me more determined.

I would turn eighteen soon, and she couldn't stop me, I said.

'Look, your father and I can only guide you, what you decide to do with your life is up to you,' she said.

And that was exactly what I did.

Only the manner in which I did it was something that neither my parents nor I had foreseen. I didn't mean for it to happen that way. But it did. I had started something over which I had no control, even though I thought I knew what I was doing. I was pretty certain too that it was what I wanted. At that point of time, I was the happiest person on earth, and I was delighted at the turn my life was taking.

The world was mine to conquer and I was ready to fly.

Chapter 10

Suchi couldn't stay the whole summer with me. Perhaps if she had, things would have been different. She might have prevented what happened. But she wasn't around. Ammu aunty had a fall and had to keep her foot in a cast for three months. She wasn't able to stand without crutches and she needed help even to get around. We were both upset when we heard, and I wanted to go back to Kerala immediately with Suchi, but both she and Ammu aunty wouldn't hear of it.

'No way—you have just got a fabulous opportunity—perhaps an opportunity of a lifetime. Also, it is not so serious that we both have to rush there. The doctor has said it is a clean fracture and will heal. Just that she needs to rest, and needs help. Once I leave for the US, I will hardly get to see her, so it's fine. I will go back to Kerala and be with her. You go model and appear on the cover of a magazine, okay?' Suchi said.

Little did we know then that her words would prove to be prophetic.

After a month, my mother's apprehensions and resistance gave way, once the ladies in her circle started recognising me.

They were slightly in awe of me and I enjoyed all the attention. I was hailed as the freshest face of the season in modelling circles and more and more work started coming my way.

They would send a vehicle to pick me up and drop me from shoots. I was beginning to feel like a star. It was all very novel for me. Ankush called me up to congratulate me on my success. He said his uncle was very pleased about the discovery.

'And you know what, my uncle said I get half of the agency commission—isn't that cool?' He sounded pleased.

While I was aware that they got a percentage of what I made for very assignment that came my way, what I did not realise was that he was involved in the financial transactions as well.

I don't know why it made me feel like he was using me. Till now I wanted to believe that what I had with Ankush was something special. I had felt the connection in that kiss when we were at the waterfall in Kerala. But now, in Mumbai, the memory of that kiss seemed distant. I wanted it. I longed for it. I wanted that magic. I wanted to feel the way we felt that day. And this money and commission that he was talking about made me feel uneasy. It was probably petty on my part to feel that way, but no matter how much I tried to brush it aside, that little niggling feeling wouldn't go away.

I brought it up with him during the next phone conversation.

'Don't be naïve—that is how these things work. The cut on the agency commission just happened. I never expected my uncle to offer it to me. And hey, why should I refuse?' he asked.

I didn't know what to say to that. He was right. There was no reason for him to refuse.

'Do you know how many girls would be willing to do

anything—and by that I mean just *anything*—to even get a chance to have their portfolios looked at by my uncle? And here, all of it has been offered to you on a platter. It isn't like you had to go through the casting couch or been subjected to the many lousy things that go on in the industry. I have been there throughout, haven't I?'

I didn't know what to say to that either. Now he was making me feel stupid that I had brought it up in the first place. But I did not like his implying that he had done me a favour and that I had to be grateful to him. I had never asked for it in the first place.

'Okay Ankush, let's just forget I said anything,' I said, trying hard to make that uncomfortable feeling go away. But it remained.

Work was never-ending, and I was always in demand. That felt terrific, even though I found the actual shoots very mundane and boring. I modelled for a soap, for a line of women's clothing, for an eye-liner, for a detergent, for a soft drink and for a bubblegum, among many others. Some were print ads and some were for television. The agency ensured that a steady stream of offers came my way, and I was kept busy throughout the day.

Once we were done at the shoot, I never hung around or went out with the others. I didn't much enjoy their company, and mostly I just wanted to escape to the peace and quiet at home. I didn't enjoy either smoking or drinking, which is what most of them did when the shoots got over. Weed was rampant too, but I did not want to try it at all. There'd been enough opportunities at Hilda's, but I had never wanted to go down that route. I realised early on that I was very different from the girls who desperately wanted to have a career in modelling. I heard so many stories of their struggles. Gradually the other girls stopped inviting me, stopped even asking me out. I was the resident recluse—the one that didn't fit in.

So after my shoots for the day, I would head straight back home, log in to Yahoo Messenger and chat with Manav and Suchi simultaneously. It was pretty much the same routine repeated day after day, with the only minor variation being that sometimes it would be just Manav I chatted with, as Suchi would be busy with her family.

Ankush was never big on chatting and he had never been fond of e-mailing either.

'I would rather pick up the phone and speak to you,' he said. But we never spoke as often as I would have liked.

The results of our board exams came out, and both Suchi and I did extremely well. We both got distinctions, and had got above ninety in the overall percentage.

'Wooo-hooo! St. Antony didn't let us down,' she said.

'Yes, and Ankush's mails brought us luck.'

'That was only for you, my dear,' she shot back.

My parents were very pleased with my results and my mother encouraged me to apply to all the good colleges in Mumbai. I decided to go for a BA in English literature. I couldn't think of any other course that would interest me. I was accepted at Elphinstone, one of the oldest colleges in the city. Luckily it was located in south Mumbai. I couldn't imagine myself commuting to the suburbs in the crowded local trains. I had lived in south Mumbai all my life, and when I visited home from school too there had been no reason for me to travel around. So I was relieved when I was accepted, as it meant I could be dropped and picked up in the car.

When I mentioned this to Ankush he laughed and said that I was a spoilt brat, used to luxuries, and in order to know what real life is, I should enrol at a college in the suburbs and travel by train every day. I told him that he could experience real life; I was happy where I was.

'You are happy in Mumbai? I thought you liked the hills and nature and somewhere peaceful,' he said.

I admitted that I did, but I couldn't think of any colleges in the hills. Besides, my modelling career had now taken off too.

I did miss my school life sometimes, but most of the time I was kept so busy that there was not much time for nostalgia.

My chats with Manav and Suchi continued, as did my modelling jobs. Once, in the middle of one of my chats with Manav, he said that he wanted to speak to me on the phone. So I asked him to call me and he promptly did.

'Hey, how are you?' he said and I burst out laughing.

'We have been chatting online for the past half hour, and you know that I am fine, well, hale and hearty, and yet you ask me how I am,' I said.

'It's just a habit, which I am trying hard to break,' he said, a bit embarrassed now. 'Anyway, this conversation is a bit uncomfortable for me, but I have to tell you something.'

'What?' I asked, my heart racing.

'I debated with myself, whether to tell you or not. But I felt I owed it to you, as a friend.'

'What is it, Manav?' I asked, and realised that I was holding my breath. Was he going to tell me that he loved me? That I meant something more to him than a friend?

'It is about Ankush,' he said, and I could already feel my heart sinking, the initial excitement dying as quickly as it had risen. I knew instinctively that what he was going to tell me was something that I would not like.

The words he uttered next hit me like a hard punch in my gut. 'He has a girlfriend, Vee. I don't think he has told you or even mentioned her,' he said.

For a few seconds I could not speak. And then I said, 'Oh.'

'I had to tell you, Vee. I know how you feel about him, even though you haven't actually said anything,' said Manav.

I said, 'Oh,' again, aware that I was repeating myself and sounding stupid, but unable to think of anything else to say.

After I hung up, I cried a little. Not too much, but a little. For a hope dashed. For being foolish and expecting this to lead somewhere. For thinking that what I had with Ankush was the start of something special. For being naïve enough to think that he got me the modelling deal because he had feelings for me. How stupid could I be? It was just a business deal for him.

And yet, I was foolish enough to believe I could get him.

I called up Suchi immediately and repeated to her my conversation with Manav.

Suchi wasn't willing to blindly believe what Manav had said.

'Hey listen, how do you know Manav is speaking the truth?' she asked.

'Why would he lie? What does he gain by telling me that Ankush has a girlfriend?'

'Because he has a thing for you, stupid. How silly can you be to not realise that?'

'God, Suchi—according to you, every guy has a thing for me.'

'But they do, Vee. In case you haven't noticed, you make the guys go crazy. And the fact that you look so much older than seventeen doesn't help. The poor bastards don't know what hit them.'

'Shut up, Suchi. You are just speaking rubbish now.'

'The truth is never so palatable, my friend. But you can easily get to the bottom of this. Ask Ankush directly.'

'And what makes you think Ankush will not lie?'

'You are willing to trust Manav but you aren't willing to trust Ankush? And yet you have a thing for him. How long will you keep suppressing what you feel? Just go tell him and be done with it. At the most he will say he's not interested. There is nothing much for you to lose anyway.'

What Suchi said struck a chord with me. She was right. There was only one way to find out where I stood with Ankush. I would have to speak to him alone.

My eighteenth birthday was coming up soon, and my mother wanted to throw a party for me and invite a whole lot of people. She said my dad would be there too, and asked me to call my friends. The only friends I had in Mumbai were Ankush and Manav. Earlier, the grand plan had been that Suchi would be with me and we would go out and paint the town red. Suchi and I had been very excited about it. But now that she wasn't around, I was not keen on celebrating it at all. My mother was very eager and insistent though. It was as if she wanted to show me off to her friends.

So, reluctantly I asked Manav and Ankush if they wanted to attend a boring party that my parents were throwing in honour of my eighteenth birthday. Manav said that he would come over early in the morning and wish me. But he wouldn't be able to make it to the party as they had an event at their college that day—something important related to placements, where he was a committee member. Suchi called from Kerala and said that even though she couldn't come, she was sending her representative. She said that Sujith would be attending, and whether I would mind if he brought along his girlfriend.

'When did Sujith get a girlfriend? How come we never knew about it?' I asked.

'This is a new development. Less than a month old, let's see how long it will last,' said Suchi.

'I thought you were in love with him.'

'Bah. That was ages ago. It was just a crush. I am over him now,' she said, and with that she dismissed any feelings that she had for Sujith. I wondered how she could be so sure about all this. She was so unlike me, when it came to things like this.

My parents had a long list of people they wanted to call. They were the cream of society. My father had invited all his business associates. I couldn't care less. I knew that there would be reporters too, and pictures of the party would be carried in the page 3s of dailies. There would be those sets of regulars who attended these types of gigs, and I knew everyone would be dressed up in their best.

My mother insisted that I go shopping and she even offered to go with me, which was a first. But by now, I could do this kind of shopping on my own. I knew what worked and what didn't from my numerous photo shoots. My mother gave me her credit card, and I chose a designer black dress: it was short and fitted, with a black belt and gold buckle, and a V neck. It cost a small fortune. I also picked lovely shoes to go with it, and my mother was pleased. Left to myself, I would have lounged about in shorts and a t-shirt. But of course my mother would have been appalled.

I described the dress that I would be wearing in detail to Suchi, and she said that she wished she could see me, and be with me. I promised to click lots of pictures and mail them to her.

Ankush turned up wearing a tuxedo, and he looked so

good that I found myself drawn to him over and over. I just couldn't take my eyes off him.

I greeted him shyly and asked him to come inside.

He looked around the apartment with a quick glance and then greeted me.

'Hey, It's so good to see you,' I said as he hugged me. It almost made my breath stop. It was excitement beyond my control, which I was doing my best to hide.

'You look good enough to eat. Happy birthday, sweetie,' Ankush whispered in my ear as he handed me flowers. They were red and white carnations and the bouquet looked gorgeous.

'Thank you Ankush, they're lovely.' My voice came out as a whisper, though I didn't intend it to. In that fleeting moment, I had eyes only for him, and I would like to believe that it was the same for him. A world where nobody and nothing else mattered but the two of us.

'Not as lovely as you,' he said, and with that statement, he completely swept away my heart. I am sure I turned crimson. I had to look away and have a glass of water to calm myself.

Then I introduced him to my parents and he addressed them as ma'am and sir. His manners were impeccable and he was all charm. I could see that my parents absolutely loved him. They realised that they had a friend in common with his parents, and that friend came over and all of them began chatting.

Sujith too was dressed in formalwear, as was his date, who was tall and lanky and all legs. She had worn a short purple dress and she looked sophisticated, grown-up and smart. I was grateful that I had gone shopping and was glad to be wearing what I was.

Everybody was drinking, having a great time. The professional caterers that my parents hired ensured that the hospitality was top-notch, and waiters moved smoothly through the crowd, refilling glasses and offering starters. The music was great and I had to admit that I was enjoying it all immensely.

I was also having wine officially, for the first time. We had of course had alcohol secretly lots of time in our school, hiding from the nuns. But it felt great to be having a drink openly, with one's parents.

Now, at thirty-four, I can tell you that if you combine teenagers, alcohol and a strong mutual attraction, the result can only be sex. But at eighteen, had someone told me that I would be having sex for the first time in my life, on my birthday, in my own room, while my parents were busy partying with a hundred other guests, I would never have believed them

But that was how it happened. By then I was high on my second glass of wine, and I think Ankush was having whiskey. If it was his third or fourth, I don't know. All I knew was that I wanted him. I was desperate for him. I lured him upstairs into my bedroom, on the pretext of showing him the new music system that my parents had gifted me that day. I had set it to play the Boyz II Men hit *I'll Make Love to You*. In retrospect I cringe at how cheesy my choice of music was back then. But at that point in time I loved the song and it expressed how I felt perfectly.

He smiled as soon as he heard it and said, 'But this was my move. I was supposed to take you up to my room, and play you this song, and try to seduce you.'

'That won't be necessary,' I said as I grabbed him, shut the door and kissed him hard.

That was all he needed. After that he was unstoppable.

Doing it for the first time is made out to be such a big deal, all the time. I can tell you with all honesty that it is nothing like what it is made out to be. It is a myth and hype that one feels heavenly, out of the world and something inside you awakens. In reality, after that kiss which transported me to heaven, and after we got into bed and slipped out of our clothes, it was a little clumsy.

'Hey, are you sure about this?' he had the grace to ask.

'Yes, yes and yes,' I whispered and pulled him closer, burying my face in his chest, inhaling his perfume. God, I loved this guy.

He seemed to know what he was doing. More than I did, anyway. I thought our bodies would fit effortlessly like pieces of a jigsaw puzzle, but it took a few awkward thrusts from his side, and I clutched his back and tried to enjoy it as he made love to me.

And it hurt.

I was sore when it was over and he was apologetic.

'So sorry—I didn't know it was your first time, otherwise I would have been careful,' he said.

'It was great,' I lied.

I was so happy that day. We quickly tidied up in the bathroom before anyone discovered us, and rejoined the others. Nobody suspected a thing.

After that Ankush met me regularly. I think deep down I suspected that it was only because he wanted to sleep with me, but I was so besotted with him, that I was okay even with that. I was so madly in love with him, I just wanted him any which way.

One time I tried to ask him about what Manav had said. His response was to pull me closer and kiss me on the lips.

When we pulled apart he said, 'What do you think? That I two-time? I see you and then go and see someone else?'

I kissed him back and that was the end of that discussion.

I never asked Manav why he had told me what he had.

Maybe Suchi was right. But I didn't want to know.

College was so different from school that I felt lost. The Gothic architecture of the college building itself was awe-inspiring. It felt more like a Victorian palace than a college. Most of the kids in my class had already seen some of the ads I had featured in and I could hear the hushed whispers when I walked in for the first time. I was not the kind to make friends easily. Had it been Suchi, she would have chatted nineteen to the dozen and would have had at least ten party invitations by the end of the day. But here I was, one month into college, and I'd hardly spoken to anyone. I think the guys were in awe of me, and the girls probably thought I was stuck up and snooty.

My shoots were scheduled after college hours, and Ankush would accompany me to them. He had by now finished his course, and had a couple of months before leaving for New South Wales, which was where he had been accepted. After I was done with the shoot, we would go back to his dad's house.

I loved his room. It had an entire wall done up with framed posters of many well-known Hollywood movies. Ankush told me proudly that they were all original posters. I loved lying in his bed, which was an antique with intricate wooden carvings. It was set by the window and if I looked out, I could see the Arabian Sea, lashing out, the waves beating against the rocks and then receding only to return again. I loved his wooden desk. And most of all I loved the way he took off his shirt and looked at me like I was the most beautiful woman on earth.

After the first time, it didn't feel so awkward, and Ankush was sensitive and kind. He never once told me though that he loved me or that I meant anything to him. I was too afraid to ask. I did not want to spoil anything between us, and so our little arrangement continued. The topic of his girlfriend, which Manav had mentioned, seemed so irrelevant now. I was content just getting time with him. He was with me, and to me that was all that mattered.

I couldn't explain this to either Suchi or Manav and I saw no reason to. I don't think anyone who has not longed for a person so much that you are willing to do *anything* just to have even a little time with them, will understand how it feels. You crave for their company, long for a little time with them and are content even if they throw you tiny morsels of affection. You are afraid to want more, terrified that you may end up losing what you have. And so you cling desperately to the moments you do have, and that is what I was doing.

Looking back, I was perhaps substituting sex for love and the two are never the same. But the way Ankush quivered, and called my name over and over, and the way he held me later, and the way we curled up together, it had to mean *something*, didn't it? That is what I kept telling myself.

I appeared on the cover of *Glamour* exactly eight months after my first modelling job. It was the Freshest Face of the Year contest, and my agency had sent in my pictures. Suchi had joined her college in the US by then. When she heard that I had won, she called from there and screamed excitedly, saying that she was so thrilled for me. International calls were very expensive then and she had to hang up quickly. But I was elated that she had called.

My mother was over the moon and she called all the ladies in her circle as well as Neelanjana aunty, who she normally never called unless it was something important. They were all ecstatic and I basked in the glory of my victory.

After that, my career sky-rocketed like a jet plane taking off. I did several more print ads, and then I also appeared in a few music videos. Acting in them was much more difficult than doing the television ads. But I was a quick learner. Though I was fairly good at all of this, I did not enjoy it. It had been something that I was almost pushed into. The initial excitement had long worn off and now it was just work.

But what made me happy was the money. The amount I earned was incredible. I hadn't realised that modelling was so lucrative and paid this much. It was my first job and I was earning in lakhs. I felt I was the luckiest person on earth to have got this much fame and money. So many women dreamt of this—and here I was, having achieved it almost effortlessly.

Ankush said we should throw a party to celebrate. We never did.

Six weeks later, at the pinnacle of my career in modelling, I discovered I was pregnant.

Chapter 11

It hadn't even occurred to me that I might be pregnant. I was tired all the time but I attributed it to too many shoots and too much work. I seemed to have no energy left for anything, and on the days that I didn't have shoots, I would reach home and collapse on the bed. Some days I was too tired to even chat with Manav. Now that Suchi was in the US time zone, chatting with her was reserved for weekends—and most of my weekends were packed with shoots. Hence, we limited our contact to casual mails.

One morning while I was at college, I felt so nauseous that I had to excuse myself from a lecture and run to the restroom to throw up. I just couldn't sit in class and the lecturer suggested that I take the day off. When I came home, my mother wasn't there, but she had a mobile phone and I called her. She said she was at a charity meeting and she would come home as soon as it got over. By the time she reached, I was feeling better, but she insisted that we see a doctor.

I didn't want to. I told her that I was just tired and overworked, and needed some rest. But she said that we would go anyway, as she felt I needed more vitamins. She felt I was looking drawn and pale. She said it could be the haemoglobin levels and the doctor would be able to tell.

Dr Shah was our family physician and we'd all had gone to him for ages. He knew my parents even before I was born. He had a private clinic in one part of his flat, where he saw a limited number of patients. He had long retired from Breach Candy Hospital, but he was still on their board of consultant doctors. My mother called him and he said he could see us immediately, as there were no patients right then.

We left at once, and when he saw us, the first thing he did was to congratulate me on all my success. He said his wife and he were both very proud and that he had mentioned it to his daughter too, who had passed on her congratulations.

After he examined me, he said he wanted to speak to me in private and asked my mother if she would mind waiting outside. When we were alone, he said, 'When was the last time you got your period?'

That was when a cold fear gripped me. When I thought back and calculated the date, I realised that it was more than twenty days late now. I had a very regular cycle usually, and I would get it on the twenty-eighth day. But I had been so busy that I hadn't even realised it was late.

'I did not want to say this in front of your mother, but if you have been sexually active, I think we might have to go for a pregnancy test,' he said.

I wished the earth would open up and swallow me. I was mortified. But he was looking at me and waiting for an answer.

I was silent for a minute. How in the world do you tell a family doctor who has been seeing you since you were a child, that yes, I have been having regular sex.

'See, the thing is, unless we know the cause of the nausea,

we might be administering the wrong treatment. So it is important to treat the cause, not the symptoms,' he said.

I thought for a bit and then I said, 'But we did use protection.'

'No method is fool-proof. Every time you have sex there is a chance that you might get pregnant. Condom failure is very common and if you are on the pill, in case you forgot to take it, that also might affect the cycle, and increase the risk of pregnancy,' he said.

There was no way out of this mess. I had made my bed, and now it was time to lie in it.

'I guess I will have to do the test then. But I do not want to tell my mother,' I said.

'I will leave that choice to you. But she will ask me what's wrong. I can tell her to discuss it with you. You are an adult now and it is your choice whom to share information with. As a doctor I will maintain confidentiality. But as a family friend, I would strongly recommend that you speak to your mother. This is not an issue you can handle alone,' he said.

He was right. But I didn't know how to face my mother.

When I went outside, she looked so worried and that frightened me even more.

'Is everything okay, baby?' she asked, her voice full of worry and concern.

I surprised myself by bursting into tears. I was not used to kindness, care and solicitude from my mother.

That made her even more worried. She held me till the sobs subsided.

'What happened? Shall I speak to Dr Shah?' she said.

'No, let's go home, I will tell you,' I said and she followed me out.

She held my hand in the car all the way home. I could

see how anxious she was. Maybe she thought that I had a terminal disease and didn't want to tell her there. Maybe she was praying. I had never seen her like this. Also, my mother had never held my hand. Not even as a child. She was always too busy for me, and now I was having a difficult time getting used to a mother who was around.

When we reached home, I said, 'Ma, here is the thing. I might be pregnant. We will have to do a pregnancy test. Dr Shah has prescribed it.'

I will forever remember the look on her face as her expression slowly changed from a look of worry to one of horror and shock, as what I had just said slowly sunk in.

For a while she did not speak. She went to the dining table, sat down and poured herself a glass of water. She was taking deep breaths. As though trying to calm herself down.

I felt anger, sadness, pain and fright all in equal measure. I knew logically it was my choice, my body and I hadn't done anything wrong. Yet, I felt that I had let her down terribly.

'Why? What was the need? And who is it? That boy who came home?' she asked.

'Yes Ma, and I ... I love him.'

At least I think it is love.

'Eighteen and you love him?' she spat out the words.

'Is there an age for love?' I shot back.

'What the hell do you know of love, Vipasha? How in the world can you sleep with someone in the name of love? How ... how could you?'

'The same way you cheated on Dad and slept with whoever you slept with.'

There are some truths you should never say. No matter how much it bothers you, no matter how much you want to blurt it out, no matter how important you think it is to say it, it is best buried, suppressed, killed. Saying the truth out loud will only cause a pain so lacerating, so wounding that it will be impossible to heal. But I was too young, frightened and in a massive state of shock to comprehend that. I wished the instant I said them that I could take them back. And tell her that I didn't mean them. That the words had come out harsher than I'd intended. But I was angry and hurt. I was lashing out. I was defending myself.

As much as I didn't want it, the words were out now. I had spoken the unspeakable.

And the effect that it had on my mother was hard to witness. Her shoulders slumped. She opened her mouth to speak and then she swallowed. She said nothing. I watched her as she went pale. And then she left the room.

I wanted to call out to her, to tell her that I was sorry. To tell her it was all a terrible mistake. But I found that I couldn't speak.

I went to my room and I lay down on my bed. I did not recognise the animal-like sound that came from my throat. It was a primitive cry of pain. A hollow wail. I was weeping for the little girl who had been sent away to boarding school because she had discovered her mother was having an affair. I was weeping for the child who had craved a mother who was there for her. I was weeping for the little baby that might be growing inside me. I was weeping because I was scared, confused, hurt. I had suppressed all that I felt this far and now it seemed as though all the sorrow inside me had exploded. I couldn't stop it anymore. I needed my mother now more than ever, and once again she had walked away—and this time too, I was responsible.

When I had exhausted myself crying, I got up and washed my face. Then I went to the phone and called Ankush.

'What the fuck, Vee, we used protection,' he said.

'Yes, but it may have failed. Anyway, nothing is confirmed yet. But I have to take the pregnancy test tomorrow morning.'

'Why can't you take it now?'

'Because the doctor said it has to be the first urine that should be given as a sample, for accurate results.'

'Oh... Shit... This is terrible, Vee. What a bummer. Hell, I'm sorry.'

'Don't be. It wasn't as though I didn't know what I was doing.'

'Yes, but we didn't plan this. We were so darn careful. Damn.'

'You can never be too careful in these things. That's what the doctor said.'

'Does your mom know?'

'Who do you think took me to the doctor? She isn't talking to me now.'

'Damn. Hell. I wish I could do something.'

He could. He could have come home and put his arms around me and told me that everything was going to be fine. He could have come and hung out with me and told me that we would get through this together. He could have cheered me up a little bit by continuing to talk to me.

Instead, he hung up after telling me to let him know.

The test came out positive. I think I was hoping somehow that it would not. That it was just stress that had caused my period to be late. I was hoping that it would just be a scare, and that everything would go back to the way it was. But that was not to be.

My mother's face was grim as we drove back together. When we got back home, I went straight to my room. I sat on my bed for a very long time, and started thinking.

I could hear my mother on the phone. She was yelling and I listened. She was speaking to my dad. They were blaming each other now.

'If only you made the time to stay at home a bit more and be a real father to her, instead of the absentee father that you are now,' she was yelling.

He must have made similar accusations, for she now said, 'Much more than you, anyway. You better take the first flight home now. This isn't a joke.'

I stayed in my room the entire day and did not speak to her at all. I thought long and hard about what was happening. On one hand I had a career, which I did not much enjoy. After the initial excitement of being photographed and appearing on billboards, it wasn't anything much. It was just a job. Though I had earned quite a bit from it.

On the other hand, there was a real, live child growing inside me. I did some quick mental calculations. I could provide for the baby for at least two or three years. I wouldn't have to work. I had a nice nest egg. After that, I didn't know what I would do, but I was certain that I would be able to do *something*. Yes, I had definitely not planned for this baby. But then I hadn't planned for a career in modelling either.

That had just happened. The same way this had happened too.

After I got over the initial shock of actually being pregnant, I began feeling a flutter of excitement. The only time I had thought about babies and things like that was in biology class, when I had thought about what a marvellous thing nature is—that one human being grows inside another. Now it was happening to me.

I switched on the computer, went online, and began reading up about girls who got pregnant when they were teens and the ones who decided to keep their babies. There were many such stories. They were heart-wrenching. In all of them, there was one common factor—that the baby meant something to them. It was the same for me and I instantly felt a kinship with all these girls. They were all from foreign countries though. None from India. That was only natural, given that having a baby out of wedlock was such a big taboo in our culture. But that did not bother me much.

The more I read, the more convinced I was that keeping the baby was an option. The more I thought about it, the more convinced I became that it was what I wanted to do. I would have this baby. There was no other option as far as I was concerned.

My father arrived later that day.

It was only when both of them called me to 'have a talk' that I realised how firm I was about not getting rid of the baby. But my parents had different views. They were now talking about where to get the abortion done. They hadn't even asked me what I wanted. They had decided that it was best to get rid of it. No way was I consenting to that.

This was my body, my baby, my choice and my life.

'You both don't get it,' I said. 'I am keeping this baby.'

They tried their best to talk me out of it.

That was exactly what Ankush had done too, when I had told him about the test results coming out positive. He was certain that the baby would be an interference in our life.

What was 'our life' anyway? Furtive meetings at his house? He was headed to New South Wales for his course. Where did that leave me? He also made it clear that he was not ready to be a father. I felt differently though. If he wanted to walk away, it was his choice. I couldn't force him to stay. But I had made up my mind.

Ankush tried his best to convince me that it was 'just a foetus' and it wouldn't feel anything.

'Look Vee, you can't screw up everything simply because you are too pig-headed to see reality,' he said angrily.

'Shut up Ankush. For me this thing growing inside me is what is real. It is a part of you. This is a part of what we shared. It is a gift. I don't care what you think, I am having the baby.'

After that, almost every time I spoke to Ankush on the phone, we fought. He went on and on about how irresponsible and selfish I was being.

How can wanting to have a baby be selfish? He said I was only thinking of myself—what about him, his parents, my parents. I replied that everyone who wanted to be a part of the child's life was welcome. But I was capable of raising the child myself.

Shortly after that I stopped taking his calls. Despite how I felt about him, it was too much negativity for me to handle. They say that pregnancy makes a woman mad. Perhaps it is true. All I knew was that I did not want to hear Ankush going on and on about how crazy it was to try and have this child.

My parents stopped talking to me after that. For them, the choice I was making was incomprehensible. They made it clear that they would have nothing to do with the baby once it was born. I said that I was okay with that.

I had never planned my life. I never had goals, dreams or ambitions. I had gone along where life had taken me. I was certain that I would find a way.

What it would be like, I didn't know yet.

And I was about to find out.

Chapter 12

My parents, I think, were paranoid about what society would say. So they did not give up easily. Every now and then I would be subjected to a 'talk', which was what I termed these sessions. I don't think my parents had ever spoken to me this much my entire lifetime. I was now getting the attention that I'd craved all these years, but it was not the kind that I wanted. The more they tried to convince me that it was a bad idea to have a baby, the more determined I became. We had countless rounds of arguments, talks, threats. I wouldn't budge. In the end they gave up on me and let me have my way. I was too adamant, too head-strong and so darn sure that I would have my baby, come what may.

My mother had boasted to all and sundry about her daughter's modelling career. How could she now tell them that she was expecting a baby and had every intention of giving birth to it and marriage wasn't even on the cards? It would be the ultimate scandal in the society she moved in. My mother made it clear that I was not to publicise it or speak of it. She also emphatically stated that she wasn't going to tell anyone in her circles about my pregnancy. She wanted me away from Mumbai, away from prying eyes and wagging tongues.

Honestly I didn't care much. I was in a state of excitement, mixed with nervousness, and also trying hard to cope with all the unwelcome things like nausea, tiredness and general mood-swings which a pregnancy brings. I bought a book on mother and baby care. The book had real photos, and showed the changes that would take place every week during the pregnancy. It explained in great detail what to expect, what the body would undergo, how many times check-ups were needed and a whole lot of other things. I began devouring it hungrily. It soon became my bible and I would every now and then look up things in the book. I was amazed that, right now, my baby was just the size of a pip! How is it possible, I thought. A couple of weeks later, it would be the size of a grapefruit.

My baby was my new project and I threw myself entirely into it, the way I had thrown myself into modelling. The funny thing was, I was happy about it.

My parents decided that they would arrange for me to have the baby at a hospital in Kodaikanal. There was a convent situated in an ancient twenty-acre property, which also had a hospital right in its precincts. My father said that Dr Shylaja, who headed the gynaecology and obstetrics department at the hospital, was one of the best in the country and that I was in good hands there. He knew people connected with this institution and all of it was arranged briskly with just a few hushed phone calls. My parents had decided that it was where I would live till the time of delivery. I did not have a choice or a say in the matter. I was okay with that, as all I cared about was that I was keeping my baby.

It was a beautiful campus, full of trees and greenery. It also had a seminary. Dad had a couple of close friends in Kodaikanal, with whom he was in business with as well. Kodai was a place that they were familiar with and comfortable in. That had partly been the reason they had chosen to send me to boarding there. Now, it had the added advantage of being far removed from their circles in Mumbai. I found it ironic that just six months back I had been a student here, and now I was a college drop-out, having a baby at a hospital not far from my school.

I don't know how I would have got through those days, had it not been for Suchi's and Manav's calls and the library that I discovered, within walking distance from the convent campus. It was a moderate, privately-owned one, a part of a well-known chain, where one had to pay reading charges per book. I did not mind at all. They would let you keep the book for about two weeks, and the plan that I opted for allowed me to borrow five books at a time. It was here that I re-discovered my love for books. Through books, I explored other worlds, other ideas and different minds. Most times I would go through one book a day. Sometimes, it would take me two or three days, but the maximum a book lasted was not more than four days.

I had a lot of time on my hands and so I fell into the world of books. I read and read and read some more. I discovered the old classics. I devoured Charles Dickens, Jane Austen, Hemingway and Orwell. I read the newer authors like Arthur Hailey and Irving Wallace. I read books about women, books about history, stories of courage, autobiographies, and many more. They inspired me. They gave me perspectives I had never thought of. I read every single thing that I could lay my hands on—even if the authors were not well known or famous. I began seeing the world through their eyes. I read a novel about a childless couple and their several attempts at having a baby, and how much they longed for it. When the wife gave birth, after many years of waiting, the child was a stillborn. It made me cry and I felt I was so very fortunate to have this baby. I began going to the convent chapel to pray that my baby would be healthy and that everything would go well.

The nuns at the seminary were used to me by now, and apart from the usual pleasantries, they asked me no questions. This was like an exile, an isolated life. There was no television on the premises and my only form of entertainment was the long walks that I took, and the books that I read. I also began spending time at the orchid garden maintained by the nuns, which housed more than three hundred varieties of orchid plants. It was breathtakingly beautiful and being there filled me with a sense of peace. The convent had four dogs and they followed me around. It reminded me of my school days, and I would feed them, just like I had in school.

There was a common telephone in the hall leading to the rooms, and Manav called almost every other day without fail. Suchi called every weekend. When I had first mailed Suchi about the baby, she had freaked out. She, like the others, had tried to tell me what a bad idea it was. I told her that I had stopped taking Ankush's calls, and if she went on about this, I would need some space from her too. I think that hurt her a bit. She did not mail or call for three weeks after that. Then she called, and by then she had accepted my decision, even though she probably didn't understand it.

I had no access to the Internet, otherwise I would have emailed and chatted with Suchi and Manav. And because there was no access to the net, I began writing them letters by hand, which I would send by post at the post office on my daily walks. I was familiar with the area, having studied there. I never bumped into anyone from my school, even though each time I went out for a walk, I expected to. I had decided that if I came across anyone, I would tell them the truth—that I had dropped out of college to have my baby.

Suchi never replied to any of my letters. When she called she would mention that she had received a letter, but that her course work at college kept her so busy she was unable to reply. Manav would send me cards in response to each and every letter of mine.

'I can't write like you do, hope this makes up for it,' he once wrote in one of the cards.

In another he wrote, 'Yesterday is but a dream and tomorrow is a vision, But today well lived can make every yesterday a dream of happiness and every tomorrow a vision of hope.'

The words made me think. I was sure hopeful of tomorrow. I did not know whether I had lived well or not, but I knew that I was doing exactly what I wanted to do. For now, that was enough.

In another, he wrote, 'It happens for a reason.' I loved that card. It had a picture of sunlight shining bright through the dense foliage of trees. I stuck that on the wall facing my bed, so that I could look at it over and over.

I clung to both Suchi and Manav. I wrote to them regularly and they were both very understanding and supportive. Ammu aunty, after getting over the initial shock of my pregnancy and my decision to have the baby, became an ally. She too called me regularly and I found comfort in talking to her. She was always patient, offered helpful tips, and regularly pepped me up.

I was thankful for tiny blessings that came in the form of friends.

Manav called one morning to say that he had a dry run at his management institute. I asked him what a dry run was and he explained it to me. He said since he was in the final year of his course, about eighty to ninety companies would visit the campus for placements and the entire procedure would happen over one week. This meant twenty companies a day would be at the campus. The placement committee had to make sure that each company got to interview its shortlisted candidates. Though it sounded simple, it was a huge operation, as they had to ensure that each candidate got to interview with each company that he/she had got a notification from. It had to go perfectly, as nobody would tolerate their chances of landing a coveted job in a particular company getting screwed up because of logistics. So to ensure there were no mistakes, a handpicked team of fifteen people had dry runs, the simulation of the placement process, on a daily basis, two months in advance. The place-com (the placement committee) would pick these fifteen people and they would also make sure that the senior control team, which was the batch that was getting placed, taught the junior control team the whole process, as they would be doing it the following year. A chart would display a record of who would be where, at what time and it had to be updated constantly, on the basis of what was happening, who was being interviewed, how long the interview was expected to last and all of that.

It was after that conversation with Manav that I began to increasingly feel that I had lost out on a good education. Manav would talk about so many things, and I yearned for the kind of knowledge that he was getting. Also he would soon be placed and he would be earning well. Meanwhile, Suchi was pursuing the course of her dreams and she would have a career too, when she graduated. Almost everyone who was my age was in college, and here I was holed up in a convent in Kodaikanal, waiting to give birth to a baby. I wasn't even a graduate. In school, I was as smart as Suchi, or perhaps smarter. But now I felt terribly inadequate, and for a few weeks I didn't speak to either Suchi or Manav. I didn't know how to explain it—whether they would even understand. After all, this was a choice I had made.

I missed Ankush like crazy. I longed to speak to him. I wanted to tell him about my pregnancy—about how it was progressing smoothly, about how I had adapted to life at the convent, about the books I read, about my walks and a lot more. But I could neither send him a mail nor could I call him. I knew from Manav that he had already left for Australia, for his course. Manav did not tell me anything more about Ankush, nor did I ask. What could I have said anyway? It wasn't like Ankush was going to change his mind about the baby.

One day when Manav called, I couldn't contain myself and asked why he had said that Ankush had a girlfriend. Manav was quiet for a while. Then he said that he had seen Ankush with someone at a coffee shop but he wasn't certain.

'What? You weren't certain and yet you told me so casually? How could you do that?'

'I don't know, Vee. I felt I had to tell you. I am sorry,' he said.

There wasn't anything I could say after that. He had apologised. Besides, it was not as if I'd broken up with Ankush because of what Manav said. And Manav had been such a devoted friend. So I let it go.

My mother had stopped calling me completely. I felt miserable about it but there was nothing I could do. As long

I was a model, appearing regularly on magazines and such things, she was happy to show me off. The moment I made a decision to have a baby, she had shunned me. What kind of a mother was she? I could not understand how a mother could be so selfish. None of my friends had mothers like mine. In one of the books that I read, there was a lady who abandoned three children and ran away to pursue her career in Broadway. If my mother had done this for a reason, I could at least try to understand that she was chasing her dreams. Here, it seemed to be just pure selfishness and nothing else. There was no other way to explain her behaviour. For her, she came first. I swore that when I had my baby, I would never do to my child what my mother had done to me. I would be a hands-on mother. I would be involved in everything that my child did. I would never send my child away to a boarding school, no matter how prestigious it was or how great the education. I would read a lot to my child, would do things with him/her, and would be a firm but kind mother. There were so many things that I planned.

My father, on the other hand, called each week without fail, and I was very surprised. He had never called me while I was in school. He seemed to be worried and enquired about my health each time, asked if I was okay, asked if the food at the convent was agreeing with me and asked if I needed anything.

One day, both my parents landed up in Kodai. It was a pleasant surprise. I met them in the visitor's hall, as visitors were not allowed inside the convent. It was odd meeting them, as by then I was in my sixth month of pregnancy and I was beginning to show a little bit.

My father was very emotional and I had never seen him like that. I think there were tears in his eyes. He hugged me and asked if I was okay and I managed to nod. I had to hold back my tears too. My mother hardly spoke. I think she was still angry. They took me out to one of the nicest restaurants in Kodai, which had a terrace that overlooked a valley full of Kurunji flowers that had just started blooming. These flowers are found only in the Nilgiris and they are beautiful. The hotel staff asked us whether we would like to sit indoors or on the terrace, and my father opted for the terrace from where we could have a view of the hills. They set us up at a table amidst the terrace garden under a pergola which was full of many varieties of bougainvillea in bloom. It was a profusion of colours—orange, white, pink—and it felt right out of a picture-postcard. The sun was mild and there was a cool breeze blowing. It was a wonderful change from the convent. The meal that we ordered was fabulous and exotic. At the end of it, I excused myself to go the restroom, which I was doing a lot these days, one of the side effects of pregnancy, and when I was walking back, I couldn't help overhearing the conversation between my parents. They had no idea that their voice carried across clearly and I could hear every word being said.

'But you can't just forbid her from coming home. Come on, she is our child and we have to be there for her,' Dad was saying.

'I have had enough. I am tired of this. What if something happens to her? Or the baby? What if we have to re-live that whole nightmare again? You know what we went through and I can't face it again. Hell—I know how hard it is. What the hell does she even know about raising a child? If she is a child, she should listen to us. She had a great career going and she was doing so well.'

I stood rooted to the spot, unable to move. So, my mother

thought that having me was a nightmare? That was so darn hard to hear. Her words hit me like an axe to my chest. That explained a lot. I felt faint and I held on to a chair that was right next to me and sat down. The noise of the chair moving alerted my father and when he saw me sitting inside, he rushed to my side and asked if I was okay.

I said that I just needed a glass of water, that I'd felt faint, and hence had sat down. He signalled to the waiter for water, and after I gulped it down, he escorted me back to our table. I was having a hard time keeping my emotions hidden.

I don't think my parents realised that I had overheard the conversation. My father asked if I wanted to come back home and have the baby there. He said that they would both be okay with it, and they would support me. My mother looked away as he said it.

I took a deep breath and then told him that I did not want to do that. I said I had adjusted to my life at the convent. Also, Mumbai held too many memories for me—I would be reminded of my modelling days, the shoots, the places I went to with Ankush, Suchi and Manav. All of it seemed like another lifetime now.

Strangely my father understood, and after the meal, they dropped me back at the convent. My father hugged me and this time I could not hold back the tears. He said he would be in touch regularly and to call him anytime, if I changed my mind. I told him I would be fine. Then he handed me a gift—it was a mobile phone. It was already activated and he said he would take care of the bills.

My mother had not said a word all this time. She said 'bye' as she got into the taxi with my father. She never looked back, even though I stood there, waving to my father, as the car turned round the bend, went down the hill, becoming a small speck, barely visible.

Later I thought that it was like my life was divided into two parts. Part one was over and the curtains had come down. Part two was what was waiting to happen.

Chapter 13

If you asked me to list all the life experiences I have had till now in the order of most ecstatic to the least, I would say that the moment of giving birth to my son is undoubtedly the happiest moment of my life. It was the most awe-inspiring, humbling and the single most powerful experience I have ever gone through. I had never thought I would give birth alone, though. I honestly expected at least my father to be there, if not my mother.

But my father was in the UK, and though he had expected to get back in time for the birth, that was not to be. Ammu aunty arrived the day after I delivered. That was a big surprise. I was overjoyed to see her. Once she came, she quietly took charge and allowed me to rest. She said she would stay with me for three or four days, and then return to Kerala. She also said that Suchi was coming the following week to India for about fifteen days, as she was between semesters. I was so happy.

Manav called and said he had succeeded in getting placed in a company called Futures Capital, in Bangalore. He had narrowly missed getting selected by HUL, which was what he had been hoping for. He had made it to the final round of three shortlisted candidates though.

'Congratulations on the placement,' I said.

'And congratulations to you on an even bigger placement in life. I cannot believe you are now a mother,' he said.

'I can scarcely believe it myself. But you just have to look at him, Manav. He is so darn tiny. He is like a little doll. His hands look so fragile but he grips my finger so tightly. He is simply amazing.'

'God—I have to see him, Vee. But I guess I will come once your parents and the early visitors leave. That way, when the initial excitement dies down, you will still have some company.'

'Since when did you become so thoughtful?' I asked him.

'I have always been thoughtful when it came to you,' he replied, and that brought tears to my eyes. This whole giving birth business turns you into a mush of hormones and I got teary-eyed so easily those days. It was as though I was viewing the world in a new light. Till now, life had been all about I-me-myself, and now I was completely responsible for every single thing this tiny human being who was entirely dependent on me, needed. It overwhelmed me.

My parents arrived the next evening. This was the first time my mother was meeting Ammu aunty, even though they had over the years spoken to each other on the phone. The contrast between them couldn't have been more stark. Ammu aunty was holding my son (god, it gave me goose bumps just to be able to say that) when my parents walked in. Her grey curly hair was slightly dishevelled and she had knotted it into her usual careless bun. She had also tucked her pallu to one side and did not care much that her cotton saree was slightly crumpled. She was cooing to the baby and it seemed as though he was smiling. My mother wore an immaculate, white, lace, expensive dress, matching high heels, designer diamonds.

When she greeted Ammu aunty I could sense the disdain on her face. Thankfully Ammu aunty was blissfully unaware.

'You have a beautiful grandson. Congratulations. Meet your grandmother,' said Ammu aunty, still talking softly to the baby, and greeting my mother at the same time.

'Goodness, no. I don't want to be called "Grandmother". It makes me feel so old. Besides, we haven't decided about the baby, have we?' said my mother.

I was outraged. What did she mean by that? Ammu aunty was absorbed in the baby, and I don't think she heard.

'Thank you for coming. But if you don't mind, can we have a word privately with our daughter?' said my mother.

'Of course,' said Ammu aunty. She said she would wait outside and walked out with the baby.

I was furious with my mother. She should have spoken to Ammu aunty a little better and not treated her like house-help. She could have, at the very least, thanked her for coming here and looking after me.

'What the hell, Ma. How could you ask her to step out?'

'God, Vipasha—you are too young. How will you handle this?' said my mother, ignoring me.

'I will manage,' I said.

'I think it is best if we give it up for adoption. See, it is still not too late. I have made enquiries, and I know places.'

I was speechless. Shocked, that she could even suggest it. She hadn't understood me at all. Couldn't she see that, for me, this baby was the most precious thing I had ever had? He was my treasure, my joy, my world, my everything now. Couldn't she tell from the way I was so possessive and protective about him? This was the first time in my life that I had been certain about anything. I wanted this child. But what could you explain to a person who refused to see?

'Look Ma, I know you do not approve, but I am keeping my baby. You can be sure that I won't ever come to Mumbai and live with you, if that is what you are worried about. I will raise him, I will manage. Now I suggest you just leave. It is time for the baby's feed.'

My mother looked at me and then walked out without a word.

My father stayed back.

'Whatever you decide, it is fine. I just want you to be comfortable. Anything you need, any amount of money you need, just ask me. I have set up a bank account in your name and will keep making deposits. I want you to be comfortable. It is not easy, raising a baby alone.'

'No Dad, I do not want your money. It is okay. I will manage. I haven't yet figured out how, but I will,' I said.

'Anyway, here are the bank account papers. Everything pertaining to the new account, including the ATM card, is there. Anytime you want, please withdraw money. Please take care Vipasha, and look after yourself,' he said, as he placed a large envelope bulging with papers on the table beside the bed. Then he kissed me on the forehead.

I nodded. But I was certain that I would never use my parents' money. I had a tidy sum from my modelling. I would invest that and use the interest while I did something to earn money. I had chosen to be an adult and I didn't want any charity—not even from my parents. This was one thing I was determined about.

Ammu aunty came back with the baby.

'All okay?' she asked.

'Yes, everything is fine. Don't worry about it,' said my dad. He thanked her for coming and looking after me and then he took my son from her and carried him. It was very hard not to cry. I did not fight back the tears. I had never seen my father like that, and the tenderness I saw in his eyes as he looked at his grandson that day is something that is forever etched in my memories.

'Have you decided what you want to name him?' asked my dad.

'Aryan,' I said. I had decided on it a couple of months back. If it was a boy, I would name him Aryan, and if it was a girl, she would be Mallika. I liked old-fashioned, traditional names.

'Aryan, the noble, illustrious one. A good choice,' said my father, and I smiled.

It is quite strange how human relationships pan out. Throughout my childhood, and while in school, my father was just a figure who breezed in and out of my life as he zipped around the world for his business meetings. Now he was making an effort to bridge the gap of so many years with me. I could see that my pregnancy and the birth of the baby had touched something deep inside him, as well as my mother. The only difference was that both of them were handling it very differently. He was embracing it, welcoming it, and she was running away.

'So the arrangement with the convent was only for till such time that the baby was born. I think it is best if you come back home with me, Vipasha. Aryan needs all the care now. The first two years are the hardest,' Dad was firm.

'No Dad. I don't want to.'

'If it is about your mother, I will make her understand.'

'I don't want to come back. I want to give this child the best of what I can. I want him to be raised in an atmosphere of love—where he is welcomed, wanted. Home is not the best place, Dad.'

Ammu aunty immediately said that I could stay with her in Kerala.

'My home has seen the birth of at least eighteen children. Everyone in the family, including Suchi's father, was born there. The wooden cradle which has been passed down for generations is still there. And do you know, we used the same cradle for Suchi and all her brothers?'

Till this day, I am yet to come across a more generous soul than Ammu aunty. In the end I convinced my dad that it would be okay if I stayed with them, till I figured out what I wanted to do and how I would manage.

While I was pregnant, I had thought about it, and my plan had been to put the baby in a crèche when he or she was about four months old and then take up a job. But I know now that the decision had stemmed out of ignorance. I did not know how powerfully gripping maternal instinct can be. This comes to the fore only when the baby is born. I now felt like a mother lion, fiercely protecting her cub. I couldn't imagine leaving him in anyone's care. And so I ended up spending the first year of Aryan's life in Kerala, in Suchi's home. The large ancestral home, in a tiny village in Kerala, where Suchi and I had spent so many summers, giggling, growing up, sharing secrets that only the closest friends do, was now also home to my son. Suchi said it was the most awesome thing to have ever happened, and she was delighted about it.

Because Suchi's parents were very well off, they had tons of help around. The best part was that everyone loved Aryan. He soon became the favourite of every single person there. A little child transforms everyone, and even the grumpiest and the oldest house-help stopped by to smile at Aryan. They all took turns carrying him, walking him around the large rubber estate, showing him cows, goats, butterflies, millipedes and many insects which are common when you live on an estate in a forest. It was the most peaceful time of my life. I had never felt this loved, this welcomed, and I couldn't have asked for a better home for Aryan.

Suchi's family had been so kind to me and I wanted to do something for them, in return. I had time on my hands, as I had plenty of help with the baby. After observing how the whole rubber estate worked, I suggested to Ammu aunty that I could help set up a welfare association for all the workers. Uncle felt it was a wonderful idea as, up till then, nothing had been done, apart from the extra incentives in cash given to them during festivals like Onam.

So I worked with Uncle to streamline a welfare scheme. We introduced various things like medical aid, housing subsidy, educational stipend, merit awards and awards for exceptional achievements in sports as well as arts. I did a lot of work and Uncle said that I deserved a salary for all that I had done. Of course, I refused. It was the least I could do for them—after all they were hosting me and Aryan. I hated to think that I was taking charity, and this way I was glad I was able to do something useful for them which benefitted so many labourers and brought down the attrition rate.

Manav had now started working in Bangalore, and he visited me in Ammu aunty's house. She welcomed him and treated him to a scrumptious Kerala meal with thoran, pullisherry and many other delicacies which he loved. I had by now picked up the language, and could converse in it, and Manav was surprised.

'You seem so much at peace here, Vee, and how well you have blended in. Don't you miss your life in Mumbai?' he asked.

I took a moment to reply.

'Strangely, no, Manav. I had never felt great about my modelling career anyway. All of it was so fake, so make-believe. But look at the people here. How warm they are. How genuine. I have never had any of this before. I feel wealthier than when I was making all that money modelling in Mumbai. You are right about your observation. This life does give me my peace,' I replied.

Aryan, who was in Manav's arms, chuckled then, and Manav laughed and said that Aryan would turn out to be a fine young man, and to just look at him—he was already agreeing with his mother. I smiled.

Then I asked Manav about Ankush. After Aryan's birth, I didn't miss him as much as I had when I was pregnant. Aryan kept me occupied all the time. Looking after a baby is such a time-consuming business, and I didn't know when the day started and when it ended. It was an endless round of feeding, bathing, cleaning, sleeping, singing lullabies, walking him around, talking to him, showing him things, and the next day the cycle would start all over again.

Manav said he too was not in regular touch, but he knew that Ankush had completed his course, and decided not to come back. He was working in a recording studio in New South Wales and he was also learning to be a DJ and he seemed to like what he was doing.

'Have you ever mailed him, Vee? You know—to tell him about Aryan's birth?'

Manav had never spoken about Ankush to me before, and neither had Suchi. As far as they were concerned, Ankush was a closed topic. I too had never raised it with either of them, till now.

'As far as I am concerned, anyone who does not want Aryan in their lives does not deserve a place in my life. I don't care, Manav. The day he asked me to get rid of the baby—it was over for me then anyway. Let's not talk about it anymore, please. I won't bring it up again.'

Though I wouldn't admit it to him and even though I had convinced myself that I did not miss Ankush at all, deep down, I still felt a hollow pain when his name was mentioned. It was a dull jab, the kind you feel when you are reminded about something that you have learned to live with simply because there is nothing you can do to change it.

My father visited me thrice while I was in Kerala. He came when Aryan turned three months old, he came again when he was seven months old and was crawling on all fours, and he visited once again on his first birthday, by which time Aryan had learnt to walk. We celebrated it at home by cutting a cake. My mother never called, never visited. My father watched Aryan proudly. Each time he came he would carry extravagant gifts for Ammu aunty and her family, which I thought was a very nice gesture on his part. He would also get many things for Aryan.

It was around this time that I began to think about what I wanted to do next. However much I enjoyed being with Ammu aunty and her family, I knew I couldn't stay there forever. I had to do something with my life. Besides, I was now itching to get going and to resume life. I was getting too comfortable here at Suchi's place, and I couldn't endlessly live with them, even though they were the epitome of kindness. Uncle had now appointed a manager for the labour welfare association that we had set up and hence my role there was very limited.

I wanted my own life now. A life with Aryan as the centre, of course.

There was simply no other way for me.

Chapter 14

Suchi called to tell me that she had just started the third year of her course and one of the requisites was a fifteen-week internship with a landscape architecture firm which would expose the student to professional practice. She also had to submit a final internship portfolio, and an internship assessment letter from the person she interned with. Suchi wanted to do it in India, and she had been accepted at an architectural firm in Bangalore which specialised in landscapes. She was going to rent a service apartment for the duration of her stay, and she urged me to visit Bangalore, along with Aryan. When I mentioned it to Manav, he said I should definitely do so, as it would be a nice change for me and all three of us could get together.

'Actually both of you can stay with me. It is a large apartment, it has two bedrooms and loads of space,' he said.

But Suchi preferred to stay in the service apartment she had found in Indiranagar, as it was very close to her office. Manav lived in Whitefield, and that would mean a forty-five minute commute for Suchi. Both of them took turns in asking me to come to Bangalore and visit them.

'God knows when we will get another chance like this, Vee. Come on, it has been so long,' she said and I decided to go.

Suchi met me at the airport when I arrived. I was shocked to see how much weight she had put on since the last time I'd seen her. She had also dyed her hair a light shade of brown. Aryan had grown so much since she had last seen him, which was when he was only a few weeks old. He had just learnt to run and he was cuteness personified as he tumbled along in that bumbly way that toddlers do.

'Oooooooh—just look at him Vee, isn't he adorable?' she said as she picked him up and kissed him on both cheeks and hugged him tight.

And then she turned towards me. 'And god—look at you, Vee. Not a single soul will say you've given birth to a baby. You have to tell me what you have been doing.'

'Ammu aunty is so sweet. I leave Aryan with her while I jog around the whole estate,' I said smiling. It was true. I had started off by walking, and soon my stamina had increased, and I had begun jogging. The pregnancy pounds had quickly dropped off, and I was now lithe and fit.

'God, in the US everything is so darn large. They don't have any normal sizes for anything. And now look at me—I have become large too. You need to coach me on losing weight, Vee,' she groaned.

It was during that summer internship that Suchi fell in love with Prakash. He was the guy she was interning under, and she declared on day one that he was the most intellectually stimulating guy she had *ever* met.

The next evening Manav came over, and both of us ribbed Suchi about Prakash. We quizzed her endlessly on all the 'intellectually stimulating' things Prakash had told her that day.

'Shut up. I just went for a cup of coffee with him,' she said.

'Oooh, so things have progressed to coffee. Oh my my!

That was quick,' I teased her, using the sing-song voice that we used in school when we discovered who a girl had a crush on.

'What rubbish,' she said. But she blushed and that was a giveaway. Manav immediately pounced on the chance.

'Oh you know—the cup of coffee that we drink—let me tell you intellectually stimulating facts about it. Our brain has adenosine which can only hang out with certain receptors and this makes us drowsy, but when caffeine shows up, it attaches itself to the receptors so that adenosine cannot. The pituitary gland thinks this is an emergency and so it orders the adrenal glands to produce adrenaline. It also bumps up the dopamine levels and hence we get a caffeine high. See Suchi, was that intellectually stimulating enough for you?' asked Manav.

Suchi threw a cushion at him and we all exploded laughing. Aryan did not know what was going on, but seeing the adults laughing, he joined in the laughter. Then he promptly threw a cushion at Manav and that sent us into helpless fits of laughter again.

This was exactly like old times. Manav was in his complete geeky element. The last time we'd had this much fun was at Essel World. Ankush was present then, and it seemed eons ago. It brought a lump to my throat now—here was Ankush's son, laughing with all of us, and I wondered for a moment if Ankush ever even thought of him. Then I pushed the thought out of my head. I was here now with my friends and I did not want to spoil the moment by pondering about the past.

Sometimes, it is best that the past stays buried.

Things between Prakash and Suchi progressed exponentially that summer. Manav and I met him at Suchi's place within four days of her starting her internship. We were both surprised at how fast he had agreed to come over to her apartment, and meet her friends. Looking at both of them together, it was obvious to me at that instant that this was a relationship that was meant to be. It was like they *fitted* well together, like pieces of a puzzle coming together.

He was tall, dark, well-built and had a beard. He had a slow manner of speaking. It was as though he thought a lot before talking. When he spoke, it was in a voice so low that one had to listen carefully to hear him. It was obvious from what he said that the guy was extremely well-read and knowledgeable on a variety of subjects. Suchi had told him all about me, and Prakash said a solemn hello to little Aryan, who promptly put out his hand and ran it over his beard, which made him smile. It was love at first sight between Prakash and Aryan, and to my surprise, Prakash spent a lot of time reading to Aryan from the board books that I'd carried along.

'It's wonderful that you're reading to him at this age. Very few parents do that,' Prakash remarked.

'Oh, I have been reading to him since he was six months old. I love books myself. In fact, I once read a book on pushing human potential and one of the things mentioned in it was early reading and how important it is,' I replied.

'Oh yes, it completely is. It stimulates mental growth and gets those brain cells running,' said Prakash and he went back to reading to Aryan.

Each time Prakash came over, he would spend more and more time with Aryan. I could see that Suchi longed for exclusive attention from him, even though she never said so. I called up Manav and told him how I felt and asked him what he thought. He promptly told me to come and stay with him for a few days.

'You will be doing them a favour,' he said.

I told Suchi that I would like to spend a few days with

Manav too, and Suchi agreed without protesting too much. I think she too sensed that I wanted to give them some space.

Manav had sent me a card that said, 'It happens for a reason', and now I have come to believe that it is true. The reason may not be obvious immediately, but increasingly I feel that we are all pawns in the universe's grand scheme of things. Had I not stayed with Manav that summer, I might never have started Paw-Factor. It was at Manav's home that I got a clear sense of what I wanted to do.

Manav lived on the fourteenth floor of a very large multi-storeyed apartment complex which also housed several offices, including his. Most of the people who stayed in the complex were employed in these offices. The complex had a lovely park for toddlers, and that was where I would take Aryan once Manav left for work. Aryan still needed his morning nap, as well as his nap in the afternoon so, at around eleven-thirty each morning, I would return from the park, bathe him, and then he would go to sleep.

It was during this time, when I sat sipping a cup of tea on Manav's balcony, that I heard the whimpering of a dog. The whines were piteous. It was as though the animal was in trouble. From the sounds, it seemed like it was coming from the flat downstairs. I looked at Aryan and he was still fast asleep. I placed some pillows on either side of him, so that even if he rolled over he wouldn't fall out of bed, and then quickly went downstairs and called out to the security guard in the building and told him about the situation. He said that a single guy lived in the flat below Manav's, and he had got a dog about a month back. I told him that the animal was whimpering, and he came upstairs with me. I took him to the balcony and the cries had grown louder. With a little manoeuvring the guy lowered himself on to the balcony downstairs, from Manav's balcony. I held my breath—if he missed his footing and fell down, it would be a straight drop of fourteen floors. From the balcony, he managed to prise a French window open, and then entered the house. The puppy had wedged its head into the space between the wooden handles of a sofa and was stuck there. The security guy called out to me and told me the situation. He told me to come downstairs and that he would open the door. I went down, and together we managed to free the puppy. It was a Labrador and was adorable. I was afraid to leave the pup alone in the flat and so brought it with me to Manav's house. I asked the security guy to inform the owner when he returned. I gave him two hundred rupees for his efforts. I was so happy that he had helped me rescue the pup. He initially refused to take it and then when I insisted he gratefully pocketed the money. When Aryan woke up from his nap, he was delighted to find a puppy in the living room.

When the owner of the pup returned he was touched and grateful that I had taken the trouble to rescue his pet. He said he was a huge dog lover, and this had been one of his worries when he had got the pup. He, in fact, had a crate for the pup, but that day the pup had managed to get out of it. He told me that it was rare to find someone who cared about animals like I did, and that nobody else would have taken this much trouble to rescue an animal. He was now worried about the pup's safety. I told him that I wouldn't mind looking after the pup while he was at work, and he said that was a big favour and he would hate to impose, and so he offered to pay me for dog-sitting. He said there were several people in this residential complex who needed dog-sitters and it would be a great boon for those who worked, yet wanted to have pets. He said that if I started a dog-sitting service, he would definitely be a regular customer.

That little Labrador pup had inadvertently shown me the way for my new career, if it could be so called. The owner of the pup had given me a lot to think about. When Manav came home that evening, I told him what had happened and also told him what the dog-owner had suggested. I mentioned that I was toying with the idea.

'It is perfect, Vee. You should go for it! There is nothing like this in India right now and you will have the first-mover advantage. Dog-sitting is a huge business in foreign countries, and you can be the pioneer in India,' he said.

The more I thought about it, the more it began to make sense. I did not have any educational qualifications to pursue a corporate job. I did not want to take up modelling anymore. It was tough and demanding, and also I had a child now. Besides, it would mean relocating to Mumbai and staying with my parents and there was absolutely no question of my doing that. I also wanted a job that would allow me to have Aryan around. So dog-sitting it would be.

'Paw-Factor. That is what you should call it. It's a splendid name,' said Manav.

'It sure is unusual. But ... what if it doesn't take off?'

'What if it does?'

'I don't have anything to lose, I guess. And I can't stay with Ammu aunty forever.'

'You can stay here as long as you want, Vee, and I don't even mind you keeping as many dogs as you like.'

'No, Manav. I am done living off other people. During my pregnancy it was at the convent, and after that it was with Ammu aunty. I think it is very generous of you to offer, but you have no idea what you are letting yourself in for. It is so difficult just to have a child in the house. Your lifestyle changes completely. And in addition to a child, there will be the dogs that I am looking after! Please Manav—there is a limit to generosity and friendship. You have your life to live.'

'I mean it, Vee. Stay here with me. I don't just say stuff unless I genuinely mean it, you know.' He seemed a bit hurt.

'I know, Manav, but I just can't. I need to make a life on my own.'

He walked towards me and cupped my face in his hands.

'I … I would love to make a life with you, Vee, if you will let me. I ... I love you.' His words were barely a whisper.

They took me by complete surprise. I didn't know what to say. So I removed his hands and turned away.

How could I tell him that I did not love him that way? That he was a great friend but I could not marry him. I just hadn't thought of him *that* way.

'Just think about it, okay? I don't want an answer straight away. Please do think it over,' he said, and I told him I would, even though I knew that the answer was a clear no.

Manav was a friend—a good, supportive friend. And I hadn't thought of marriage. As far as I was concerned, what I wanted to do was to find my footing in life, and raise my child. I hadn't even found a career yet. I was tired of living with other people. I just wanted a life of my own, with only Aryan and me in it. That was all I wanted. Adding other people would only mean complications.

Next time I met Suchi, it was just the two of us, apart from Aryan of course. I told her I wanted some time alone with her, without Prakash, and we met at her apartment, which is better than meeting at coffee shops or anywhere else when you have a toddler. Suchi and I discussed what had happened at length. Suchi said that Manav was a great guy and I ought to reconsider my choice. I lost my temper with her then.

'Look Suchi—the way I look at it, if I marry Manav even

when I clearly do not love him, then he is just a meal ticket for me. And that is a terrible thing, don't you get it? If I wanted that, I could have easily swallowed my pride and gone back to Mumbai, and lived in the lap of luxury with my parents. But that is not what I chose to do. That is not who I am, Suchi. If my closest friend does not get this, then who will?'

'Sometimes I feel you are much too independent. So what if you are depending on other people? No man or woman is an island, Vee.'

'It is easy for you to say. You have always had the comfort of a family that loves you. It is different for me. I don't want to go back home, nor do I want to exist on the kindness of other people. We all carve our own paths, Suchi, and I have chosen mine.'

'A path where you have thrown away a promising career, dropped out of college, have a baby, and have no visible job prospects.'

She had stated the truth so bluntly and it was hurtful when she hurled it at me like that. Yes, those were the choices I had made. But no matter how close you are, there are some things you never say to a friend, even if you mean well. You never know how much it can wound them, perhaps decimate them.

Though I was hurt, it did not knock me down. I took the punch well.

I told her with firmness that I was clear about what I wanted, and yes, I knew that they might not be conventional choices. In fact, they might not even make sense to her, as it probably wasn't what she would have chosen. But they were important to me and I was sticking to them. Suchi understood, or at least let it go, and she hugged me.

Then she made us both some tea and we relaxed in the

living room talking about men and life. She told me that she was certain that Prakash was 'the one', as far as she was concerned. She would wait for him to make the first move though.

'Fingers crossed, Vee. You never know how these tricky things called relationships can go. One minute you are inseparable, and then things change and you move on,' she said.

'Don't worry, it will all work out. I can just see that you two were meant to be,' I replied and she hugged me again.

When I got back to Manav's place, I thought a lot about my future, and the more I did, the more it seemed like dog-sitting was the way forward. I started spending long hours online, reading about dog-boarding facilities the world over. When Aryan took his naps, I drew up plans of how I would want it to be, the things that had to be taken into account, and the resources I would need.

Manav encouraged me a lot. He said if there was one thing that he had learnt in his business school, it was that you had to be passionate about what you did, and your heart had to be in it. Maybe Manav was right. When I was modelling, my heart wasn't in it, and that was why I hadn't enjoyed it.

That evening, Manav and I took Aryan to the park in his apartment complex and the security guard who had helped me rescue the pup beamed at me.

'See, even the security guard has flipped for you. Everyone falls in love with you, Vee. You are so beautiful and fragile, it just makes every single person want to rush to you and take care of you,' said Manav and smiled.

Except Ankush. It didn't make him want to take care of me. It made him want to run.

I was quiet for a while. The sadness must have immediately

reflected on my face, for Manav said, 'Hey, don't look so forlorn.'

Just then Aryan fell down in the sand and I rushed to pick him up. It saved me from thinking about Ankush and about Manav still wanting to make a life with me.

I simply wasn't ready.

My father flew into Bangalore on business the following week. After Aryan's birth, it was as though he were making plans just so he could see his grandson. I could see the worries and stress being replaced by happiness and joy on my father's face during the time that he spent with Aryan. I was seeing a side of my father that I never knew existed. I wished my mother too would just let go and reconcile to the fact that I was a mother now. Then I would have been happy. But it is rare that you get what you want in life.

I discussed my business plans with my father, and he gave me a splendid idea. The family home that was lying locked up in HSR Layout could be put to good use. Neelanjana aunty wasn't likely to come back to India. She had met someone in the US, after years of being single, and it looked like she would settle there.

'Move in there, Vipasha. At least it will be occupied and looked after. Also, it is large enough for the kind of project that you have in mind. And you are the legal heir to it, you know. Unless of course Neelanjana didi decides to have a baby at the ripe old age of fifty-seven,' my father said and chuckled at his own joke.

He was right, of course. It was the perfect solution. The family home had anyway been locked up for so many years.

As a little girl, I had been fascinated by it and had wished that I could live there someday. Now my wish seemed to be coming true.

The following month, I moved to Bangalore and that was how Paw-Factor was born.

In the initial days, I struggled for good help. Between looking after Aryan, taking him to the doctor when he fell sick, his vaccinations, his food and his routine and also trying to run Paw-Factor, life was extremely demanding and on most days I would flop into bed, exhausted, dreading having to wake up the next day. But I persisted as I had no other choice.

Manav knew how hard it was for me and he visited me every now and then and helped in whatever way he could. One day he mentioned to me that the security guard who had helped me rescue the puppy told him that his uncle from his native village in Maharashtra was looking for a job. He had lost his entire family in the Latur earthquake and now wanted to come to the city. He was willing to do any job. He was currently staying with him, but ideally wanted something where he could live on the premises. And that was how Jamu kaka walked into my life. That turned out to be one of the biggest blessings for me.

'See how things happen, Vee. Had you not interacted with that security guard that day, he would not have even thought of approaching me. And you wouldn't have got your Man Friday,' Manav once said.

'Yes, Manav. Every single thing that happens to us, does happen for a reason,' I had replied and he smiled, pleased that I still quoted those words which he had once sent to me.

Jamu kaka was a great handyman, and he transformed the neglected, overgrown foliage that surrounded the house into a beautiful garden, full of flowers and trees. He loved animals and he was brilliant with the dogs. He adopted Aryan and me as his family, and in him we found our perfect support system.

I learnt a lot about the business over the years and, along with Aryan, Paw-Factor too grew. Slowly and steadily. In the initial years, I could not afford to pay Jamu kaka much. But he never complained. He was happy to have a place to stay and to have found a purpose in his life. He was healing from a great grief and I was coping with the reality of my choices. It was a good synergetic relationship, the kind you rarely find in life. I felt lucky to have him around. Later, when the business started doing well, I raised his pay to about three times of what he had been earning. He totally deserved it. To my surprise, he said that he did not need that much. He said Aryan was a growing boy and to keep the money for him. I was touched.

Till Aryan was about four, Manav still had hopes that I would relent and agree to marry him. But I was too busy raising a young child. Finding a perfect pre-school for him was not an easy task. I did the rounds of many pre-schools, after making appointments with each of them. I spent a day in observation, Aryan in tow, understanding their teaching methodology, their staff, and all they offered. I ended up choosing a nice Montessori house, not too far from my home.

Manav would come over every now and then, and we would go for an ice cream or a stroll in the park. It was a nice change for Aryan, and because my social life was non-existent—most days I was too busy running Paw-Factor, and looking after Aryan took its toll—I went along whenever he came, even though I felt I should withdraw from him. I didn't want to lead Manav on or give him any false hope.

Eventually Suchi completed her course in the US and she relocated to India. By then Prakash had proposed to her, and she had accepted. Initially her parents hadn't been too happy as Prakash was older than Suchi by twelve years. I spoke to Ammu aunty and told her what a great guy Prakash was. When they met him, they were convinced about the match. I went to Kerala, along with Aryan, for the engagement ceremony and also for the wedding. Everyone at Suchi's place fussed over Aryan and exclaimed at how much he had grown. It was a lovely break for me as well. Jamu kaka managed Paw-Factor well in my absence. Manav too attended the wedding, as did Sujith and all her cousins.

It was at Suchi's wedding that Manav told me that he had interviewed with a German company. If he got the job, he would be posted in Berlin. I wished him the very best and told him that I hoped he would get the job. One part of me was sad: if he went, I knew I would miss him. He was the only real friend I met somewhat regularly. But another part of me felt that, with some distance from me, he would gradually get over me and find a nice girl and perhaps fall in love with her.

The following week, he got the job. He was to leave for Berlin in two months, and every single day before he left, he would come over and hang around with Aryan and me. He was always full of praise for all that I was doing. He said he loved how Jamu kaka had managed to transform the place.

The day before he left he asked me if I had re-thought my decision about our life together. I said I had given it enough thought and getting married to him was not an option for me. I felt miserable as I said it, but there was no other way.

Meanwhile, satisfied customers spread the word, and soon more and more people wanted to board their pets at Paw-Factor. We hired two additional hands and Jamu kaka oversaw them. Most days we boarded about twelve to fifteen dogs. Sometimes the numbers went up to twenty. During holiday season, we had to hire additional help as the usual numbers doubled and we ran to full capacity. Holidays was peak time, and one had to book months in advance to get a spot at Paw-Factor.

I was content and happy in my tiny world. However, the depressing feeling that my education was incomplete kept gnawing at me. Though I felt sad about it, I couldn't do anything much as I had bigger things to worry about, like Aryan's school.

When the time came for him to go to school, my father helped. We chose a school where the emphasis was not solely on academics, but also on other things like sports, having a well-rounded personality, a love for nature, and many such things.

When Aryan reached class two, my dad said that my mother had filed for divorce. He was sad but seemed resigned to the fact. I said that I was just surprised it hadn't happened earlier, having seen how it was over the years.

'Everything has its time and things will happen when they have to,' said my father.

That same year, as soon as her divorce came through, I got a call from my mother. I was surprised, because seven years is a long time and I had closed that chapter in my head. I couldn't accept a mother who seemed not to care. As far as I was concerned, it was Ammu aunty who had fulfilled that role in my life. My own mother was simply a glamorous, distant figure, who breezed in and out of my life, as per her whims and fancies.

'How are you, Vipasha?' she asked.

I replied that I was fine, and so was Aryan, even though she had not asked.

Then she said that I had probably heard of the divorce from my dad. She said she would be getting married to a guy who was in the film industry. She also said that his family was well-known and that they knew Ankush's family, with whom they'd been friends for years. She wanted to know if I would come for the wedding, but without Aryan.

I replied that I had never left Aryan alone anywhere since the time he was born and I didn't intend to now. She said that the reason she had asked was because there was someone she thought would be a good match for me. It was the nephew of the guy she was getting married to. He was a divorcee and had a four-year-old son.

That was when I told my mother to fuck off and stop interfering in my life. What gave her any right or authority to match-make for me? Had I asked? What qualified her to even be my mother?

'Just because you gave birth to me doesn't mean you are a mother. Being a mother is so much more,' I yelled and slammed down the phone.

She had tried calling a few more times after that, but I never answered. As far as I was concerned I had shut the door on my mother, and I intended it to stay that way. I hated her. And I had cut the umbilical cord.

She died two years later. It was her new husband who called me to tell me. I was stunned at the suddenness of it, a bolt from the blue. He said that it was a cardiac arrest. She had been fine that morning but had not woken up from her afternoon nap. Dad called shortly afterwards.

Her death was a huge shock to me and it left a strange

sense of emptiness inside me, but even when I saw her body, I couldn't bring myself to cry. I did not take Aryan to the cremation. I left him in Jamu kaka's care and flew to Mumbai for the day. He hadn't even met my mother and I saw no point in dragging him along. For me, her death was the final closure in what had been one of the most disturbing relationships in my life. All I wanted from her was a little bit of love and acceptance. I remembered the time when she had taken me to the doctor when I was pregnant. I remembered the time she had told all her friends about my modelling success. And as hard as I tried to muster other memories of her, all that came to my mind was bitterness and anger. Even in her death, I couldn't forgive her. So deep was my pain.

When Aryan reached class five, he wrote an entrance exam to his current school, one of the most coveted educational institutions in the country. I was overjoyed when he cleared it and was admitted. My annual income made me eligible for a bursary, and I accepted it. There was no way I would have been able to afford the full fees unless I took money from my father, which I steadfastly refused to.

Several more years passed and the closeness between Suchi and me multiplied manifold. She was heartbroken when she discovered that she couldn't have any children. They'd tried all kinds of treatments for several years and had now accepted the fact. Prakash was more than willing to adopt a child, but Suchi didn't want to.

Now that Aryan was in school full time, I had a bit of time on my hands, especially in the morning. Suchi had been steadily gaining weight and had joined a gym. But she hated the instructors there.

'They don't understand my body, Vee. They just act like

it is a boot-camp and treat me like some new recruit in the Indian army,' she complained.

'Come on, they are not your best friends to understand you and train you. Their goal is to get you in shape.'

'I know, but I hate them. Listen—why don't you train me? You are so fit even after having a baby. And you understand exactly what I want.'

'I am not even qualified, Suchi! I just know instinctively what will work.'

'That is precisely what is needed. You have always been in shape and look at the way you have bounced back after childbirth. How long will it take for you to get a proper qualification anyway? And now that Aryan is in school full time, you do have some time on your hands, don't you?'

She had a point there. I had always been interested in fitness, but getting professionally qualified had never occurred to me. The thought of going back to studies appealed to me. At least it would be something more than just having class twelve as my educational qualification.

Suchi assured me that I would make a great gym instructor, and she pushed me to do a course. She found out all the details about it. It was a hundred-hour course with both theory and practicals, where I had to work in a gym, and would take me about three months. I completed the course and thoroughly enjoyed it.

I never trained Suchi though. She was too inconsistent and just not motivated enough to stick with a weight-loss program that required discipline and an iron-will.

About a year later, Manav wrote to tell us that he was getting married to a German girl. I was happy for him. Exactly what I had wanted had happened. Yet I felt a sense of loss.

Suchi said that deep down maybe I regretted not marrying

him. I knew that was not true at all. Manav was not the guy for me. Yet, he had been there for me unfailingly whenever I needed him. Up to now, it was like I was a big part of his life. But with his marriage, of course that would change. He would start his family, move on with his life and I would probably cease to matter to him anymore. I consoled myself that I had Aryan and that was all that mattered.

Life chugged along, safely, smoothly, comfortably. Aryan went from one class to the other, always scoring perfect grades. Suchi and Prakash were around for him all the time. Prakash started coaching him with his math and he was amazed at how quickly Aryan learnt. He was also popular in school, regularly receiving invitations to birthday parties and having his friends over every now and then. Aryan was enthusiastic about every single thing, happily taking part in all the extra-curricular activities in school.

I couldn't have asked for more. I was content, raising Aryan, running a successful business, and leading my life. I did feel every now and then that something was missing but that never bothered me enough to do something about it.

Everything had been good. Up till now. Now my business would be associated with two dead dogs. And it wasn't even anything that I could have prevented. This had been my life, my main occupation, the thing that gave me most joy, and it had received a massive knock.

I dreaded facing the next day, not knowing how to handle it, not knowing what to do. It was a colossal blow and I did not know if I had the strength to face it alone.

Chapter 15

The telephone ring feels like it will penetrate my brain and drill holes into it. It sounds like it is coming from the inside of a hollow drum. In my sleep-drugged state, I have no idea where the phone is. I have a hangover the size of the Eiffel Tower. My head hurts, my throat is parched and it is with great difficulty that I prise open my eyelids and pick up the phone, which I locate under the body-pillow on my bed that I am hugging, and hence it is right next to my ear.

'Maa, where are you? I have called at least five times and you didn't answer the phone,' wails Aryan.

That's when it hits me. God—I was supposed to have picked him up so he would have time to change and leave for school. I look at the time. It's half past seven. Damn—there isn't enough time for him to come back home, get ready and then reach school.

'I'm so sorry Aryan, I overslept. I'll have to bring your school uniform with me to Vishok's house and you can get ready over there and leave,' I say as I get out of bed, grab my handbag and the car keys, put on my sandals and throw on a jacket over the spaghetti top that I have slept in, all at the same time. Then I quickly throw Aryan's uniform into a bag and step outside.

Jamu kaka, as dependable as ever, has already fed the dogs and is playing with them.

I drag myself, all groggy eyes and dishevelled hair, into the car, and it is with great effort that I manage to drive to Aryan's friend's house. Aryan is waiting impatiently for me at the gate, along with his friend, who is ready and waiting for the bus.

'Thanks Ma,' he says as he grabs his school uniform from my hand and rushes inside to change.

'Just in time, Aunty—the bus will be here in the next five minutes,' says his friend and I heave a sigh of relief.

'Ma, are you okay? You look upset,' says Aryan when he emerges, changed and freshly scrubbed.

'Hmmm, yes, I am fine. I'll see you in the evening. You have a nice day, sweetheart,' I reply, not wanting to get into the details of the previous day with him. I wave him off, and drive back home.

When I get there, I see that Jamu kaka has kept a cup of tea and a plate of biscuits ready for me. I thank him and settle down in my usual spot, which is the wicker armchair on the veranda. As soon as I open the city newspaper, what hits me is the caption:

DOGS DIE IN LOCAL KENNEL. DOG-LOVERS BEWARE.

It is front page news and I am aghast at what has been reported.

> Two dogs died and three more were admitted to a veterinary hospital in the city yesterday. The tragedy unfurled at Paw-Factor, which is an upmarket boarding house for canines and

which calls itself a pet-resort. The owner of the dog who died is distraught and has not ruled out the possibility of suing for negligence.

When contacted, the owner of the pet resort, Vipasha Mishra, said it could have been due to poisoning but could not provide additional details and was later unavailable for comment. Vipasha Mishra is a former model who appeared in several advertisements.

The veterinarian who treated the dogs, Dr Saurabh, said the dogs were dead on arrival and had ingested poisoned meat.

Paw-Factor is one of the premium boarding houses for dogs in the city, and it is difficult to obtain a place for pets unless booked months in advance.

The dog owner, Mrs Mehra, said her pet Shiro was like a son to her and she is devastated by the loss. What is surprising is that the animals were hastily buried before the owners even had a chance to see them. The owner of the other dog who died was unavailable for comment.

Animal rights organisations in the city have expressed grave concern and will be investigating the matter. But no amount of investigation can bring back the dead dogs. 'An ounce of prevention is worth a ton of cure,' goes the adage and it seems to ring true in the case of Paw-Factor.

My heart sinks. There is no mention of Damodar at all. The fact that the dogs have been deliberately poisoned has conveniently been left out. And how in the world did they dig up information about my modelling days? That was sixteen years ago. And what did they mean that the animals were hastily buried. Don't they know that there are no morgue facilities for animals in India, and a dead dog, especially one that has been poisoned, quickly rots and the stench would be unbearable had we not buried it? And what the article does not say is that I am shattered by the loss too. I am deeply devastated, but there is no mention of that anywhere.

I feel sick and I hurry to the toilet to violently throw up the tea and biscuits. I don't want to face this.

The phone rings and I decide that in case it is the press, I will ignore it. But it is Suchi.

'Vee, don't even read the papers,' she says.

'Too late, I already read it.'

'All?' she asks.

Good lord—that means there are more. I have seen only the local city paper. This means that every newspaper must be carrying the news in their city sections.

'No, only *Bangalore Buzz,*' I say.

'I am coming right over. I'll cancel all my meetings for today. Hang on.'

'Hey, listen, it's okay. The dogs are let free as it's their play-time, and I am fine. It's not like I have gone to pieces.'

The thing is, Suchi dislikes the dogs licking her or even coming towards her and this is the time that all the dogs are let free. If she comes over, it will be hard to get her inside the house unless I lock the dogs up and I don't want to do that. This is their exercise and grooming time, and Jamu kaka as well as the hired help have got their hands full. Besides, I am in a rotten mood and I don't want to talk to anyone.

'Are you sure? It's no trouble,' she offers again.

'No Suchi. Don't cancel your meetings. It's fine.'

As soon as I hang up the phone calls start. The word has spread all over. Most of the customers want to know what happened. I explain wearily to each one, repeating the same story over and over again. I say that I am deeply sorry, and it was definitely a case of deliberate poisoning. Yes, the necropsy reports had come in, and yes I will be figuring out what to do next, and yes, their dogs are safe.

There are about three animal rights groups wanting to meet me. I tell them to come over. I decide to meet them all at the same time so I don't have to repeat myself. I know what I am going to say. They all turn up one after the other, and now a group of nine people is sitting with me. I tell them in detail what has happened. Then I show them around Paw-Factor. I explain the extreme care I take when it comes to the dogs. I show them the pristine kennels with curtains, clean bowls of water and the green surroundings. I show them where the food for the dogs is cooked, and explain how I would never have given raw meat to them. I introduce them to Jamu kaka who is busy playing with the dogs, and they can see how much he loves them. I explain to them how devastated and shattered I am and how much the media has twisted the facts. They understand perfectly when I tell them that I couldn't possibly have waited for the owners of the dogs to arrive before burying them. I tell them about Benjamin and Mary-Elise who are in Cambodia, and who do not even care that their pet has died. I tell them that the Mehras haven't even given me a chance to explain and I also tell them about Damodar. How he hated the dogs, how he had complained incessantly, and how he had marched into my home several times over the last three years and created scenes, because of the dogs. Then I take them to my drawing room and Jamu kaka serves them lemonade. I show them the necropsy reports. By the end of it, they are convinced about my side of the story.

'I can understand how stressful all of this is for you,' says a short, curly-haired lady who sports a nose ring and thick glasses.

'Yes, it's been terrible. I'm thinking of approaching the police and filing an FIR against Damodar,' I say.

'Let me be honest, we work for animal rights, and trust me, they aren't going to bother. Nobody values an animal's life in India. Hell, they don't even care about humans, how will they bother about the animals? My sincere advice to you, strictly off the records though, is to avoid it because it will be an utter waste of time. Besides, how will you ever prove that it was he who poisoned the dogs? It could have been anybody. And I don't think the police will even bother to spend time and resources to investigate this, as it's just animals that have died,' she says.

'So what do I do then?' I ask her.

'The sad truth is we cannot do anything. We as animal-lovers rally for the living ones, and try to make their lives a little better. I am glad we made this trip. At least our misconceptions have been cleared. We wish you the very best,' she says and they all leave. I am glad that they have been so understanding and that they are on my side and could see the facts for themselves.

The owners of the dogs I am boarding are not as understanding though. They are emotional, angry and visibly upset.

By noon, four have turned up and cancelled the rest of the stay for their dogs and taken them away. By evening all the dogs have been taken away by their respective owners.

For the first time since I started Paw-Factor, it is empty.

When Aryan comes home that evening, there are no excited yelps to greet him. He is taken aback. He wants to know what happened and I wordlessly hand him the newspapers.

He silently reads each one.

'God, Ma, when did the press come? And how dare they write such bullshit. And why didn't you tell me before I left for school?' he demands. The anger on his face and the indignation in his voice makes me want to hug him.

I am silent.

'Why didn't you tell me, Ma?' he asks again.

'I didn't know myself that it would be so bad, Aryan. They were here yesterday, while you were at Vishok's place. I didn't think that this is what they are going to report. I saw no point in worrying you too.'

'The … the bastard. I am going to kill that asshole,' he says and before I can stop him he marches off to Damodar's house.

'Come back, Aryan,' I call out wearily. I have no energy left to go after him.

He comes back in about five minutes.

'The fucking bastard … the asshole … the prick ... aaaaargh,' he says and kicks the wall.

'What happened, Aryan?' I ask.

'You know what? The house is empty, Ma. The bloody asshole—he has moved out.'

I stand rooted to the spot. So, it was all planned. He had done it deliberately. Had the dogs been such a nuisance for him, he could have easily moved out without killing them.

What was the need to poison them? I am so upset that I am barely able to breathe.

My hands tremble and I call up Suchi. She picks up as soon as it rings.

'Come over, Suchi. The dogs are all gone. And Paw-Factor is over.'

She is silent for a few seconds.

'Vee, I'm in Mysore—I have some meetings here. I'll come as soon as I can though and head straight to your place, okay? I'll probably get to your place around dinnertime. Just hang in there till then.'

When I hang up, I burst into tears. Aryan puts his arms around me and comforts me. The tears just do not stop. My whole body shakes.

After a while I stop sobbing and Aryan and I sit silently in the drawing room facing each other.

There is nothing left to say anymore.

Chapter 16

Saurabh calls in the morning and asks if I am fine. I tell him that yes, while I am upset, I will get through this. I don't sound convincing at all and I think he senses it too. He says he has read the newspaper reports, and to not bother about them too much.

'It is just the media. They will lose interest soon. Do not pay attention to it,' he says. His voice is calm and it comforts me. At least I am able to talk about it with him.

'I know but it is hard to not think about it. This is something I have built from the scratch. It has been my world for so many years now.'

'I can come around after work today and check on the other dogs,' he says. And that sends a fresh wave of pain through me.

There are no more dogs. All of them have gone.

Then I realise that he *wants* to come and *wants* me to invite him over. I am so weary that I just want to drop down dead and go to sleep. But, to not invite him after everything he has done so far would be churlish and so I hear myself saying, 'Please come over Saurabh. But, this is not to check on the dogs. Just to have a drink again. And you can meet my friend too, she will be here.'

'Oh, in that case shall I defer my visit to tomorrow? And are all the other dogs doing fine?'

I intentionally hadn't said anything about the other dogs because I didn't want to talk about it. The wound is too raw, too exposed. But he has asked me a direct question now.

'No more dogs, Saurabh. All the owners have come and taken them away. Paw-Factor might be shutting shop.'

Each word feels like a kick in my gut. But this is the truth. It can't be kept a secret forever. Sooner or later I will have to face it.

'Oh,' he says. And then, 'I will see you this evening, around eighty-thirty. Is that fine?'

'Yes, drop in and stay for dinner.'

The best way to handle pain and disappointment is to bury oneself in work. I have already taken a day off from the gym, and I don't think Mahesh will be too happy about giving me another day off. Besides I don't want to disappoint my clients. Sheetal, who is in her early forties and a mother to two teenagers, is showing good progress. Her older son is Aryan's classmate. I had met her at a parent-teacher's meeting at school, and she was impressed at how fit I was. I had told her a few things to follow and that had helped her. Then she asked me if I would be her personal trainer, and after a quick word with Mahesh, she had started training at the gym. From seventy-five kilos, I have managed to bring her weight down to sixty-eight. What I have targeted for her height (she is five foot four) is fifty-five kilos. Sheetal thinks that will be impossible to achieve and is thrilled already at the amount she has lost. I know from experience that this is the most delicate time. If I don't monitor her closely, she is likely to regain weight from complacency.

My other two clients had come on Sheetal's reference.

Mahesh was okay with it, as long as I gave ten percent of what I charged them to the gym. That way the gym made something over and above the membership fees being paid. I saw no sense in it, as, if it hadn't been for me, they wouldn't have joined the gym in the first place. But since Mahesh owned the gym, there was no way I could argue with him.

My second client, Ashok Das, has hired me just for fitness, and not for weight loss. He is an industrialist in his late sixties. He does not need a personal trainer. He is remarkably fit for his age and is a regular at the gym. But he says he feels better working out with a trainer. My third is the balding Mukul Shah who works for a corporate organisation and would like to lose some weight. He has lost about four kilos so far, and he needs to be monitored too. I suspect he has hired me more for my looks than my professional qualifications as a certified fitness instructor, but whatever it is, it's my job to see that he is fit, now that he is my client.

So I drag myself into the gym, and try and carry on as usual, even though it feels like there is a huge grey cloud hanging over my head. All of them have read the papers too, and it drains me to explain the same thing over and over again to each one separately.

Yes, the dogs were poisoned.

No, there is no use filing an FIR.

Yes, I am devastated about it.

Mahesh has either not read the newspapers or he does not care about my life outside the gym as he does not mention it at all. I am thankful for that.

I am permitted to do my personal workout only when I am done with my clients or before they arrive. For the duration of my duty-hours, I have to hang around, in case anyone needs help using particular equipment.

Exercise is supposed to make one feel good, but today no matter how much I try to throw myself into the routine, and no matter how much I try to cheer myself up by playing some fabulous workout music, my heart isn't in it. At the end of the day, I am glad to be able to leave and reach the comfort of home, where Jamu kaka is waiting with tea and biscuits.

I tell him that Suchi and Saurabh will be coming over for dinner and he helps me rustle up a meal comprising spicy roast potatoes, grilled chicken and a pasta, which is easy to make. The pasta is laden with calories, and on most days I would have avoided it. But just now, I need the comfort of carbohydrates. I will work out and burn them off another day. Today I crave comfort food.

Jamu kaka tells me that he was free the whole day and it felt odd as he had nothing to do. I tell him that it hurts me to look at the empty kennels. We both understand each other's pain. Though we talk about it, it brings no solace.

Aryan tries to cheer me up when he comes back from school, but there is nothing that can be done. Also, he has numerous projects to work on, so I put up a brave front for him and pretend that I am fine, while actually I am dying inside.

When Suchi arrives, I am so happy to see her that I hug her. She has brought me flowers, and two bottles of wine.

'It is such a change to see this place without dogs,' she says and I wince. She immediately realises the insensitivity of that remark, and hugs me and says, 'So sorry Vee, I know how terrible this is. That was stupid of me to make that comment.'

I forgive her almost instantly. If there is one thing about Suchi that I have to admire, it is her guileless honesty and how she immediately expresses what she thinks, even though it may not be what I want to hear. Our friendship has always worked that way.

Saurabh hasn't arrived yet and Suchi and I have already finished a bottle of wine between us.

Aryan has left us alone. He's had his dinner and is busy with a project in his room.

'Prakash is travelling out of the country for a conference, otherwise he would have joined us, but that's fine, it just means more wine for us,' Suchi said as she poured two glasses of Shiraz for us. She is trying her best to get me out of the darkness that I have descended into.

Then we proceed to finish the bottle, while talking about everything except Paw-Factor. Having made that mistake as soon as she walked in, she is now sensitive enough to avoid the topic. But that is only for a while. The magnitude of what has happened is so great that it is impossible *not* to talk about. And sure enough she brings it up.

'Look Vee, for you at least this is a business that has died. It is fixable. Unlike my bloody uterus. It can't hold a baby. And do you know how much that hurts?' she says now.

She usually gets emotional when she talks about her inability to conceive. There is so much sadness inside her but she rarely expresses it. I feel wretched when she says this though I realise that she is trying to cheer me up by pointing out that she is in a worse place. I put my arms around her and tell her that I am sharing Aryan with her anyway, and I don't know how I would have managed had they not been around for me.

Suchi is quite high on the wine by now. I can tell by the way she giggles and the slight slur in her speech. But it is only because I know her so well. An outsider who is meeting her for the first time would probably not be able to make out. She cannot handle wine at all, and I know she is drinking just to give me some company and because I like it.

That is when the doorbell rings. Jamu kaka lets Saurabh in, and he walks in to join two emotional, slightly drunk women. The large cheerful yellow Asiatic lilies that Suchi got me are now perched on the breakfast counter in a blue glass vase, with a slight chip on the edge, which happened when I washed it the last time. Saurabh immediately notices the flowers and tells me they are lovely and I introduce him to Suchi as my best friend, my soul sister and someone who makes my life complete. He smiles at the introduction but I do mean it with all my heart. I tell him that we have grown up together and we are indeed like sisters, though not related by blood.

He nods, but I don't think he gets it. Anybody who hasn't had a close friend like that would not get it, I suppose.

'Sit down, sit down, good Doctor. Vee has told me all about you,' says Suchi as she offers him her hand.

Saurabh shakes her hand formally and says, 'Hello Suchi, pleased to meet you,' and somehow that makes me smile.

He is wearing a dark blue shirt today and has paired it with light khaki trousers and brown shoes. He has made an effort to shave and looks dashing.

'So tell me something, Doctor, in all your years of veterinary practice, have you come across animals who cannot conceive?' asks Suchi.

'Shhh, Suchi, shut up. This is not what you ask someone you meet for the first time,' I say.

'No, but he is a doctor and he ought to know and I want to know too,' she says.

Saurabh does not even find the question odd. He thinks carefully and his brows are knitted in thought. He looks good when he does that. Good lord—am I getting attracted to this guy? This guy who speaks complete formal sentences and has—what had he said, I try to remember, and then it comes back to me—a mild case of Asperger's syndrome?

I am overcome with an urge to read up all about it. I discreetly take out my phone and Google it. I quickly learn that it is a development disorder that often goes undiagnosed until late childhood or sometimes even adulthood. It is mistaken for social awkwardness, as it involves impairment in social skills, communication and sensory processing. It falls under the Autism spectrum of disorders and mild cases are usually very hard to detect, and yet when detected can be managed and there are plenty of resources for people with this syndrome to have meaningful relationships and successful careers. There is even a list of careers most suited for people with Asperger's and I see that veterinary medicine is one of them.

No wonder his manner of speech is odd. I now understand him a bit more. It must be a huge effort for him to meet us. I am touched at the effort he has made for me.

Saurabh is earnestly answering Suchi's question now. 'Of course there are cases of infertility in animals too. It is of concern only if the animal is used primarily for offspring reproduction, such as in farms. In case of home pets, many owners prefer to get the female neutered and it is also recommend for a variety of reasons, if you have no intentions of breeding,' he replies.

Suchi nods solemnly and takes in everything that Saurabh says. If she finds his manner of speech oddly formal, she is either too drunk to notice it or too polite to point it out.

Then she says, 'Ah, but here is the thing—I cannot breed even if I want to.'

I wince.

But Saurabh does not even raise an eyebrow.

'Is it because of a condition you have? Have you tried treatments?' he asks.

'Hey—this is not normal conversation for people who are meeting for the first time. Please Suchi, can we lay off the topic?' I ask. I don't want Suchi to discuss this as it will only make her sadder. This has happened a couple of times in the past when she has got too drunk. Then she gets hysterical and it is only with great difficulty that we can calm her down.

But Saurabh does not know this and so I can't blame him for not cutting the conversation short. Besides, it is Suchi herself who has brought this up.

'Blocked fallopian tubes, which then got treated. And now they can't find the cause. It is just unexplained, and there are no tests that I haven't done and no treatments that I haven't tried. God just doesn't think I am good enough to be a mother.' There is a slight difference in the tone of her voice now, one I recognise from past episodes.

'Enough Suchi, let's not talk about this.' My tone is firmer this time.

Then I grab Saurabh's hand and take him aside. 'Please, don't talk to her about this. She tends to get extremely upset and we have already had one bottle of wine between us,' I say.

He nods and then says, 'Look—amazing wooden beams on the ceiling. Is it antique? It looks so beautiful.'

It takes me a few seconds to register what he is asking and then I realise that he is trying to change the topic. So I enthusiastically launch into how I always wanted this house even as a child. How beautiful I had found it, and how I never thought that I would end up living here.

He nods, and Suchi too is distracted. She talks about how

lovely it is to live in an old house, and describes her mother's home in Kerala.

I pitch in, and then the conversation goes on to other things. Saurabh tells me about his native village in Thanjavur. His mother is a north Indian from Punjab and she fell in love with his dad, a south Indian, and married him. Most people predicted that she wouldn't last in a small south Indian town like Thanjavur. But they are the happiest couple he knows, and she has lived there for more than thirty years now. The way he describes their love story makes me think how rare happy marriages are. I have seen far too many bitter ones and too many break-ups.

And so the evening passes. They both appreciate the meal I have cooked. By the end of it, I am definitely feeling better. The sadness is still there but it is not as dark as before. I am glad that Saurabh has come over.

It is close to midnight when they get up to leave. Suchi is quite drunk but she has a driver who has been with them for more than five years now, and so I know she will reach home safely.

'I would have loved to stay longer, Vee, but I have a meeting at eight-thirty, and it is at the other end of town. I can't miss it,' she says.

'It's fine, Suchi. I'm glad you came. I'll be okay,' I say and hug her.

Then I hug Saurabh too. The contact with him surprisingly sends a jolt through my body, even though it is a very formal hug. I wonder if he felt it too.

Later, as I lie in bed, I pick up my phone and send him an instant message: *Thanks so much for being there. It makes all the difference. Feeling good now.*

I wait and wait for him to message back. I check my phone

at least fifty times in the span of half an hour. But no reply comes.

And then I feel like the biggest fool in the world, to have sent him that message.

Chapter 17

The next morning too, I wait for Saurabh's reply to my message. But he doesn't text back. I wonder why people don't reply to messages. I know he has seen it as the Instant Messenger shows me that it has been read. I wonder what is going on in his head.

Life feels very empty right now. Aryan has gone to school and since my gym timings are eleven-thirty to three-thirty, I have a lot of time on my hands in the mornings. Without Paw-Factor to occupy me, I feel lost. My usual day would have begun with clients either checking in dogs or checking them out, supervising the cleaning of the kennels, the airing of the bedding, and also seeing if each pet has fresh water and whether they have eaten properly.

It is the middle of the month, and I do not see any point in holding on to the hired help. I give them two months' pay and tell them we no longer need their services. While on the outside I appear matter-of-fact and brisk, inside I am shattered. There are so many angry posts on the wall of my Facebook page and there are so many people who have made nasty, rude and downright mean comments. It is as though people on social media derive some sadistic pleasure from kicking someone who is already down.

No matter how often I delete the posts, more keep springing up all over the Internet, especially with the news clipping from the *Bangalore Buzz* that had alleged negligence in huge bold headlines that occupied half the page. I curse the social media and the Internet. My mind goes back to the time when social networks hadn't taken over our lives. Back then, if a disaster such as this had happened, it would be written about in the newspapers, and then forgotten after a couple of days, when the old newspapers went into the rubbish pile. But now social media makes it all so permanent. Anyone who googles Paw-Factor anytime from now will see a mention of a case of negligence. Which would naturally mean that they will not make a choice to board their pets here. I feel a tightness in my chest even thinking about it.

I keep checking my phone to see if Saurabh has replied to my message. My heart sinks further when I see that he hasn't. I so want to hear from him now. His strange formal manner, his detached, almost emotionless way of speaking, his calmness, is what I need. I wonder what he is doing at this very moment. Does he see more dogs on a regular basis or does he treat other animals too? I realise that I know nothing about his work-day, his routine, or anything much about him at all, apart from the Asperger's. I consider messaging him a second time with some inane stuff, just so that I can hear from him. But I can't think of a single thing to ask him without appearing silly.

Finally I cannot resist it anymore, and so I take the direct approach. I message him saying, *Hey, did you get my message last night? It was great having you over.*

I know it is a stupid thing to do. If he had wanted to reply to me, he would have done so last night itself. I know that my message has been delivered and read.

Now I keep checking to see if this message has been delivered, and I don't even realise that I am absentmindedly chewing my nails.

There is a single tick mark next to the message and then it turns into a double. So I know the message has been delivered to his phone. Then I see that he is online.

His display picture is one where he is wearing a business suit and he looks handsome.

There is no reply again, and I curse myself for having given in and sending a second message. This makes it look like I am chasing him. Which I probably am, but I hate to do that and now it is too late.

There is nothing much to do till I leave for the gym, and so I walk out of the house and wander around the garden, something I haven't done in ages. Jamu kaka follows me around, pointing out a pumpkin patch, and showing me how the pumpkin has just started growing. Then he shows me the beans. He also proudly points out the brinjals, cabbage and radish. I hadn't even realised that there were so many vegetables growing in the garden. Every now and then Jamu kaka would pick some vegetables that were ready to be harvested and we would use them in the kitchen, but till now I hadn't bothered to actually step outside and see the little farm that he has created. I am quite surprised now.

But it still does not take my mind off Paw-Factor. The more I think about it, the more hopeless seem the chances of reviving it. So I tell Jamu kaka to remove the curtains from the dog crates, and to dismantle them.

It all seems so final.

He asks me what to do with the feeding bowls, the grooming

brushes and everything else that we use for the dogs. I tell him to just collect everything, put them in cartons and clear all the rooms. He asks if the business is dead, and whether or not we can continue. He says that everyone will forget about this incident after a few days, and that I should keep it open.

I don't have the heart to tell him that I am convinced about my decision to close the place and what he suggests is not so simple. As far as I am concerned, this is a devastating thing to have happened to a business like mine, which functions on the trust the dog-owners place in me and their comfort levels with me. Once that is gone, it is nearly impossible to get back.

Also, I don't know how to explain the power of the Internet to him. I can't even bear to look at the nasty comments posted online about Paw-Factor. Some have even gone on to say that the earlier positive reviews which appeared there were paid. That outrages me. I have never ever paid for a review. It has always been through word-of-mouth that our reputation as a top destination for dogs had spread, and now it is the same word-of-mouth that is killing it.

No one wants to risk boarding their dogs with me. I guess it is like a residential property where an earlier occupant has committed suicide. Nobody wants to rent it anymore, and even a sale would fetch only a very low rate.

Here, I can't even drop my prices. It would only send out signals of desperation. The faster that I accept that it is over, the better it is. I try to explain all this to Jamu kaka, and he nods, but I don't think he gets it.

My phone rings, I make an almost crazy dash to the veranda, where I have left it on the chair. It could be Saurabh. Maybe he is the kind of guy who is not comfortable with messaging. I remember reading somewhere that there are many men like that.

But it isn't. It is Suchi.

'Hey, how are you? You doing okay?' she asks.

'I don't even know how I am doing anymore, Suchi,' I reply honestly.

'Listen, I know this is probably not the right time to mention this, but Nimish called me. He seems keen on seeing you. But he isn't sure about calling you up. I think he is trying to get some kind of a feeler from me. Would you like to go out with him?'

I had almost forgotten about Nimish. The events of the past three or four days have been life-changing, to say the least. I now remember that he was pleasant and well-mannered, and seemed intelligent as well, when I met him at Suchi's place for dinner.

Why not, I think. It can at the very least provide a distraction for me, and I know I need that big time.

'Sure, please tell him to call me or text,' I say.

'Oh my god, someone has actually agreed without a fuss. I can't believe it,' says Suchi.

In the past, whenever a guy she set me up with wanted my number, I would never agree this easily. Then Suchi would cajole me, force me, plead and beg me to give the guy another chance and I would then agree. He would text me and ask me out for a date which would be at some fancy restaurant. Then when we went out, I would usually discover something about the guy which would completely put me off. There would, on very rare occasions, be a second date or a third. Suchi and I would then dissect the guy in minute detail. Suchi would say that I am fussy and fastidious and I would tell her that she doesn't understand me. After that, we would discuss what I want in a guy—which according to me was not much, but which according to her was nearly impossible.

'You want your men to be caring, charming, well-read, intelligent, humorous and also crazy about you. How can you get all of this in one super-combo?' she asked me once.

'Well, I am not desperate. I don't need to have a man in my life, unless he happens to have everything that I want. I have my own life, and my own little world. It is you who is desperate to see me hooked,' I had replied.

Which was true, of course.

Which is why Suchi is surprised that I so readily agreed to letting Nimish contact me. I wait around a bit more, and there is no message from Saurabh at all. I decide that I am definitely not messaging him a third time. There is a limit to desperation too. It is now time for me to leave for the gym. I go a little early before my clients arrive, so I have time for my own workout.

My workout today is slightly better than yesterday. Today is my legs day, and I usually dread it. But today, the pain of working those muscles actually proves to be comforting, because thinking about Paw-Factor is even worse. I didn't know till now that physical pain is always easier to bear than a mental burden. I focus now on my oblique and transverse abdominals and check my pose in the mirror as I prop my upper body on my left forearm, and raise my hips so that my body forms a straight line from my ankle to the shoulders. I finish my reps for all the exercises, shower and then fill in the register that records my in-time and out-time. Mahesh usually signs it every two days.

Once my clients come, I am able to totally forget about Paw-Factor, and I think that is big progress. Yesterday I could barely focus, but today I am able to concentrate on what is happening. Sheetal tells me about how the school field trip this year is to Himachal Pradesh and how much her son is looking forward to it.

'Hasn't Aryan mentioned it to you?' she asks, resting between her dead-lifts.

'No, I don't think he has. I didn't even know about it till now.'

'It's a twenty-day trip this time, and the last ten days they will be building a school in Himachal Pradesh. The exchange students from Spain are joining them and it is a UN-funded project. Isn't that awesome?' she says, beads of sweat dripping from her forehead, but her eyes glistening with enthusiasm. I sometimes wish I could be as excited as she is about a child's school trip. While I am happy that it is something useful, it isn't sending me into raptures of ecstasy. I am so different from her in my approach to parenting. I guess I have bigger things to worry about.

My phone rings, and this is one of the rare times that I have forgotten to put it on silent.

'So sorry,' I say as I rush to press the mute button. But I cannot resist seeing who the call is from. Maybe it is Saurabh. But it isn't. It is from Nimish, which is what the app that I have installed on my phone to show the caller tells me. I would have to call him back later and explain that I don't take personal calls while at the gym.

I finish with both Mr Shah and Mr Das—just the usual without any variations. One of the regular gym clients wants to know whether she should run at a constant speed, or whether she should vary it. She has started coming only recently. I tell her to run at eight kmph for two minutes, walk at four kmph for a minute, six kmph for the next, and then again drop back to four kmph. Once she recovers her breath, to run again at eight kmph for two minutes and to continue this pattern for twenty minutes.

'This way you are fooling your heart into working harder, but with less effort,' I tell her, and she smiles.

As I'm heading back home from the gym, I put the sound back on my phone and also automatically look at my missed calls and messages.

There is one from Suchi. *Chin up and carry on, this too shall pass*, it reads.

There are none from Saurabh. The first guy I messaged twice in years and he doesn't reply. It makes me feel like I am a stupid teen instead of the mother to a teen.

When I get home, I automatically check my mails, and I am so darn surprised to see one from Manav, that I nearly drop my tea. The last I heard from him was when he had sent his wedding invitation. I had replied congratulating him and he hadn't written after that. Neither did I. I have always felt slightly guilty for turning him down.

I wonder what he has to say now, after all these years.

I begin to read:

Hey Vee,

How are you? It's been just over ten years now I think, if I remember right. I think I last wished you on Aryan's fourth birthday, and later left for Germany. I remember I sent you my wedding invite.

I read about Paw-Factor online. I am so sorry about what has happened. Whatever it is that has happened, I am certain that it was not negligence on your part. You were too passionate, too diligent about it, and so was Jamu kaka. How is he, btw? Is he still with you?

Anyway, the reason I write today (well, I can't call it a reason, but I use that for want of a better word) is that I got a mail from Aryan a couple of days back. It took me by surprise. He asked me for Ankush's e-mail id. He said he wanted to contact him.

I know I am probably betraying Aryan by letting you know that he wrote to me—but I think you have the right to know. I also think he has the right to contact his father if he chooses to.

I thought about this a great deal, and then I sent him Ankush's contact details. But I haven't said anything about Ankush. I think that is a call that Ankush has to make himself. I have been in touch with him, on and off, and he knows you live in Bangalore, and own Paw-Factor. I haven't given him any other details, just like I haven't given you any, as both of you are mature individuals and I don't think you need a middle-man.

But I thought I should warn you that I have replied to Aryan.

Eva and I are happy—or at least we are still together, which means she must be happy with me ☺. We are childless by choice. She is working on her thesis on early child education in developing nations for her PhD program. My career is going well, and I have been appointed the CTO of my organisation. While it is a lot of responsibility, and a whole load of additional work, it is great. I am not complaining.

We plan to visit India soon, for some

research Eva needs to do. We'll be spending two days in Bangalore. If you want to meet, let us know and we can catch up.

My numbers are at the end of this mail. Send me yours too, if it has changed.

That's all for now.
Manav

Chapter 18

No matter how well parents think they know their child, they don't. They might think that they are very close to the child, that the child confides in them completely, that they understand their child better than anyone else, but often that is wrong. Most parents do not want to believe that their children change when they turn into adolescents. They cannot accept that their children can now think on their own and will no longer mouth the opinions that the parents have instilled in them, but instead will form their own. I know this is true, out of experience. But this is the first time I have been forced to confront it.

Manav's mail has come as a rude shock to me and has taken the wind out of my sails. Till now, I thought that Aryan was my baby, my child, with whom I shared a close relationship and whom I knew like the back of my hand. I thought I could predict his every emotion, his every mood, and even before he spoke, most times, I knew what he would say and how he would react to something. We were a team—it was him and me, always together. And now to think that there is a whole new side to him which I haven't seen or know nothing about, frightens me.

How did he find Manav's e-mail id? Why does he want to contact Ankush? Why hasn't he spoken to me about it? What else is there about him that I don't know? At what age do children stop confiding in their parents and turn to others?

These questions whiz through my head, as I wait for Aryan to get back from school.

I have decided that I will be calm about it and have a talk with him and find out what is going on in his head. When he comes home, it is with great restraint that I force myself to first ask him if he is hungry and offer to make him a snack. He doesn't even sense that I am bursting to ask him something. He wants me to make him a double-egg omelette as he is hungry. I force myself to focus on chopping the onions and I start making his snack. I also make him a cup of coffee, which is actually more milk and less coffee, but he doesn't mind. He says he played basketball and the other team won. He also says that his physics teacher is no good, as he rushes through the portions. I listen to him without any comments. He is busy eating and does not even notice my silence. He is oblivious to my inner turmoil.

I wait for him to finish his meal. When he's done, I say, 'Aryan, why did you contact Manav? And how in the world did you get his e-mail id? Why didn't you speak to me first?'

He is drinking his milk-coffee and stops mid-sip.

'Whoa Ma, slow down. That's a whole lot of questions,' he says.

He doesn't even seem affected by my knowledge of what he's done. He is acting as though it is the most natural thing in the world.

'Aryan, I want answers. This … this hurts me, you know,' I say.

He seems surprised. Then he says, 'Sorry Mom, I thought

you would be mad if I told you I wanted to contact Dad. In the past, you have always brushed aside the topic whenever I tried to raise it with you. I could sense that you would always become upset even if I as much as asked you a question about him. I stopped asking because I couldn't bear to see you upset. But it has been gnawing me from the inside. We were doing a project on genealogy and ancestry, and I felt kind of empty. I couldn't possible ask Suchi aunty, as the next thing she would do is call you. So I thought I would write to Manav. I meant to tell you that I did, but then a whole lot of things happened, the dogs died and everything. So I never got around to it.'

Aryan has always addressed Manav by just his first name, and never as Manav uncle, as that was what Manav had taught him when he was a toddler. But I am surprised that Aryan even remembers Manav.

'But you last saw Manav when you were about four or maybe five. You haven't even seen him since. How did you remember him?' I ask.

'That night when we were out for dinner at Suchi aunty's place, I had gone upstairs to her study. I finished my PPT quickly and I didn't want to come downstairs and join you all, as I found that guy Nimish very boring. So I was going through Suchi aunty's books, looking for something to read, when I found old albums in her bookcase. There were some wedding photos of Suchi aunty and Prakash uncle. There was a picture of me as a toddler, and in most of the photos, I was being carried by Manav. Then I remembered how he used to come over often. My memories were vague, but the photos refreshed them. I also found his wedding invitation in that album. So I got to know his last name. I Googled him and found his profile on Linkedin, as well as on Facebook. The photos helped. He hasn't changed much at all Ma, he looks just the same. I dashed off a mail, and then next thing I know, we had got that phone call about the dogs from Jamu kaka. Then I never got a chance to tell you about it.'

'Why didn't you just Google your dad then?'

'He must have a phobia for social media. He doesn't seem to have a profile anywhere online. You have no idea how much I have looked. Also Mom, I don't know what he looks like. You haven't even shown me a single picture.'

'That is only because I do not have one myself, Aryan. I wish I did, but I don't. It just never occurred to me then to take photographs. We didn't have digital cameras or cameras on our phones at that time.'

'Hmm. I wish you did.' There is sadness in his voice.

I go around and hug him tight.

His explanation seems fair enough. It was done more on an impulse, without much thought, and when he explains it, it doesn't seem like a deliberate act of connivance and betrayal, which was how I had perceived it. Somehow that makes me feel better. I tell myself that it wasn't that he wanted to hide it from me. It was just that he delayed telling me.

'Oh Aryan, I didn't know finding your dad meant so much to you.'

'It does, Ma. I want to know what he is like now. And I know you can't answer that.'

That brings a lump to my throat. How did this child of mine have the maturity to understand something that I myself haven't been able to come to terms with? I still don't know what I feel about Ankush. I only care for Aryan, and while at nineteen I was in love with Ankush, I don't think I am anymore. He is just a bit of my past. Or at least that is what I tell myself, ignoring the dull pain that I feel even to this day when his name is mentioned.

I just nod, not trusting myself to speak.

'Don't worry, Mom. It's fine if he doesn't want to be in touch with me. But I wanted to at least try to know him and meet him at least once. I hope you understand.'

I didn't.

Why would he want to know a father who hasn't even bothered to get in touch for the past fifteen years? What if he rejects Aryan, just like he did me when he knew I was pregnant? I don't want Aryan to go through all that hurt and agony. Why isn't Aryan happy with what he has and all that I have done for him? Why does he want to contact Ankush?

And here I was, thinking that I had done a darn good job of answering his questions about his father and a splendid job raising him as a single mother. Now I feel somewhat inadequate, as though everything that I have done for Aryan this far was not enough. I have done my best to raise him well. I have been a great mother—or at least that's what I liked to believe. And now this child of mine is going in search of his absent father. I don't want him to.

'I would rather you don't contact your father. Ever.'

There, I have said it. I have expressed what I want but have never voiced.

'Why?' There is defiance in his tone as well as indignation.

'Because he has never contacted me all these years, never asked about you, and doesn't even know what you are up to. He has never been a father to you.'

'So maybe it is time to start making amends now. I want to give him a chance.'

'But I don't, Aryan. Our connection with him is over. I don't believe in second chances—there is nothing in common anymore.'

'Your connection, Ma … *yours*. You are free to break all

ties from him. But I am still his son. I share the same blood, the same genetic traits. I want to know what he is like. Is he like me? Does he like music as much as I do? Where does he live, what has his life been like, what does he look forward to most, how does his typical day go, what does he like to wear, to eat.... I want to know all of that, Ma. I want to ask him why he left us and if he has ever thought of me. And also, Ma, I don't have to believe what you do. I have my own beliefs and I think second chances do exist.'

I don't know what to say. Of course Aryan has a right to know his father. But somehow I didn't think this moment would come this soon. I had, in my mind had this notion, that perhaps when Aryan was twenty-six or twenty-seven, living on his own, he might try and contact his father. But I was obviously wrong.

'Aryan, have you ever considered the possibility that he may not reply to you? And that maybe, as far as he is concerned, we are a closed chapter.'

'Maybe Ma, or maybe not. But how will I ever know unless I try? And the break-up, it happened so many years ago. Isn't it silly to hold on to grudges for that long? I want to know what happened and why he left us.'

I am silent for a long time. Then I decide that I have to tell him the truth.

'He did not leave us Aryan. It was me. I broke up with him.'

It is hard for me to tell him this.

'What?! And all these years you let me believe that it was *he* who walked out. What the hell, Ma....' he gets up, goes to his room and slams his door shut.

I just sit in silence in the drawing room. I want to tell him that I never led him to believe that. He has just got that idea into his head himself. Till this moment I did not even realise that I became defensive when he raised the topic of his father. Now, after this talk with him, it seems to me that he is right. I felt so bad about Ankush, that I buried it deep down. I hated talking about him, and somehow this message has been sent out strongly to Aryan, even as a child. No wonder he never asked too many questions. It must have been eating him up inside. I feel terrible now.

Maybe I should have tried to contact Ankush earlier. Told him about Aryan.

But that would have seemed like I was begging him to come back, and using Aryan as a weapon. That was the last thing I wanted to do. Also, Ankush knows my e-mail id. He could have also easily mailed me.

After thinking about all of it for a while, I am overcome with an urge to speak to Manav. So I check the mail and then look at the time in Germany. They are four hours behind India and it would be twelve-thirty in the afternoon there. Which means Manav is probably at work.

I key in his number and wait with bated breath till he answers.

And when he does, he sounds exactly the same. Just as he did all those years ago.

'Vee, I knew you would call!' he says and he sounds so happy.

'Manav, you know me a bit too well,' I reply and I am smiling now.

'How have you been? Life treating you well?' he asks.

'I guess we all get our knocks. I've just got a big one now. I am down but not out.'

'That's my girl!'

I smile again. *His girl?*

He used to say that all those years ago, and he still does. I don't comment on it though.

'You know, you sounded formal in your mail,' I say.

'Oh! Is that so? Wait a second, let me read it again.'

There is something wonderful about old friends. They know everything about you, have been a part of your life for so long, that you can seamlessly pick up right where you left off. With Manav, it is as though the years have dropped off just like that. It is as though he never went to Germany, never got married, and it feels like old times, when he was in the same city.

I hold on and I hear a few clicks, and then he says, 'Yes! You're right. I didn't realise it, Vee. Maybe it was because I was thinking about Aryan, and how to tell you about this development.'

'I just had a talk with him, Manav. He wants to find Ankush. He seems determined.'

'I know. And I don't think it would be fair for you to stop him. Let him do what he thinks is right.'

'What if Ankush rejects him and does not respond?'

'He won't do that.'

'How do you know? How can you be so certain?'

'Because he asks me about him every time we speak. It isn't often, but he does ask about you too. I think he wants to get back in touch with you, Vee.'

'What?! I don't believe this. He has my e-mail id. Why hasn't he mailed all these years?'

'I don't know, Vee. I guess it is hard for him. He feels horrible about what happened all those years back. He had been quite persistent about asking you to get rid of the baby. What would he say now? "Hi—I want to meet the baby that I asked you to get rid of?" Come on, Vee. It isn't so simple and you know it.'

I know it. Of course, I know it. It is for the same reason that I have never mailed him. I felt there was a huge wall of ice between us. I existed this side in my little world, secure and content with Aryan, Paw-Factor and my gym. He was on that side, and as long as I didn't think about him, it was fine.

Now with Paw-Factor having crumbled, and Aryan wanting to reach out to Ankush, there is a gaping hole in the wall. And it is growing larger and larger. I am so afraid that it will somehow engulf me completely. I have no idea where it will take me but I am terrified nevertheless.

I think Manav understands, because before he hangs up, he says, 'I'm here for you, Vee. Don't worry. Nothing has changed.' He speaks very softly, but I hear it clearly.

At this moment, I could hug him.

Instead I say bye, hang up and wait for what is to come.

Chapter 19

Some things happen to you when you least expect it. I had waited and waited for a reply from Saurabh and had given up hopes of getting any. Now, out of the blue, I get a phone call.

I pick up the phone, wondering what he wants to say after so many days.

'Hello, Vipasha,' he says and his tone is as formal as ever.

'Hi, Saurabh. How are you?' I am slightly guarded.

'I was wondering if we could meet. For a cup of coffee perhaps?'

This is a pleasant surprise. What is he playing at? Blow hot, blow cold?

'That would be nice. When do you want to meet?'

'How about right now? May I come over and pick you up?'

'Now?'

'I mean at about ten-thirty? We could proceed to Cream and Coffee. Would that be convenient for you?'

I think it over for a moment. This seems a bit sudden. But then, it is not as though I have anything to do. It would definitely help me to not brood about Paw-Factor. So I agree and tell him that I will drive to the café myself as I can go to the gym after that.

'I shall await your arrival,' he says and I smile.

Even though I have interacted so much with him, I wonder if I will ever get used to his formal way of speech.

I quickly shower, and pick out a dark blue wraparound skirt and a pretty white blouse to wear. I style my hair with a hairspray. Then I apply a light, barely-there lipstick. Next I line my eyes and use mascara. It has been so long since I made the effort to look pretty and I feel ridiculously happy as I drive off to meet Saurabh. He is already there when I enter the café and I spot him straight away.

'Hi there,' I greet him as he stands up. I move towards him to hug him, but he quickly steps back and says stiffly, 'Hello Vipasha,' and he doesn't even smile.

I am a little surprised at this, but I dismiss it as something I might have imagined and I sit down as the waiter has pulled out the chair. The place is done up in cane and wicker furniture and has an earthy feel with a terracotta floor and indoor plants everywhere. The atmosphere is light and cheerful.

Saurabh does not speak for a long time. I wonder what it is. The waiter takes our orders, a cappuccino for me and mocha for him. He is very quiet and so I tell him about how much I miss Paw-Factor, and how it was a very large part of my life. I also tell him about how the animal activists told me that it would not be a great idea to file a police complaint and how angry that makes me feel. The waiter returns with our orders and I am happy to see a little heart in my coffee, made with the cream.

Saurabh is silent. I can sense a kind of reticence about him and so I ask him if everything is fine.

Then he says, 'I am afraid I cannot meet you anymore, Vipasha.'

'Oh,' I say, befuddled.

What does he mean by that? Is he dumping me? We aren't even in a relationship for him to dump me.

'I have realised that, over the last few meetings, you might have developed an emotional attachment to me. I have mulled over it and I have come to a conclusion. I am afraid I cannot fulfil your expectations. Under such circumstances it is best we do not see each other again.'

I have no idea what has hit me. What in the world is Saurabh saying? When have I ever demanded a relationship from him? And here he is talking as though we have been living together for ages, and now he wants out.

'Saurabh, I have no idea what you are talking about,' I say, and he is flustered. That is when I notice a thin film of sweat on his forehead. He fiddles with the napkin now.

'I am sorry, Vipasha. I might have completely misread the signs. This is hard for me.'

Actually he hasn't misread the signs. He has got it spot-on. I was definitely thinking that something was brewing and he has caught on very quickly. But most men would never take the trouble to meet and clarify things. I know that I should be a little more understanding as I am dealing with someone who probably struggles in a social situation. But I am smarting under the bruise of rejection. It is the first time someone I hoped to have a relationship with is turning me down.

All my life I have had men chasing me and falling over themselves to get a date with me. And now, when at last, I begin to genuinely like someone, I am being turned down by a him. I find it difficult to accept.

'I am sorry that it is hard for you. But I never even thought we had anything going on between us like that,' I lie.

'I am terribly sorry. Please forgive me—it is because of my

condition. I … I might have misread the signs,' he is unable to meet my eye and he fiddles with the spoon.

'No, that's okay. I understand,' I say and look away.

I now want to get out of there as fast as possible. I try to make small talk. Saurabh is extremely uncomfortable now and it looks like he too would like to leave.

We finish our coffee in silence.

And then we part ways.

When I get back home that evening I read up more about Asperger's syndrome. I read about how difficult it is for people in a relationship to handle partners who have Asperger's. I read about how emotionally unavailable the men who have Asperger's tend to be, and how it would take a huge amount of understanding to be able to deal with it. Perhaps this was what Saurabh had been trying to tell me. Given his condition, to must have taken a great deal of thought for him to have done this. And I had been so curt and abrupt with him, dismissing it so easily, pretending it never mattered to me.

There are some relationships that never take off. All the ingredients for a successful one exist—but various other factors interfere and sometimes it dies even before it has a chance to blossom. There is nothing you can do about it.

Saurabh is someone who came to me at a time of need. He fulfilled a certain obligation and his role ended there. And in any case, it is not as though he led me on into a relationship and then dumped me. I rationalise all this in my head and yet I feel rejected and helpless in my heart.

Perhaps he will message me later and want to see me again. Maybe we can be friends. But for now I have to let it lie. As bad as I feel about it, I have no other choice.

About a week later, I am having my evening tea on the veranda when Aryan shoots out like a bullet looking for me. I can see that he is fighting hard to hold back his emotions. It is a mixture of joy, sadness, anger and excitement. He has never been like this before. He paces up and down the length of the corridor, even accidently knocking a potted plant over, and I ask him to be careful and watch his step.

'Ma, are you mad at me?' he says and I know he isn't referring to the plant.

'No Aryan, how can I ever be mad at you? Well, not for long anyway and you know it.'

'I want to tell you something but I think you will flip it.'

'I won't.'

'Promise?'

'How can I promise something without knowing what you are going to say?'

'Then I can't tell you.'

'Okay. Fine.'

I am taking a gamble hoping to call his bluff but I know that he is bursting to tell me. Of course, I am right. I haven't raised him for fifteen years for nothing.

'Okay Mom—I will tell you, but please be calm and try not to yell at me, okay?'

I take a deep breath.

'Okay. What is it?'

'I heard from him.'

'Who, Aryan? Manav?'

'From Dad.'

'Oh,' I say, and then my throat goes dry.

Ankush has actually replied to Aryan.

'Are you upset, Mom?'

I am not even able to speak. I just shake my head.

'What did he say?' I ask, after a while.

'You know what, Mom, he has another name. That's why I couldn't find him online. He used to be a cool DJ, Mom. Then he founded his own company. And now he is a multi-millionaire. Have you heard of Moonbeam? He owns it, Mom! He owns it. Can you believe that? How cool is that?' He speaks fast, barely pausing for a breath, the words shooting out like racing cars.

He is also jumping up and down with excitement.

Ankush founded a company? Moonbeam? What kind of company is that? What is he into? I have never heard of it.

'What does Moonbeam do? And what did he say?'

'God, Ma! I cannot believe that you don't know Moonbeam. How can you not?! They are the guys who brought John Adam to India, and also Metal-Heads and Spinning-rex. Remember you wouldn't let me go to the concert because you were worried I was too young? All my friends went. And how cool is it to say that it was my dad's company who brought them to India.' Aryan is bouncing all over the place now.

'Aryan, calm down,' I say. 'Has he indicated in any way that he even wants to have anything to do with you? How can you just go around telling people that he is your father? Do you even know how he feels about it?'

'Ma, he is super-cool. He is delighted to have heard from me. He said he has been wanting to contact me for many years, but was afraid you wouldn't let him. And now that he has got my mail, he wants me to go and visit him in Australia! He is keen to meet me, Mom—and he says he will send us the tickets and everything.'

'Wait wait wait.... Slow down, Aryan. This is proceeding too fast for my liking. What does he mean, he wants to meet you and he will send tickets? How can he presume I will be okay with it? He hasn't even reached out to me—and he makes you an offer and you happily go along with it, is it?'

I am a bit upset with Aryan now, the way he is raving about Ankush with stars in his eyes. I wish he wouldn't. But he is too elated, too overjoyed and too darn happy to have heard from him. He is dancing with excitement—whether it is the excitement of hearing from his father, or whether it is the 'coolness quotient' that teens associate with DJs and anything to do with what they term 'cool music', I don't know.

'No, Ma. It isn't like that at all. It is not like I am rushing off to meet him. I just thought it was nice of him to offer.'

'Where was this niceness all these years?' I cannot help saying. This sudden turn of events, where Ankush seems to have dropped back into our lives like a nuclear bomb, is something I cannot easily adjust to.

And here is Aryan, eyes shining bright, excitement writ on his face, telling me all about Ankush.

'Ma, do you want to read his mail? Will you feel better then? It isn't what you think at all. I never expected to hear from him and I am just amazed that he has actually replied, and the icing on the cake is that he wants to meet too. He could have just ignored my mail, you know, and carried on with his life. There was no need for him to respond even.'

Exactly. That would have ensured fewer complications for me. But I don't say that to Aryan. I don't want to be a damp squib. But I do want to see the mail. I am curious to know what he has to say. I also want to know what Aryan wrote to him.

'Are you sure you won't mind me reading the mails?'

'Come on Ma, if I did, would I offer?'

'Okay, show them to me,' I say and Aryan goes and fetches my laptop from inside the house.

He logs into his account and opens the mails and says, 'Here Ma—read them for yourself. Then you will know what I mean.'

I cannot believe this is happening. All those years back when I had decided to have my baby, I had never even thought that there would come a day when he would be independent enough to contact his father on his own.

The mails are in chronological order, the latest ones on top. So I scroll down and I read Aryan's mail to Ankush first.

Dear Mr Bhargav,

This must be the strangest e-mail you have ever received. It is definitely the strangest one I have written. I am addressing you as Mr Bhargav as I am not sure how you will respond to this mail.

I don't know where to begin.

So let me start by introducing myself, as that is what you do when you meet someone for the first time. Of course, we haven't met yet, but I am hoping we will, after you read this mail.

My name is Aryan and I am fifteen. I got your e-mail id from a friend of yours—Manav. Manav is my mother's friend too. My mother is Vipasha Mishra, and I think by now you would have guessed where I am getting at with this e-mail.

My mother does not know that I am writing to you. I have always been curious about you, but have never got any information from anybody. I tried Googling your name, and it is the first time I have found a person with no presence on the Internet. Hence I thought it would be best to ask you directly.

Where do you live, what do you do?

I am based in Bangalore and I would like to meet you once, even though I know that my mom will be very upset if she knows. She is the one I am closest to, and I share a very strong relationship with her. So you know how big a deal this is to me.

In case you don't want to meet me, then you can ignore this mail and we can forget I ever wrote. I promise you will not hear from me again.

I am hoping though that you will reply.

I just want to see the man who is my dad. Just once.

Aryan

I read the mail and there are tears in my eyes now.

Aryan stands behind me and puts his arms around me.

'Mom—I am sorry if I upset you. I never meant to,' he says.

'It's okay my baby,' I say.

I haven't called him my baby since he was eight or nine.

I can't believe this is happening. I am holding my breath and my heartbeats have multiplied. My hands tremble ever so slightly as I scroll up and read Ankush's reply.

My dear son,

It took me about four days to recover from

your mail and hence the delay in response. To say that I have thought about nothing else for the last few days would be an understatement. Let me also tell you that I have thought of you several times over the last many years, but they were always fuzzy thoughts. It was like you existed somewhere in my past. But now with this mail of yours, everything has changed.

I saw the display photo that Google displays next to your name, in your mail, and I am stunned. My heart is filled with pride. I must say that you resemble me a lot when I was your age—or at least I think so.

Fifteen years is such a long time. I have done some pretty stupid things when I was younger, but I think the thing I regret most is not even trying to meet you. I could have if I wanted to, but didn't. In my defence, I was lost and I didn't know what I wanted out of life, like most people I guess, but that is no excuse for my actions. 'Most people' don't have a son that they never speak to for fifteen years.

Well, you asked me what I do and you also mentioned that it was the first time you came across someone with no presence online. That's probably because you have googled my real name, which is not the name I am known by. Please google DJ Anka and you will get all the details about me. I think the music I made was popular when you were about four or five. You may not even have heard my tracks. I moved on from there, and I founded Moonbeam. We are the company that brought musicians like John Adams and Metal-Heads to India. Now, those, you might have heard of!

I shuttle between Australia, where my company is based, and the US, London and India, where we also have offices. I come to India very often, as almost all the big gigs that happen there are organised by us. In Bangalore, we have a tie-up with a local radio station, as well as with an event management company, and hence I would most definitely come to Bangalore very soon.

I would like you to come and visit me in Australia though. It is a very beautiful place, and I have a lovely home, overlooking the ocean, and no one to share it with. That is a long story, which we can talk about when we meet in person.

Please forgive me for not being a part of your life all these years. It is something I deeply regret.

I lost my father two years ago and my mother about five years ago and I feel terrible that they both passed away without even meeting you. I have lost too much in life, including a chance to share your growing years, which I was too young to understand then.

I am overwhelmed that you have taken the first step forward and also deeply grateful that you seem to bear no grudges against me. I have to thank your mother for that.

I do want to make amends, and I hope you will give me a chance.

All my love
Your dad

I read Ankush's mail and I begin to sob. I cry for all the years that have gone by. I cry for not reaching out to him earlier. I cry because I have denied Aryan the chance to meet his paternal grandparents. I cry because I never knew that Ankush was capable of feeling this deeply. I cry because I have shut out a big huge world for Aryan, to which only I held the key. And yet neither Aryan nor Ankush seems to blame me at all.

'Mom—here,' says Aryan as he hands me some tissues and I blow my nose into one and wipe my tears.

'Aryan, I am so sorry if I came across as defensive when you asked about your dad. I was only trying to protect you, my son.'

'I know, Mom. I have never accused you.'

'You haven't, but I feel terrible.'

'Leave it, Ma. You can't change the past. Just google DJ Anka—read what it says. Woooo—I can't believe it, Mom,' he says.

So I google DJ Anka and I too am blown away by what I read:

Anka Vega is one of the wealthiest DJs in the world, and he's getting even richer. The former night club DJ, who also used to perform with the band River Storm, founded

Moonbeam in the year 2007 and still owns 8 percent of the company. The revenues topped $1 billion for the first time this year, placing his personal net worth at $1.6 billion, up $100 million from last year.

The increase in Vega's fortune can partially be traced to the rise in the popularity of Western music—more specifically, the success of the Eternity World Tour, a joint venture with the Metal-Heads estate. Since its October debut, the show has grossed over $2 million per night across eighty-five show dates, with hundreds more to come.

Vega isn't part of the music business in the traditional sense—he doesn't own a record label or a publishing company—but he's one of a handful of moguls on our recently-released billionaires list, benefiting from the increasing value of music. Overall music sales are steadily rising and the top fifty global tours grossed 4.7 percent more than last year.

The University of New South Wales awarded an honorary doctorate to Anka Vega in 2012. The year before, Anka took the Ernst & Young Entrepreneur of the Year award for both levels: Australian Capital Territory as well as Queensland.

In 2011, he also received the Entrepreneur of the Year Award from New South Wales Association for Industry and Commerce. The same year, he was recognised by *Time* magazine as one of the fifty people who have made an impact on the music industry worldwide. He has also been honoured by the Condé Nast group as part of the Never Follow Program, a tribute to creators and innovators.

'Whoa—that is something!' I exclaim.

'Isn't it?! Imagine him being my dad. Now you know why I am so excited.'

While I am happy that Ankush has responded positively, I am also filled with dread. How will anything that I do ever be enough for Aryan now?

Ankush is a multi-millionaire. He probably has multiple homes across the world. He is a mogul, and magnate and a big success story.

And here I am, a failed entrepreneur, and a part-time gym instructor, trying to raise a teen in a ramshackle old ancestral house that belongs to her dad and her aunt.

What in the world have I made of my life? What have I achieved so far? I don't have a house of my own. I drive a second-hand car. No college degree either.

Suddenly I feel old. Very old. And I feel a complete failure.

And no matter how much I try to convince myself that I still have Aryan, and that I have raised him well, that little voice in my head which constantly reminds me of my present reality refuses to shut up.

Chapter 20

A few days later, as I am serving Aryan his breakfast, he says, 'Ma, you know Dad and I have exchanged some more mails after that.'

'Hmm ... okay.' My response is cagey, cautious.

I have tried not to think of Ankush these last few days, but it is hard. Suchi had been right all along. I should have simply met more guys, dated some more men, and found a Mr Right. Ankush may not have affected me as much then. Right now I am in a place where I want to forget him, but am not able to. All this while, I had learnt to deal with it by just refusing to think about him at all. But now, with Aryan contacting him, the floodgates have opened. It is like I am being punished for having suppressed the memories all these years. As much as I do not want them to, they are streaming out. I remember every single detail like it was yesterday, and it is as though these sixteen years never happened. Aryan's voice cuts through the thoughts running through my head.

'He is awesome, Ma. He is coming to India in two weeks. Have you heard of Zedmau?'

'No.'

'He is like the coolest DJ ever—he is simply the best. He's

performing in Mumbai, Delhi and Bangalore, and Dad's company is organising it. Guess what Ma, I am getting VIP tickets. Dad and I will be in the VIP enclosure. Then after the concert, I get to go backstage and meet him. Dad has already spoken to Zedmau and he is cool with it. How awesome is that? My friends are going to be so jealous.'

How easily the word 'dad' rolls off Aryan's tongue. He seems so happy to keep saying 'Dad this' and 'Dad that'.

Ankush is actually coming to India. I can scarcely come to terms with it. I have Googled his images, and he looks slightly older, his hair is greying a bit and he has put on a little bit of weight. He used to be so lanky. But he isn't unattractive; in fact he still looks so darn handsome that I feel my stomach knotting up. I am not sure I even want to meet him. I won't know what to say. I have no idea how to handle this new development in my life either. So I decide to focus on what Aryan is saying. He is now talking about how it will be easy to get into the concert because of the VIP tickets.

'Hmm, and what makes you think you have got permission to go for this concert?' I say.

'Mom! You cannot say no this time. I am going with Dad.'

'You know what, Aryan, "Dad" hasn't raised you. I have—and I don't think he has any say in this matter,' I say, making inverted commas in the air. I know I am being childish, but his saying 'dad' each time he refers to Ankush annoys me big time.

But Aryan is so elated that it doesn't affect him at all.

'Oooh Ma, you are just jealous,' he says and he laughs as he kisses me on the cheek and runs off to catch his school bus.

Maybe I *am* jealous. I give up everything to have this baby, raise him for fifteen years and then, in walks 'Dad' who is able to give him things that I can't. And my son is so happy about it. How is that fair?

I call up Suchi and ask her whether she has any meetings in the morning. She says she doesn't. I have had both Mr Shah and Mr Das cancel their personal training sessions today, and hence I can go late to the gym. I am glad that Suchi is free as well.

'I am coming over then. I need to talk. Keep some lunch ready for me,' I say as I quickly pack my gym clothes, deciding that I will leave for the gym from Suchi's house.

Suchi's home is always a comfort zone for me. Her maid lets me in and tells me Suchi is in the kitchen. There is a lovely aroma wafting in the air and I know she is in one of her 'cooking moods'. It will be high-calorie, fat-laden stuff that she is making for sure, but I also know that it will be delicious.

I walk up behind her and shout 'BOOO!' and she screams and nearly drops the stuff that she is cutting.

I laugh at her shocked expression. Then she gets over the surprise and recovers her breath and she too laughs.

Then she says, 'God, Vee. You gave me such a fright. What an idiot you are.'

'I know, Suchi, I feel like a prize idiot right now,' I reply. She nods knowingly. That's the thing with Suchi. She gets me without my having to explain anything.

'Hmmm, come, let's sit down, have some tea and talk,' she says and calls out to the maid to serve us some tea. She leads me to her Zen terrace garden, upstairs, off her bedroom. This is the place we always head to when we want to talk. Or at least talk about something that has upset one of us.

Suchi has done up this place beautifully, with tall bamboos and all kinds of flowers like azaleas, daisies, lilies, chrysanthemums and roses. It also has a little lawn and a water body, and there are beautiful garden accessories like stone mushrooms and carved frogs scattered at strategic locations, adding to the serenity and beauty of this space. The garden was even featured in an interior design magazine once, as an example of what could be done on a large balcony or a small terrace.

We sit on the swing for a while in silence. Then the maid serves us our tea. It is cloudy and cold and the tea is comforting.

'We have come such a long way from our school days, isn't it Vee?' she says as she gazes towards the light blue sky, laden now with greyish white clouds. It is the kind of weather that makes you want to reminisce and talk about the years gone by.

'Yes, we indeed have,' I say and then I am quiet again.

'So are we going to talk or are you just going to sit in silence? What is bothering you?'

'Ankush.'

'Aaah—Ankush. I knew he was trouble right from the moment we spotted him at that ice cream parlour all those years ago. But why are you thinking of him after all this time? I thought that was a closed chapter?'

'I thought so too. But it turns out I am wrong. He is coming to India, and he wants to meet Aryan. More than that, Aryan wants to meet him. And every second sentence that Aryan utters these days starts with "when Dad comes". It is awful and I am burning with jealousy. I have never felt this jealous before.'

'What?! What are you saying? When did Ankush get in touch?'

'About a week back.'

'And you tell me only now!'

'He did not get in touch with me, Suchi. He wrote to Aryan.'

And then I tell her the whole story of how Aryan had found Manav's photos, how he wrote to Manav and how Manav got in touch with me, and then how Aryan wrote to Ankush. I fill her in on how successful Ankush is now and how miserable I feel.

'Good lord. What else have you been hiding from me? You didn't even tell me you spoke to Manav.'

'I'm telling you now.'

'After a whole week? And I thought I was your soul sister. The one you confided in.'

'You are. That's why I am here now. I needed time to come to terms with it myself. I don't want to meet Ankush. I am thinking that maybe I can drop Aryan here, and Ankush can pick him up from your place. That way I am not involved.'

'Hmmm.'

'What is "hmmm"? What do you feel?'

She is quiet for a while. Then she says, 'Look Vee, you may not like what I am going to say. But I am going to say it anyway. I think you are taking a terribly naïve head-in-the-sand approach to things. It isn't going to work. At nineteen, you made an adult decision—to have a baby and raise him. And now, at thirty-four, you want to run away from meeting the father of your child? It will be uncomfortable, yes. After all, it was you who cut him off. But you can't run, Vee. You have to face him. And if I am to be even more honest with you, I can see that you have never ever got over him. You still hold a torch for him and that's why you don't find any guy good enough. How many guys have you met over the last so many years? Ever wondered why you did not click with any of them?'

I don't say anything in reply. I just sip my tea. Now I wish that I hadn't asked her for her opinion, even though a part of me knows that she is perhaps right.

'See, I would never tell you something that I thought wasn't right for you. Nor would I sugar-coat anything just to make you feel good. I guess you know that.'

'I do, Suchi. But sometimes I wish you would lie,' I say and we both smile.

'He may not even affect you the same way that he did. You might be holding on to a chimera of him. Maybe he is fat and ugly now. Go meet him and then release him from your soul. You will feel better.'

'I am not holding on to any chimera. I Googled his images. He is still so darn attractive, Suchi.'

'Ooooh—so madam has checked out Ankush. Ankush and Vee, sitting on a tree…' she starts off in a sing-song voice, the rhyme that we used to recite to tease all those girls in school, who had crushes on guys.

The whole rhyme went this way:

(girl's name) and (boy's name) sitting in a tree

K.I.S.S.I.N.G.

First comes love, then comes marriage, then comes a baby in a baby carriage

Sucking his thumb

Wetting his pant

Doing the hula hula dance.

Suchi sings the whole song in the exact tune that we did in school and it is hilarious.

I laugh and then I reply, singing back to her, in the same tune, that in my case, it was the baby first and then the carriage and no matter who I met, there was no marriage.

'See, you have to chase the guy aggressively. Otherwise how will they know they are in love with you?' says Suchi helpfully.

'Last time I did that, I got pregnant,' I reply and we both giggle.

Later at the gym, I think that while the visit to Suchi's home hasn't solved anything, at least I feel lighter. I will have to meet Ankush, of course. It was a silly idea to think that I could avoid him altogether. Then I think that, yes, maybe Suchi does have a point about seeking out guys to meet. I usually never make the effort.

That is when I remember Nimish's call. So I text him, and tell him that I am at the gym every day from eleven-thirty to three-thirty most days and hence couldn't take his call.

He replies almost immediately. *No worries. Will call you after that*, he says.

Okay, I reply.

Shortly after that Sheetal arrives and I start her off on strength-training.

'I have never used these in my life,' she says, eyeing the dumbbells that I have lined up for her. I have chosen the lightest ones for the lateral curls, two kilos, and for the bicep curls, the two-and-a-half kilos so that she gets a hang of it.

'God—I have never used these,' she repeats.

'I'll show you how to do it,' I say, and I proceed to tell her that it will increase her lean muscle mass, boost her metabolism and help her burn more calories. I also tell her that, after a while, cardio alone is not enough and now that the initial weight loss has taken place, it is important to maintain it and also add weight- and resistance-training which I will be introducing later. I also explain to her how important form is while doing the exercises, and that she should not slouch. I start her off with just ten reps, and when I want her to do another set, she flops down on the bench and says she just *cannot*, and that she feels her arms burn.

This is the biggest challenge for most personal trainers—

knowing how much to push the client. Today I decide to let her be. I tell her that it's fine for a start, but we will slowly build the intensity, and she nods glumly.

I laugh and tell her that she will thank me later when she is showing off her arms in a sexy strapless dress, and that cheers her up somewhat.

Almost as soon as my gym session gets over, Nimish calls. It is as though he has been waiting to call me.

'Hey, Vipasha. How is the lovely lady doing today?' he asks.

Minus two. That was a bit too smooth an opening with someone you have met just once, and are speaking to on the phone for the first time. You need to be a little more formal.

'I'm good. How are you?' I reply politely.

'Now that I have spoken to you, I'm great,' he says.

Ugh. Minus four. And I can't believe that I had found this guy interesting at Suchi's home, the first time I met him. Why in the world had I thought that he seemed decent?

Then I hear Suchi's voice inside my head, telling me that I dismiss guys all too quickly. And so I decide to give him another chance. He doesn't mess it up this time.

'I would like to see you again, Vipasha. If you want to see me as well, that is. How about I take you out somewhere nice?' he asks.

That was perfect. Maybe I should give him a chance. Maybe he was just nervous and was trying to mask it by acting smooth.

'Sure, I would like that,' I reply.

He says he is travelling on work for four days but he would like to see me as soon as he is back.

So we fix the date, about a week from now. He says he will pick me up from home and we can decide where to go later.

And that is how I find myself going out for a date, the day that Ankush is supposed to land in India.

I discover that only much later though, when I tell Aryan about the dinner plan with Nimish.

'But Ma—that is the day that Dad lands in India,' he says.

On a little more probing I discover that Ankush's flight gets here in the morning.

'So that is fine then. I will be going out only in the night,' I tell Aryan.

But I can see that he is not happy about it.

'Dad said that maybe we could all go out for dinner,' he says.

'Aryan, I think your dad should have asked me first if I had other plans or not, before making a decision,' I reply firmly.

And I am more determined now to go out on that date with Nimish, just so that Ankush knows I am not sitting around waiting for his grand arrival.

Chapter 21

No matter how much you think about certain things, nothing prepares you for the shock of actually facing it, or going through it. My meeting with Ankush after nearly sixteen is one such event.

Aryan is at school, when Ankush rings my doorbell on Friday morning and greets me with an enormous bunch of white and red carnations.

I nearly die of shock.

I knew he was landing in India, but I thought he would first check into his hotel and then wait for Aryan to come back from school before messaging him, to set up a meeting. But he has, instead, landed up at my doorstep.

I have just finished breakfast, and have not even changed out of my night clothes. Heck, I'm not even wearing a bra. My hair is uncombed, there is not a trace of make-up and I am wearing the oversized t-shirt and shorts that I went to bed in last night.

'Hey, Vee, so good to see you after all these years,' he says as he hands me the bunch of flowers, and kisses me on the cheek.

I am mortified and of course embarrassed to be looking this dishevelled. He looks immaculate. He is wearing a dark blue shirt, pale cream trousers, brown suede shoes, a leather belt that matches the shoes, and a very expensive-looking watch. His cologne is woody, distinctly masculine, and he smells great. His hair is cut stylishly short and he looks every inch the successful businessman that he is.

He smiles at my confusion and amazement, and his eyes crinkle at the corners. He looks even better than he did all those years ago. I feel my heartbeat whipping up a drum roll and my stomach churning at his presence. He looks more handsome than the pictures I have seen of him.

'Good lord ... you ... you could have called,' I say, unable to think clearly.

'Yes, but then it wouldn't have been a surprise, would it? And maybe you would have refused to see me? This way you didn't stand a chance. May I come in?' he smiles.

God, he is still just as charming as he was.

'Please,' I say as I step aside and gesture to the drawing room. The carpets have been rolled up by the maid who is still cleaning, there are newspapers and magazines lying around, and on the breakfast counter are some of Aryan's schoolbooks, which he had asked me to put away as he rushed for school. There are coffee mugs that haven't yet been cleared and wilted flowers.

Damn. I wish I had tidied up a little bit.

'Excuse the mess, I wasn't expecting any visitors,' I say.

'Not at all, and hey, Vee, you look absolutely beautiful,' he says, looking into my eyes, and I can feel a tinge of colour creeping up my face.

I could kick myself. This is unbelievable. I see him after all these years and I blush at a compliment he gives me, instead of being all cool and unruffled. This wasn't how I had planned it at all. In my head, I had visualised him coming to my home when I was all dressed up, maybe in a lovely dress, and as he rang the doorbell, I would say bye to Aryan, and walk off with Nimish for my date, leaving him staring.

So much for fantasy.

Instead, here I am looking like a homeless hobo and at the moment, my cleaning maid is dressed better than I am.

'Give me five minutes,' I say as I rush to my bedroom and shut the door.

I quickly run a comb through my hair. Then I take a skirt from my cupboard. No—a skirt will seem like I am trying too hard. So I put it back. I can't decide what to wear. And he is waiting just outside. After much indecisiveness and deliberation I pick a pair of pale blue shorts that fit me well, and a lacy dark blue top. I quickly do my eyes with eyeliner and mascara and then dab on a hint of lipstick. I can't believe I am doing this. Dressing up at ten-thirty in the morning for someone I didn't even want to meet in the first place. I do it all in record time, to the accompaniment of my heart thudding wildly. When I am finished, I am happy with what I see. The make-up isn't over the top, and yet it makes a big difference. This is more like me. At least I can face him now, without worrying too much about how I look.

When I step outside, into my living room, Ankush is looking at the snaps of Aryan and me over his various birthdays, which are part of a collage that Suchi had made and gifted to him on his thirteenth birthday. I had got it framed, and hung it on the wall outside the kitchen. He turns around when he hears me, looks at me, whistles softly and says, 'Wow.'

I am a bit flustered. It has been so many years since I felt shy and it feels strange, yet familiar. This is exactly how I used to feel when I was with him all those years back.

'You know what, Vee, you haven't changed at all. You look

exactly the same. You haven't even put on an ounce of weight. It's simply unbelievable. It is as though you have stopped ageing.'

'Thank you, you look good yourself,' I say and ask if he will have coffee and he says he will. This feels so bizarre and yet so normal.

'So much has happened, Vee, and yet nothing has changed. How is it possible?' he says as he walks around and sits on the bar stool at the breakfast counter, watching me make the coffee.

'A lot has changed, Ankush. How can you say that nothing has changed?'

'You know what I mean.'

I do. But I don't want to admit it so easily.

'No, I don't know what you mean.'

'I think we both know it, Vee.'

I don't know what to say to that and so I ask him if he would like to go to the garden, and he follows me while I lead, our coffee mugs in hand.

Jamu kaka is around, and I introduce Ankush to him as a friend, and Jamu kaka greets him. But I think Jamu kaka immediately knows that this is not just a friend. Though he doesn't say anything, I can see that he is silently checking out Ankush, giving him an 'is-this-guy-good-enough-for-my-madam' kind of a look. I guess he senses something is up as it is not every day that I bring a man over, to show him the garden.

Jamu kaka proudly gives us a guided tour. He isn't fond of flowers though. He considers growing them a waste of time and resources.

'*Paudhon ka koyi prayojan hona chahiye,*' is one of his favourite sayings—that plants have to be of some use. Having been raised in a farm, he prefers growing stuff that we can use for our cooking. He takes us through the patches of red amaranths, spinach, capsicums, runner beans, tomatoes, cauliflowers and potatoes. He has also planted trees—the hybrid variety he clarifies—that have flowered and given fruit in just three years he says proudly. Showing people around the garden is clearly one of Jamu kaka's favourite activities.

Ankush nods and smiles with polite interest, all the while his eyes rarely leaving me.

Then we go back to the veranda and sit down facing each other.

'Shall we go out for lunch? We have a lot to catch up on,' he says.

Then I look at the time. God, it's nearly eleven o'clock.

'I have to be at the gym in half an hour. If I don't rush now, I will be late,' I say.

'Miss your workout for a day, Vee. I think a meeting after so much time warrants that.'

'I wish I could, but currently that is the only job I have. Didn't Aryan tell you that I work as an instructor at a gym?'

'Oh. He did not. In that case, you better rush,' he smiles. I don't know if he is mocking me or if he is serious. Even after all these years, I still can't tell.

'Sorry to leave so soon, Ankush, but I have to go.'

'Join us tonight then? I want to take Aryan out.'

'I have a date.'

'Oh!'

And as childish as this is, I feel a small amount of satisfaction at this tiny sting I have delivered and I make a mental punch in the air.

You ignored me for almost sixteen years and so I am going on a date. So there.

'What about immediately after the gym then?'

'That seems workable.'

'Okay, I'll wait.'

'Here?'

'Yes, why not? If you don't mind. I want to see all the photos that you have of Aryan over all these years. I have missed out on such a lot.'

'It was a choice you made, Ankush. You could have come back any time you wanted.'

'But you had shut the door on me, Vee.'

'You could have knocked.'

'I was busy getting knocks. And I was frightened about being in a relationship when I wasn't even ready. Besides, you would have never forgiven me back then.'

'I know. Maybe I was a bit too hard on you. I was young and foolish.'

'So was I. And a lot happened with me too. Life changed in ways I never expected. I have been through a difficult time these last four years.'

'I want to hear all about it.'

'And I do want to tell you. Everything. Why do you think I came by early to spend the day with you? I was hoping we could talk.'

'Don't you have any work to attend to? I would have thought a man with your success would be terribly busy, rushing from one meeting to the other.'

'I now have an efficient team that does everything for me. I just have to oversee things once in a while. I'm past that stage where I have to slog, which I did of course in my early years. It's all on auto-pilot now. I don't have to do the actual work. I get it done.'

'Aaah, the small perks of being the super-boss of a very large empire.'

'Of course. It has to have some advantages, right?'

'Right. So let me change and head off then. I'll be right back, okay?'

'Okay. Wherever you go, whatever you do, I will be right here waiting for you.'

And then he goes on to sing it, a very poor imitation of Richard Marx. I smile.

'Ha ha. Do you remember it?'

'Of course I do. How can I forget? We had played it on a loop that crazy afternoon when we made love.'

'Four times. You were incredible.'

'I still am.'

'How would I know?' I can't resist saying that, even though I mentally kick myself.

'You will have to take my word for it. Or see for yourself,' he winks.

I melt at his words and his voice, and before I change my mind and decide to give the gym a miss and stay with him, I tell him that I truly have to leave, which I do after changing and handing him a huge bunch of albums that have hundreds of photos of Aryan and me over the years.

And even before I reach the gym, I realise that I am madly in love with Ankush.

Perhaps I always was.

He was right.

Nothing had changed.

Some people never really leave. They remain in your heart.

But I don't know if he feels the same way I do, or if he is being what he was all those years back—the 'good friend' who probably never loved me at all but liked me enough to bed me several times. And has now come back as he is the father of my child, and he wants to see Aryan.

I don't know what is going on inside his mind, but that doesn't stop my heart from doing a merry jig and a smile from depositing itself permanently on my face at the fact that he is there, in my home, waiting for me to get back, going through all the pictures of my son and me, piecing together those parts of our lives that he has missed.

And for now, that is all that matters.

Sheetal's workout has been rescheduled for an hour later than usual. I finish with my other clients and I have fifteen minutes before Sheetal arrives so I do my cardio quickly, even though it is against gym rules. Today I want to finish at the gym as quickly as possible and get back home.

I am excited about Ankush being here and I now do not want to go out with Nimish at all. But then it would not be fair to Nimish if I cancelled. Also I don't want Ankush to think I am a pushover. He walks back into my life after so many years and I am waiting for him with a red carpet. No way. Also I have no idea what his life is like now. He may not even want a relationship with me, and might have come back only to see Aryan.

If that were so, he wouldn't have wanted to spend the day with you.

Maybe he wanted time with me only to tell me all that has happened. Then another fear creeps in. What if he wants joint custody of Aryan? That possibility hadn't occurred to me at all. Being the father, he would of course have rights over Aryan. I have no idea what the legal implications are. Can an absentee father just walk back into someone's life, and claim their progeny? Then I tell myself that I am over-analysing this thing, and I would soon know why he wanted to spend time with me.

Sheetal arrives even before I complete my cardio, and so I get off the treadmill without even a proper cool-down.

'You're early,' I tell her.

'Yes, my meeting got over earlier than I expected, and so thought I would head here. What are we doing today?'

'Weights. We will focus on your arms and biceps.'

'No!'

'Yes. You're getting the hang of it. Now warm-up first, and then we will start,' I tell her and point to the treadmill.

I make her do cardio for about ten minutes and then tell her to go and get the weights.

She gets them, and I start her off on bicep curls.

I am counting and it is on the eighth rep that there is a dull thud and a second later I scream in pain.

'OUCH! AAH ' I yell and everybody who is working out turns to look.

A dumbbell has landed on my foot. Initially I think it has slipped out from Sheetal's hands, but then I realise that she is still holding on to both dumbbells and looking at me in horror. A guy who was doing bench presses with dumbbells has now jumped up from the bench he was lying on and looks horrified.

Nothing much registers after that. The pain is so excruciating, I see stars.

'Oh god ... I am so sorry ... I have no idea how that slipped,' he says and is now next to me, trying to help me.

I am in agony. I clutch my right foot and, holding the guy's hand, hop over to the nearest bench and sit down, scrunching my eyes in pain. I have worn Vibrams today, and I wish I were wearing my Nikes instead. Vibrams offer no protection whatsoever and the pain now rips into my body, shoots up through my feet and reaches my chest. It is so bad that I find it hard to breathe.

I am not even able to put the foot down.

Mahesh walks over to me and examines my foot.

'I think it might be a fracture. We'll have to get you to a hospital. I'll take you. Do you think you can walk to the car?'

I try to put my foot down, but the lacerating pain is too much to bear. I'm convinced I've broken something.

Damn. And just on the day that Ankush is waiting for me at home. I ask Sheetal if she can get my bag, and she runs to bring it.

'It's okay. Accidents happen,' I say to the guy who is still apologising profusely.

I remember reading somewhere that sixty-eight percent of all gym injuries are because of dropped weights. At that time I had wondered how someone could be stupid enough to drop a free weight. Now I know. Maybe he hadn't wiped the sweat off his palms before picking up the dumbbells. Maybe he had pushed himself a bit too much while doing the reps and his arms gave way. There are a hundred maybes in retrospect.

But right now, more than how it happened, I can only think of the pain that is ripping me apart, making me want to yell.

I call my landline at home and tell Ankush what happened.

'Oh god, Vee. Are you okay?' he asks.

'I don't know. I think I've broken something. We're going to the hospital to check.'

He says he has a car at his disposal and that he will be right over. It's easy to give him directions since the gym is practically down the road from my place.

I tell Mahesh that my friend is coming over and about five

minutes later Ankush calls to say he is waiting downstairs. Sheetal and Mahesh help me down the stairs. Ankush is in a chauffeur-driven Mercedes and gets out to help me. He puts his arm around me and supports me as I get into the car. I am in my sweaty workout clothes since I didn't even have time to shower after my workout.

'Sorry, I am all sweaty,' I say.

'Don't be silly. You are sexier that way. It's a big turn-on,' he says and I smile despite the pain.

'Yuck, only you can think of sex at a time like this,' I say.

It is then that I realise how comfortable we are with each other. There is no awkwardness between us at all. We seem to be like old friends who can pick up from right where they left off, both of us very happy to be in each other's company.

I am not able to explain it logically at all. All the bitter fights we had, all the angry exchanges that took place—all of it seems to have evaporated. Time has made us both older and more accepting perhaps. They say that time is a great healer. May be it has healed our bruised hearts. We haven't even been in touch for sixteen years, and yet here we are now, the conversation between us flowing so smoothly, with a perfect understanding of each other, and above all that warmth which lights up inside me each time anything to do with him comes up.

At the hospital, they take several x-rays, and we wait to see the doctor.

Fortunately there is no fracture, but the doctor says that it is a very mild lisfranc injury. My foot has swollen up enormously now, and the doctor says that I should just follow the RICE treatment—which is basically Rest, Ice-pack, Compression with a bandage and Elevation. He says the swelling should come down after that, and in case it doesn't, then we will have to put it in a cast. He asks me to wait for about three to four days, and then come back if the swelling persists. He also prescribes a painkiller.

And then Ankush helps me back to the car.

In the car he looks at me and smiles and says that I will not be able to go on that date after all.

'And you're happy about it?'

'Of course. I feel bad about your foot though. But see? You were destined to spend time with me,' he says.

'Hmmm, I better cancel with Nimish,' I say. I call Nimish and tell him what has happened. He immediately wants to come over but I tell him that I have a friend with me, and he is helping me.

Aryan has reached home by now and he calls me on my mobile. I tell him that I will be home soon and do not tell him anything else.

When we reach home, Aryan is waiting for me, and the look on his face when he sees Ankush with his arm around my waist, and mine around his shoulder, as we make slow progress to the front door, is priceless.

Chapter 22

'Mom, Oh my god, What happened? Are you okay?' asks Aryan. He doesn't look at Ankush or even acknowledge his presence. I can only imagine what a huge shock it must be for him.

'Let me get inside. Someone dropped a dumbbell on my foot in the gym and by the way, this is Ankush,' I tell him. Aryan just nods.

Not the best way to get introduced to your father whom you haven't seen since birth, I guess. But this is the best I can do under the current circumstances, and so we slowly proceed inside, as I hobble in, supported by Ankush on one side and Aryan on the other.

Once I settle down on the sofa and my foot is propped up, Ankush and Aryan greet each other. They are both a little awkward with each other.

'So ... hello,' says Aryan very shyly and extends his hand.

'My son,' replies Ankush and then envelops him in a hug. After a few seconds, Aryan's arms go around Ankush, and they stand that way for at least about fifteen seconds. I am so overwhelmed that I look away, feeling almost like an intruder.

'I've missed you,' says Ankush, and I think Aryan is crying. I can't tell for sure as his back is turned to me, but I can sense it.

Aryan just nods.

'And I am so sorry … for everything,' Ankush says, his voice hoarse and low. This time I can see Aryan's shoulders shaking and I know he is crying.

There is a lump in my throat. There is joy and yet there is sadness, there is contentment yet a slight anger, there is also a little bit of jealousy because the child who was up to this moment exclusively mine, is not anymore. It is as though someone has taken a large cauldron, mixed all the emotions together and soaked me in it. Added to all this, I also feel an overwhelming sense of regret to have kept Ankush out of Aryan's life for so many years. He did not deserve that. He deserved to have his father every step of the way.

But then again—who knows—maybe there is a time for everything, like one of the teachers in my school used to say. She would tell us that no matter how much you tried to make something happen, you will not be able to until the time is right. She used to say that most problems get magnified because we over-think them, creating more problems in the process, and sometimes things take their own course. All we can do is to let it be.

After what seems like ages, they step away from each other and we sit in silence in my living room. There is a slight drizzle outside now, and I say, 'I wish I could offer to make the coffee, but I can't.' And with that the silence is broken.

Aryan immediately says he will fetch Jamu kaka and he goes off to the outhouse to call him.

As soon as he is out of earshot, Ankush turns to me. 'There, that didn't go too badly, did it?' he says.

'I don't know. He is upset, but I think in a good way,' I reply.

Now that Ankush is here, Aryan seems to be subdued and in awe of him, almost as if he cannot believe that this is happening. Without Ankush around, Aryan was jumping around in excitement, talking about the concert that he would attend with his dad in the VIP enclosure. And now, when he is here, he isn't even addressing him as 'Dad'.

Ankush asks Aryan about his school, and he tells him all about his teachers, his subjects, his upcoming school trip to Himachal Pradesh, which he is looking forward to.

'Oh yes, Sheetal mentioned it. How come you never told me?' I ask.

'Oh didn't I? I thought I did mention it, Mom. In fact, I remember forwarding you that mail a long time back, and I did tell you about it. Maybe you forgot. Anyway, we leave next week,' he says.

That is when I remember that he had indeed sent me a mail a couple of months ago. The trip was already paid for, at the beginning of the year, along with the fees, and that is probably the reason it slipped my mind. I hadn't realised that it was just round the corner.

Aryan then goes on to repeat most of the information that I know from Sheetal anyway—that it is a twenty day trip where, along with exchange students from Spain, they will help to build a school in a rural district, as part of a social service program. They will all be camping, and while it is likely to be a lot of hard work, Aryan seems proud of what he will be doing.

'It is wonderful that your school includes all these initiatives, I think it is important to give back to society,' Ankush says.

'Spoken like a true father,' the words just slip out and I see

Ankush's face go stony. I can immediately see that he thinks it was a sarcastic remark. So his retort is quick and acerbic.

'A father who was kept away from his son,' he says.

'Come on Ankush, that was not fair.'

'You know what, Vee, you always looked at things only from your point of view. Nobody else's. Did you even once pick up my calls? I remember I called about seventeen times, at the very least, before I left for New South Wales. And later, you didn't bother to keep in touch.'

'Ankush, it was a different time. I was helpless.'

'Oh, not that helpless, Vee. You managed to keep in touch with Manav and Suchi.'

'Because they understood me.'

'And I didn't? Come on, Vee. How can you even say that? You know how it was.'

We haven't even realised that we are squabbling in front of Aryan and that too barely within hours of meeting each other.

'Hey guys—cut it out. It was a long time back and there is no point rewinding and blaming each other. Mom, aren't you the one who says "it happens for a reason"? Maybe this too happened for a reason,' says Aryan.

'And how did my baby become so wise?' I reply.

'I always was, Mom, just that my wisdom was too advanced for lesser mortals like you, to comprehend or grasp,' he says and Ankush guffaws while I ask him to shut up in mock-anger.

And with that the little tension that was building up between Ankush and me dissolves. But deep down, I know this will come up once again. For now though, we have both let it go.

I tell them that since they had already planned on going out for dinner, they should continue without me. But Aryan wants to stick around, though I assure him that I will be fine.

'Let's make it special then. This is indeed a treasured day for me, as I have today met my son. We will order some food, and let's have some wine, too,' says Ankush.

When the food arrives, Jamu kaka collects it and helps Aryan set the table. Aryan has taken out the expensive cutlery—the one that we use for special occasions—and I think that it certainly is a special occasion. A reunion like this does not happen often.

Ankush tells us about his early days in Australia. About how liberating it was because nobody knew his family and the fact that he was a film producer's son did not mean anything. All this is new to Aryan. I have not given him any details at all about Ankush's family. Aryan asks him what his grandfather was like, and Ankush tells him in great detail, about his father, the movies he made, what he believed in and his philosophy.

'And back then, I was ashamed of the kind of movies he made. I hated them. I did not want to be associated with my dad's production house in any way. But later on, I understood it better. For him, it was the only work he knew. It was what put bread and butter on the table. He had the formula for a movie to do reasonably well and he didn't want to risk doing anything he wasn't sure would work. The movie business is a very risky industry and he wanted to make sure our family was well provided for.'

Aryan nods, listening intently. I wonder how much of this he has absorbed. But I can see that he is fascinated.

The wine flows and so does the conversation. It is as though father and son are making up for all the years that they have missed. Aryan has so many questions and Ankush isn't tired of answering them at all. On the contrary, he seems most happy to.

Once we are done with dinner, we shift to the drawing

room and Aryan serves us all some ice cream, of which there is always a stock in the fridge. He pours generous amounts of chocolate sauce over his vanilla ice cream and is delighted to discover that Ankush too loves his ice cream that way. I wonder if taste and liking for a particular thing are inherited, along with other characteristics like looks, intelligence, hair colour and build. Up to now, I had never much thought of Aryan's habits or traits. But now, the resemblance between Ankush and him is so striking that it is hard to ignore. Aryan seems to be delighted in discovering even the smallest thing he has in common with Ankush. He simply can't have enough of his dad.

By eleven-thirty, I tell them that Aryan has school the next day, and unless he goes to bed early, he won't be able to wake up on time.

'Chill Ma, stop worrying, I'll be fine,' Aryan says.

Ankush says that I have a point, and that he will leave. He tells Aryan that he will see him after school, the next day.

He asks me to take my painkillers, and then he leaves for his hotel.

It is only after he has left that it occurs to me that he only mentioned wanting to see Aryan—that he never said anything about seeing me tomorrow.

Aryan turns to me and hugs me.

'Ma, he is just awesome. Thanks for being nice to him. You don't hate him, do you?'

'No Aryan. How can I ever hate him? It is because of him that I have you.'

He asks me to wake him up earlier than usual the next day as he has some school work to finish. Then he kisses me good night and goes to bed.

I am unable to sleep. Ankush's visit has disturbed me big

time and thrown everything out of gear. My foot is beginning to hurt again, and so I take a painkiller, and then I call up Suchi. Talking to her always helps me make sense out of things.

She answers on the first ring itself.

'Hey, I was waiting for your call. How did it go? Has he changed? How was it?' the questions tumble out even before I have had a chance to speak.

'I don't know, Suchi. It is such a mixed feeling. And by the way, I am immobile. I hurt my foot,' I say and then go on to explain all that has happened ever since Ankush arrived.

'God, Vee. That is unfortunate. You know what they say, about bad luck striking thrice. Just be extremely careful.'

'It's a silly superstition, Suchi. How can you still believe in such things?' I am now angry with her. I had expected her to be a shoulder to cry on, a sounding board to discuss and mull things with, but she is being a doomsday prophet, warning me to be careful about bad luck.

'You too used to believe it in school. Don't you remember how much we used to pray for each other when one of us had the slightest misfortune? How can you forget? I will anyway say a prayer for you,' she says.

'School was a long time ago. People change, Suchi. Life goes on. And everything cannot be resolved by prayers,' I reply, still a little irked.

Then I tell her that I am tired and I hang up, little realising how much I would actually need those prayers.

Chapter 23

I don't hear from Ankush at all, the next day or even the day after that. I had hoped that he would want to spend both days with me. Now that he hasn't called or texted, I feel that perhaps I was expecting too much. He was here for Aryan after all, and it was naïve of me to think that he would have any kind of feelings or affection towards me.

Now with my foot injury, there is nothing at all for me to do, other than read or watch television, and I find myself thinking about Ankush constantly. The more I think about him, the more I miss him. I replay in my head every single thing that he said since he arrived, the way he spoke, the way his eyes crinkled when he smiled, and the way he was so emotional when he hugged Aryan. I badly want to know what he is up to and yet I don't want to text him. It is the same old tussle between the ego and the heart and it is the ego that wins. So I resist.

Then it occurs to me that he might have got in touch with Aryan, and so I ask him if he has heard from Ankush.

'Yes, Ma, I did get a mail. He had to leave for Mumbai for five or six days because something came up unexpectedly. The Australian company which represents Zedmau had some issue with the on-ground arrangement for the concert, and they need Dad there to sort it out,' replies Aryan.

'Oh, I see.'

'Why Mom, are you missing him?' Aryan smiles.

'Of course not,' I say a bit too quickly.

'Then why did you ask? And why didn't you ask him directly?'

'I asked as I thought he would have come and met you the next day. I don't want to ask him directly as he has come to see you Aryan, not me,' I reply.

'But he likes you Mom, I can tell.'

'Rubbish. It's just your overactive imagination.'

'No Mom, I am his son remember? I know him. I think he has come to meet you too and maybe build bridges?'

'It isn't so simple to bridge the gaps, Aryan. We aren't the same people we were all those years ago.'

'Things are only as complicated as you want them to be. Most of the time it is we ourselves who twist knots in our path. Then we spend an entire lifetime trying to untie them.'

I smile. 'And what have you been smoking? What's with all the wisdom?' I ask.

'Lines from a play, Mom. And I wrote the dialogues. Splendid, isn't it?'

It was. I had to grant him that.

Then a little thought creeps up—that he is Ankush's son after all. The creative genes had to show up somewhere.

I don't know if it is because I am immobile and have a lot of time on my hands or whether it is because of the huge changes my life has seen in the last few weeks, but I miss Ankush tremendously. It's an even more intense feeling than when I was pregnant with Aryan. I have never felt this strongly about someone. Now it is as though I cannot stop thinking of him.

Suchi and Prakash come over in the evening with a huge container of soup, which according to Suchi is the best remedy for everything.

Prakash gives me a half hug, as I am seated.

'Oh my—look at what you have done to yourself. You should be more careful,' says Prakash. He has been on a strict diet and has lost at least five kilos. I can tell just by looking at him.

I compliment him on it.

'All the credit goes to Suchi. She has been whipping up some healthy stuff,' he says.

By now Suchi has walked into my kitchen, rummaged around for soup bowls and poured me a cup. She hands it over to me and asks me to drink up.

'I don't know about soup. I need a large mug of whiskey right now,' I say.

'To celebrate Ankush coming back or to drown your sorrow about it?' she teases.

'Just to stop myself from thinking about him. It's crazy—this is like an obsessive compulsive disorder,' I tell her.

'You had never got over him, madam. And now that he is back, it is time to face the music. The music that you have been running away from for the last fifteen years.'

'Thanks a lot. That was just what I needed to hear. Move away before I pour this soup on your head,' I say, and she and Prakash, both chuckle.

My spirits lift slightly as they make conversation and we chat about everything under the sun.

Much later, after they have left, I think that what she said was right. Maybe I was running away from Ankush, and now that he has caught up with me, there is nowhere to go.

My thoughts keep going back to Ankush. What did he mean when he said that he has been through a lot too? Is he in a relationship? He couldn't possibly have been celibate all these years. Sixteen years is a long time for him to have not got involved with anyone. I badly want to know. I contemplate on whether I should call up Manav and get the details from him but then dismiss it almost immediately. This is between Ankush and me. I will have to wait for him to tell me.

The days drag on languorously. I have never in my life been this still. Even when I was pregnant with Aryan I had led an active lifestyle. But now, this immobility has rendered me strangely restless and very aware of a lot of things that I had taken for granted earlier.

For instance, it is impossible now to wear pants on my own, as it needs the balance of both feet. So I take to wearing wraparound skirts. Earlier I wouldn't think twice about taking a shower as and when I pleased. But now I am dependent on Jamu kaka to set up a bucket, a mug and a stool, and fill the bucket with lukewarm water, keep the soap within arms' reach, and to keep a towel handy. I hate to sit down and take a bath with a mug and a bucket, but if I do not do that it's impossible to manage.

My father catches the next flight to Bangalore as soon as he hears of the mishap. It is terrific to see him and it is not just because I am completely bored having read at least four novels, and seen around six movies, only two of which I enjoyed. After a while, there are only so many movies that one can watch or so many books that one can read. My father looks much older than he did the last time I saw him. He seems to have lost weight as well, and the suit which once looked perfectly fitted, hangs loose on him.

'Dad, is your diet and everything okay? You look a little down,' I tell him.

'It's age catching up. I am no longer young, you know,' he says.

'Nonsense. If that were so, then you should be looking at retirement options,' I tell him.

'I will. When the time comes,' he says and that surprises me. He has never talked about retirement earlier.

Once he has settled and had a cup of tea, I tell him about Ankush coming back into our lives. Dad is stunned to hear it.

He is silent for a moment and then says, 'Blood is thicker than water. And nothing can stop the connection between a child and its parent. No matter what you say or do, there exist ties that can never be erased, ever be broken.'

I ask him something then—something that I have held back for so many years. In retrospect, I shouldn't have asked. But the words, laced with a tinge of bitterness, slip out before I can stop them. 'What about Mom then? Why didn't I feel anything even when she died? Why did I never ever feel a connection with her? Why was it a strange sense of relief mingled with sorrow, as though an unpleasant part of my life was over with her death?' I ask.

He is quiet for a very long time. When he speaks he says that now that I have asked, he thinks it is time to tell me something that happened many years ago.

I don't want to hear it. Instinctively I know that this is not something pleasant. But he has started telling it to me now.

'You know what Vee, there is something I have never told

you before. There were six babies before you. Not one of them survived. It was heartbreaking for your mother and me to go through it over and over again. Each time we would be hopeful that our wish of having a child would be fulfilled. But each time, there would be a miscarriage. No matter how much the doctors tried, they were unable to prevent it. One child, a baby boy, was born, but only survived till he was twenty-three days old. Then he succumbed to jaundice. His cremation is the most painful thing your mother and I have ever gone through. We were broken after that. I dealt with it in the only way that I knew—I buried myself in work. Your mother would weep and weep. She stopped talking to people, stopped socialising, stopped going out. It was as though something in her had died. Then you came along. Your mother was afraid. She was afraid that if she loved you too much, you too would be taken away like all the others. She was so broken that she was afraid to even hope. It was irrational, but then what had happened to us was completely without logic too.

We did not celebrate your first birthday. It was as though we were waiting and watching. Then slowly, by your third birthday, your mother started meeting people again. By then she and I had already grown apart. It was a gap that was too large to bridge. I knew she was seeing someone. But I did not have the heart to confront her or stop her. If that little thing gave her happiness, I felt it was best to let it be. Anyway I was never around for her. I had found my release in my work and she too needed something in life to go on. She was shattered, Vee—and afraid to get too close to you. I am sorry, my child. I think we were sometimes too harsh with you. But it was only the fear of losing you that kept us away from you. Please forgive me and her too if you can. She loved you, you know.'

His voice breaks as he speaks and I am quiet for a long

time. Then I realise that there are tears streaming down my face.

'Thanks for telling me, Dad,' I say and he nods and looks away.

I wish he had told me this when she was alive. I would have perhaps understood her a bit more then and not been so bitter and disappointed with her all the time.

Of all the regrets in the world, the worst is one which you can do nothing about because the person is dead. But this revelation, in a strange way, makes me feel even closer to my father.

Chapter 24

After my dad leaves, I keep thinking about what he said. I dig up memories of my mother and replay them in my head. Now I have something else to think about, other than Ankush. I tell Jamu kaka to fetch the old photo albums from the cupboard and I pore over them eagerly, looking for pictures of my mother and me. There are very few.

There are tons of pictures of boarding school though—there is a picture of me giving a speech, winning an award for long jump, carrying the trophy when my house had come first as I was house captain. There are loads of pictures of Suchi and me along with her mother, in her home in Kerala. Looking at the photographs I realise that by being so afraid to lose me, my mother had actually done just that. Perhaps she had loved me from afar. But I had longed to be held, comforted.

'I wish you had just hugged me once, Mom, and told me that I mattered,' I say to myself in my head as I keep looking at more photos.

No matter how much I rationalise it and try to ignore it, the feeling of emptiness refuses to go away. I still feel as though something was robbed from me, even though I had got a good education and a friend for life, in Suchi. Then she had brought with her Prakash. I think about how parents want only the best for their children, and yet they act in ways that harm the child, without even realising they are doing so.

I reflect on my parenting now and wonder if I have done anything inadvertently to hurt Aryan. If I take everything into account, I don't see anything that I could have done differently. Perhaps I pampered him a bit too much, but then I have to grant that he is a well-behaved, well-adjusted child, with a lot of friends. Whatever else I might have got wrong in life, I am doing something right here.

Aryan has to leave for his trip soon. They will be camping at Barot valley and they are taking a flight to Delhi, then the Shatabdi to Chandigarh, from where they will all be travelling by bus. The students have all been involved in making the travel arrangements, as the school wants them to have that experience as well. Aryan is quite proud of it and he now regales me with details about the trip every day.

It is on the day that he is to leave that Ankush returns. My foot is much better by now and I am able to stand and walk slowly without hobbling too much, for a short period, but I am not yet fit enough to drive him to school, from where the whole group will leave. Aryan happily tells me that it is not a problem as his dad will drive him there.

When Ankush comes to pick him up, he does not come inside the house. He just waves to me from the car. I have managed to walk up to the door. Aryan has packed every single thing needed for the trip on his own. I am quite proud of how he has managed to do it all by himself. Until last year, it was I who used to pack his stuff according to the checklist given by the school. But this time he said that he would do it. I realise how, in little ways, Aryan is becoming independent and needing me less and less. Even though I am happy that he is growing, one part of me is a bit worried about what I will do once he leaves for college.

But there is time yet for that and now Aryan hugs me tightly, telling me to take care, and that he will be back very soon. He also reminds me that his mobile phone will be switched off during the day, as they are allowed to use it only between eight-thirty and nine-thirty in the night. He says that he will message me every day and I can call him then. I tell him that I will and then wish him a happy journey and tell him to have a great trip.

And with that I wave him off, as he loads the boot with his backpack and sleeping bag and gets into the car with Ankush.

He messages me the next evening and I promptly call him.

'Maaa, this place is heaven!' he exclaims and I can picture him saying it with his eyes shining and the wind blowing in his hair. I can hear the sound of the wind over the phone.

His excitement is infectious and I feel happy that he is having a great time. He says the campsite is very picturesque—they are in a lovely field in Barot valley. He describes the awe he feels when he looks at the Himalayas. He is also excited to be near thick cedar and oak forests, and a sparkling river in which he can see trout and other fish in the clear water.

'You just inhale and it is pure oxygen, Ma. I wish I could package some for you, and get this air to Bangalore. It is that good,' he says and I can almost picture the place in my head.

'Lucky you. Just take care and stay with the group,' I tell him.

'Yes, Ma. We're going paragliding tomorrow. But that's in the latter half of the day. The first half they have planned an excursion. And don't worry, Mom, they are all qualified instructors and they are big on safety,' he tells me, as though reading my mind.

That is the last time I speak to him.

The next day I am in for a rude shock, when my dad calls me up from Mumbai.

'Vipasha, have you spoken to Aryan? Is he okay?' he asks.

'Yes, Dad. I spoke to him last night.'

'No, I mean after the news.'

'What news?'

'Switch on the TV, Vipasha. A group of students from Bangalore have been washed away in the Beas river, near Mandi.'

'Oh. Hell. I will get back to you, Dad,' I say and I frantically scramble for the television remote control.

Then I see the breaking news and I am frozen to the spot.

Immediately I try Aryan's number and it is switched off. My heart sinks. I try to tell myself to stay calm, that Aryan's group is probably at this very moment paragliding, blissfully unaware of all this. But then I wonder how many groups from Bangalore would be visiting Himachal at that exact time. It is a horrible realisation and now it feels like there is a hollow where my heart was. I can't handle the tension.

I call Ankush. There is no time for egos anymore.

He is as stunned as me when he hears what I have to say, and then he says he will be right over.

He reaches my place in fifteen minutes and I am still watching the news, in a complete state of shock.

One does not know what true helplessness is, till you have a child and then you don't know if that child is alive or not. Not knowing what has happened to that one person who means the most to you in the world is the most devastating experience anyone can face. I haven't moved from the spot since I heard the news.

Ankush is as frantic as me. Gone is the easy, flirting, all-is-well-with-the-world manner. Gone is the nothing-can-faze-me attitude. I can see that he is just as tense, frustrated and sick with worry, as me.

It is an eye-opener for me, to know that he cares *this much*. So I tell him that.

'How can I not, he is my son too,' he says, but the words have a heavier weight now. I would have dismissed them had he said it when he had just met Aryan, perhaps the anger pent up over the years clouding my judgement.

But now there is no ego, no judgement, nothing. I just want to know that Aryan is safe.

And in a strange way, it is a relief to have someone who is just as worried as me.

The television just keeps showing the same footage over and over, and they have nothing more to add, other than the loud music, melodrama and the news that rescue operations have been launched.

We try every single number the school gave us of the teachers in charge, but all of them are switched off. I am not able to reach the school either. I call Sheetal and she is as clueless as me and even more panic-stricken. So I hang up and we promise each other that the moment either of us gets any news, we will let the other know.

I switch on my laptop to see if any news site has anything to say other than what the television is blaring.

'Refresh it and see if there are any updates,' Ankush says, as he sits down next to me. I go to another news site and read the same thing that I have already just read.

At least twenty-four students from a school in Bangalore are feared drowned in the river Beas near Thalot village in Himachal

> Pradesh's Mandi district after large quantities of water was released from Larji reservoir on Monday. The students were on a tour to Himachal Pradesh and taking pictures on the banks of the river, when hundreds of cusecs of water discharged from Larji Hydro Power Project's reservoir at around 10 a.m. on Monday morning.
>
> According to police, the students, eighteen boys and six girls, were heading towards Mandi from Barot on a bus when they decided to get down and walk to the riverbank to take pictures with the Beas in the background. Just when they reached the banks, a sudden, huge gush of water washed them away. Sources said Larji power project management had not issued any notice before releasing water from the reservoir.

A massive rescue mission has been launched with professional rafters and divers called in to look for survivors. Police and people from nearby villages joined in the search for the students but it was impossible to locate them in the dark. Sources said the massive current must have carried them to another reservoir twenty kilometres downstream at Pandoh. More rescue teams have been sent from Mandi.

I wish now I had been a little more patient with Aryan. I wish I had not got mad at him for the tiny things. I vow that if he is safe, I will let him go to as many concerts as he likes. I make promises to God that if he comes back to me safe, I will never again worry about his grades or yell at him. All the things I get angry with him about seem so trivial at this moment.

Every single memory of Aryan runs through my mind—the early days at Ammu aunty's house; his first steps; how delighted he was when he first pet a dog in Manav's flat; the time he grazed both his knees when he was learning to ride a bicycle without trainer wheels; his delight at seeing the ocean for the first time when we went to Goa with Suchi and Prakash; his happiness at clearing the entrance exam for his school; his pride when he was chosen as class representative; his first victory in an inter-school debate; his getting caught by the school for sneakily tasting alcohol brought by a friend, his getting a rustication, my tantrum, my tears—all of it flashes before my eyes, and I keep replaying it like a film reel on loop.

Stop it, Vee, I tell myself. *It is not like he is dead yet.*

But I can't stop.

I get calls from Suchi and Manav. They too have heard the news and are frantic with worry. I tell them that I will keep them posted. Manav tells me he will be arriving in India the next day, and his phone will be switched off for a while, the duration of the flight. He says he will call me the moment he lands. I tell him that Ankush is with me and he is glad about that.

Then I walk slowly over to the kitchen, and ask Ankush if he will have some tea. He nods, eyes moving from the television to my laptop, which he keeps refreshing from time to time.

As I switch on the electric kettle to make the tea, I fear the worst. That I may never see my son again. The sinking realisation, the anxiety and the tiny hope fluttering against a huge cage of reality, which is so many children are feared dead in the mishap, grips my throat like the noose around a prisoner's neck which the executioner is waiting to pull. I die a thousand times. I don't want to live till I know that Aryan is safe.

And yet I have to go on.

'Ankush, this is terrible, I can't take it anymore,' I say and I break down.

He is beside me in a jiffy and I hug him and weep. He hugs me back.

Both of us know that there is nothing the world we can say to each other without it sounding like empty words of reassurance. The reality of the moment is too harsh, too horrible, and to face it is a terrifying prospect.

'No more waiting, Vee, let's go there,' says Ankush as he releases me.

'Go over where and do what, Ankush?' I ask.

'To Mandi, and then we will get a clearer picture. There is no point waiting here anymore. There is nothing we can do from here, anyway.'

He is right of course. And at least it would be better than waiting around for news.

I call Suchi and tell her that I am leaving for the airport with Ankush. Then I call my dad. He has been worried, and has called me at least fifteen times now. I tell him that I will call him the moment I land.

Ankush quickly checks the flights. We'll have to go to Delhi first, from where the nearest airport to Mandi is Kullu. It is already noon now, and by the time we land in Delhi it would be around eight o'clock. There is only one flight from there to Kullu, an Air India flight, at six o'clock the next morning. Ankush books it. The other option to reach Mandi is to take a bus from Delhi, which would take about twelve hours.

'It makes sense to stay in Delhi and then take the flight

early in the morning,' he says and I nod.

I hurriedly throw some clothes into a suitcase. Ankush says his stuff is already packed in the service apartment, and we just have to make a quick stopover there, which we do.

We are very quiet throughout our journey to the airport. There isn't anything to say. And I am not able to focus on anything else. My mind keeps going round and round, thinking about Aryan. There isn't anything I can do, but I am unable to stop.

I keep refreshing the newsfeed on my smart phone, till Ankush puts a hand over it. Silently. Then he kisses my forehead and squeezes my hand. That does it. Tears roll down my face, and Ankush wipes them with his hand without a word. Then he does not let go of my hand. I lean my head against his shoulder and that is how we complete the rest of the journey to the airport.

There is a new bond between us now. The bond that only a child can create. His presence is comforting. His concern and anxiety seems to echo mine. In him, I see a part of my son. And a part of me.

Nothing he did before all of this matters. What matters is this moment here right now. He is finally the father of my son. Truly, in every sense of the word. And even though I am dying with worry, for this small moment, I am grateful too.

Chapter 25

In Delhi, we check into the Leela Palace, which is just a short drive from the airport.

'This way we save commute time, plus it is a good place to stay,' says Ankush.

'The place is the last thing on my mind. I only hope Aryan is safe,' I say.

He holds my hand in reply and squeezes it.

The bell boy takes our luggage upstairs. The 'room' turns out to be a presidential ultra-luxury suite with a drawing room, dining area and a lavish double bed. Under different circumstances I would have perhaps admired it. Now I am just too tense to care.

'Would you like to dine in the restaurant or order room service, sir?' asks the bellboy.

Ankush tips him a generous five hundred rupees and tells him that we will let him know.

'Anything, sir, I am at your service,' he says and vanishes.

'So what will you have, Vee?' asks Ankush and I know he is trying to maintain a façade of normalcy.

'I don't want anything,' I reply and I reach out for the remote of the television.

The news channel now flashes visuals of personnel from the National Disaster Response Force who have launched massive rescue operations, along with the locals. They have also managed to get footage of the water gushing in the Beas River. My hands go cold when I see it. It is like a tsunami. There is a massive, gigantic outpour of water that has filled up and swept everything in its way, in minutes. There is also the sound of people screaming. It has been twelve hours now since the tragedy struck and so far the authorities have not discovered any bodies.

Ankush watches with me, standing rooted to the spot.

Then he grabs the remote and switches off the television.

'Let's just not watch it, Vee. There is nothing we can do. Let's pray, and we will go there tomorrow,' he says.

I nod. Then I sink to the floor on my knees and clasp my hands, resting them on the bed and I pray. I pray that Aryan is safe, somehow. I pray that he is unharmed and unhurt. I pray that he was not with the group that was washed away. I also pray for those students who are missing, and beg God that they are safe. When I open my eyes, I see Ankush next to me and he helps me up, on to the bed.

Then he sits down beside me and holds me. We stay like that, in silence, for a very long time.

Then he kisses me on my forehead. I hold him very tight and bury my head in his chest.

He starts stroking my hair, and pulls me closer. I kiss him now on his mouth and he kisses me back with tenderness, care and a million emotions that cannot be named. The intensity of the emotions that flow takes us both by surprise. Once we start, we are just not able to stop, and we make love. It is slow, soft, comforting. It is as though we are clinging on to life, in the face of death. It is as though, by this act, we are assuring ourselves that we are there for each other, no matter what happens. It is a powerful thing, and in that moment we feel so connected to each other, the sweat of our bodies mingling as we cling to each other, and I start crying again.

He wipes my tears and kisses me. 'He will be just fine. You wait and see,' he says.

I don't say anything. He holds me tighter, and through the gap in the curtains, I can see the blackness of the night and a million stars twinkling.

'Vee, I don't want to lose Aryan and you. I have lost a lot in my life. Will you marry me?' he says.

I am shocked. I wonder if I heard right. Then I look into his eyes, and there is so much love, hope and tenderness reflected in them that I know I did hear right. That is exactly what he has asked.

'Marriage? Why bring this up now, Ankush?'

'Because sometimes you wait and then it is too late. You just have to do what you feel like doing, at that moment. If there is anything life has taught me, it is this. That you have to express your love, not hold back, and if you want to be with someone, you have to take that step forward and not be afraid. That is just what I have done.'

I wonder why he is saying all of this. Is it because we are in a state of turmoil, not knowing about Aryan's safety? He answers me as though he can read my mind.

'I had a daughter, Vee. And a beautiful wife. I lost Annie and Janya, together. One moment they were in this world and the next moment they were gone. It was my Islander that was carrying them, when it crashed. The pilot too died. I was waiting for them in Fiji—we were supposed to have a vacation together. The saddest part is that Annie and I had been having massive fights over my not spending enough time with them.

My business had been growing at a crazy pace and I know I was guilty of neglect. Annie used to always say that what use was money if I had no time. I would assure her that it was just for a little while more, till my business stabilised. The "little while more" never came, Vee. The next I saw were their mangled bodies.

It took me about three years to even come to terms with it. The first few months were the hardest. I went into therapy to cope. I kept wishing that I had said the million things to her that I'd always wanted to. You know, she very badly wanted to go on a Europe tour and see the Tower of London and all of those places. I kept promising her that I would take her. Mostly it is those memories—the things that you did not do that kill you later, when it is too late. And since then, if there is something that I feel like doing, I do it almost immediately. You have no idea how overjoyed I was, when Aryan reached out to me. I wasn't sure how you had raised him—whether he had hatred for me in his heart or not. And one of the reasons I refrained from reaching out was because I wouldn't have been able to deal with his rejection, Vee. It would have left me a broken man.'

I hug him tightly in response and he hugs me back.

'How come none of this is online?' I ask him.

'Because I kept my personal life extremely private. Only people close to me knew I was married. And Annie never visited India, neither did Janya. Janya was two. I used to tell them we would celebrate her third birthday in Mumbai with my parents, but they never got to see either of them.'

I hugged him again. 'Nothing is in our hands Ankush. Life takes the strangest turns,' I say and he nods.

We go to sleep that night lying in each other's arms and never in my life have I felt this connected to anyone. The bond that I had with Ankush when I was a teenager was so different from what we share now. I had no idea what love meant, then. Now I think I do. The saying that I read many years ago—Love does not consist of gazing at each other, but looking outwards in the same direction—comes to mind, and I understand it perfectly as I curl up and go to sleep with Ankush's arm over me.

We have a very early start the next day. I switch on the television as soon as I wake up, and I am horrified to discover that three bodies have been recovered and they await identification. Ankush wakes up hearing the television and my cry.

'Stop it, Vee. We are going there anyway. Get ready quickly now,' he says and we hurry to the airport. Once we land in Kullu, a car is waiting to take us to Mandi. We are quiet for most part of the journey and we hold hands throughout. It feels as though this heaviness in my heart is now a part of me. I am sick with worry, helplessness, and also I am exhausted praying.

We reach Mandi, and when we stop on the riverbanks and enquire, we are told that the bodies have been discovered at a place called Pandoh. So we instruct our driver to take us there.

When we reach Pandoh, it is virtually a media circus. There are many television cameras focusing on the crowd, and reporters screaming and trying to get 'exclusives' to their viewers. It reminds me of a time not so long ago when I faced them myself. And now here they are again under completely different circumstances. I feel like yelling at them, asking them if they have ever been in this kind of a situation where they do not know the fate of their child, but better sense prevails.

Nothing prepares me for what I see when we make our way through the crowd towards the three bodies wrapped in white cloth. The faces are bloated, misshapen, grotesque. It is at this point that I walk over to the side and throw up.

A few belongings from the pockets have been discovered and I am relieved to find that none of them belong to Aryan.

The rescue operations are still on, and there is confusion and crowds everywhere. I tell Ankush that instead of seeing this on television, we are now bang in the middle of it. How in the world will we find Aryan in this confusion and mass of humanity?

We return to the car, and that is when I see three missed calls from unfamiliar numbers.

'Ankush,' I say and I clutch him, handing over the phone.

'Call back, what are you waiting for?' he urges.

When I call I discover that the guy at the other end speaks only Hindi. So I give the phone to Ankush.

He listens intently and nods. Then he says, 'Address *bolo*,' and gestures to me for a pen, which I promptly pull out from my handbag along with the flight ticket, and he scribbles an address behind it.

When he hangs up, he is unable to speak. He sits in the car with his legs outside, holding his head in his hands and I realise he is crying.

I wish then that I could die. Everything around me seems to be fading.

I walk around the car and get in from the other side and sit down, numb with shock.

That is when Ankush turns towards me and holds my face in his hands and he is barely able to speak.

'Didn't I tell you, Vee, that he is going to be fine? He is okay,' he says, barely able to articulate the words.

'What? WHAT?' I yell.

'He is in the Sanjeevani zonal Hospital in Mandi. He was rescued by the villagers. He is okay and is now asleep but he gave them your number and they have been trying to call us since morning, but it was switched off as we were on the flight.'

I hold Ankush's hand and we hug each other and weep with relief. He is crying openly now, and then he composes himself, gives the address to the driver and tells him to rush us there.

I will never forget that sight of Aryan sleeping peacefully in the general ward, in that tiny hospital in Mandi with an IV drip in his arm. The place is filled with people but I have eyes only for my Aryan. He has a bandage on his head and around one of his arms and the doctor tells us that he swam to safety and managed to cling on to a branch of a tree, despite the current. He is one of the very few children who have managed to escape and he tells us how fortunate we are.

I send a thousand prayers of thanks to the Almighty and then I call my dad as well as Suchi. Almost immediately I get a call from Manav and I tell him that Aryan has been found and is okay.

'You have no idea how much I have been praying, Vee,' he says and I nod.

I can completely understand.

'Thank you Manav, it helped,' I say.

Aryan has to be in the hospital for a day. The doctors say that the injury on his head is not very deep and it doesn't need any stitches. The gash on his arm too seems to be healing. We shift him immediately to a private room and never leave his side.

He is discharged the next evening, and that night we travel to Mandi and check into a hotel. Aryan and I stay in one room, while Ankush takes the adjoining one.

The next morning, we travel to Kullu, take a flight back to Delhi from where we take another connecting one to Bangalore.

Aryan is in a state of shock and barely speaks except to talk about his friends. About how sudden it all was, and how he had no idea from where the water rose and hit all of them.

'One moment we were taking pictures, Ma, and the next moment, we were swept away,' he says. I hold him and hug him as he talks. A few more bodies have been discovered and there are eight deaths in all, five boys and three girls. Aryan feels miserable about it.

'I wish I could have saved them, Ma,' he says.

I keep talking to Aryan, and I know that he will eventually be okay, even though he may take some time to mentally recover from such a massive tragedy.

I feel very sad for the parents who lost their children, but there is also an overwhelming sense of relief and gratitude that Aryan is safe and sound. I can't thank God enough.

That very evening my dad flies in from Mumbai, and he hugs Aryan as soon as he sees him. Suchi and Prakash too have come over. Manav calls a little later to say that he is in Bangalore, and I tell him that everyone is at home. He asks if he would be intruding if he came over. I tell him to please join us and I invite Eva as well.

Ankush greets everyone and makes them feel at ease. When Manav comes over, they greet each other warmly. He introduces us all to Eva and I take an instant liking to her. She is blonde, short, dressed in a salwar kameez, and sports a long red bindi. In contrast, Suchi is wearing a very pretty dress and

I am in my usual shorts and a t-shirt, too beaten by the turn of events to bother dressing up.

It is as though coming so close to a huge tragedy has made us all realise the fragility of human lives and the pettiness of holding on to grudges and slights, real or imagined.

It is when I am pouring a drink for my dad that Manav walks over to me. The others are busy conversing and having too great a time to pay any attention to us.

'See Vee, how things change and turn around? Who would have imagined that we would all meet this way once again and who would have thought that Ankush would come back. You know I was heartbroken after you turned me down. I thought I would never recover from that. But then I met Eva and she makes my world complete in a way that I never thought possible.'

'So you were right after all, Manav. It always happens for a reason. Had we got married, I don't think we would have ever been happy, because while I love you such a lot, marriage was something I couldn't even imagine at that point.'

'Aaah, the typical "I-love-you-but-am-not-in-love-with-you" phrase that women throw to reject a guy gently.'

'Come on, I never told you that line. Ever.'

'You didn't, but Eva did, at one point,' he smiles.

'Really? Then what happened?' I ask, my curiosity piqued.

'She fell head over heels in love with me and decided she couldn't live without me.'

'It has to be like that, Manav. You marry someone because you cannot imagine life without them. You are willing to compromise on anything, just to have their children. You want to grow old together, carve a life together and raise children together. The world outside ceases to matter then.'

Manav smiles and slowly turns towards Ankush. Which is

when I realise that what I have just said is an acknowledgement of where Ankush stands in my life.

But there is time for that later.

Right now, there is a huge party in my home and I feel blessed to be surrounded by such loving friends and family who care deeply. I am grateful for life's blessings and as the evening slips into night, we play music, converse, laugh and reminisce about old times.

We are in celebration of being alive.

What Came Later

Vee and Ankush got married in a private ceremony in Hamilton Island in a luxurious beach resort on a beautiful, white sandy private beach. They flew in their close friends, who were all accommodated in the sea-facing rooms. Aryan was in charge of the music and did a fabulous job of being the DJ for the evening, playing all the tracks that his parents loved, including those they had played when they were teens. All the guests agreed that it was the best wedding they had ever attended.

Vee, encouraged by Ankush, enrolled for a two-year associate degree program in veterinary technology at the University of Queensland. Aryan and Vee both studied together for their exams with the mother-son team competing hard with each other, watched fondly by Ankush. Aryan got straight A's in his A-levels in the Cambridge International exams, and Vee got straight A's in all her papers too. Vee plans to study further and qualify as a doctor of veterinary medicine, while Aryan wants to apply to UCLA for his Bachelor degree program.

Suchi has now become open to adoption. They have applied to adoption agencies and await their turn for eligibility. Prakash is elated at this change in Suchi. Suchi says that it was only when they came so close to losing Aryan, that she realised what it means to love selflessly, and so what if the baby did not come out of her womb, it was raising the child that mattered. Meanwhile Suchi and Prakash continue to grow their business and have managed to expand their firm which now has its presence in five Indian cities. When it comes to garden landscaping, they are a name to reckon with.

Saurabh is still single and does not intend on getting married. He thinks the best relationship he can ever have is with his work. His hospital won a 'best practices award' and he is proud of it. Vee invited him for her wedding. He called to express his 'extreme joy at the developments in her life', but did not attend the wedding.

Nimish has started dating someone he met at one of his marathons, and things look promising between them.

Ammu aunty continues to live in her beautiful home in Kerala, surrounded by rubber trees, and when she flew to Australia to attend Vee's wedding ceremony, she was as excited as a child at Christmas on seeing a completely different world from the one she had come from.

Vee's father has now stopped talking of retirement. He has started funding start-ups and has founded an organisation that educates village children.

The family home in HSR Layout was renovated and is now being let out for home-stays and also long-stays. Jamu kaka has been promoted as the manager and chief operator in charge of the property. He has a staff of four young people to assist him and he does a marvellous job of running it.

Mrs Mehra was never heard of and neither was Damodar. Vee doesn't want their paths to ever cross again. Vee believes that some people come into your life to teach you a lesson and she says that she sure has learnt hers. Had those events not happened, she would probably never have studied to become a veterinary doctor.

After all, like Manav had once said, it happens for a reason.

A Note from the Author

Any dog lover will vouch for the fact that the world is sharply divided into two kinds of people—those who love dogs, and those who don't understand the former.

Many people in India are terrified of dogs and will not go anywhere near one. In many homes in India, a fear of dogs is instilled right from childhood, probably because there are stray dogs that run wild and sometimes attack people. To a Westerner this concept is alien, as most people in the West associate dogs with love and warmth.

Dogs like the Doberman, German shepherd and Rottweiler have been used as military and police dogs for many years now and have cracked hundreds of narcotic cases. They are also used as 'search and rescue' dogs to locate suspects or missing people or objects. Dogs also assist law enforcement agencies in detecting illicit substances, drugs and explosives. Many dogs are also used as guide dogs for the blind. Dogs are also used in therapy for treating disability, illness, disease and trauma.

Anyone who does not like dogs has to watch the movie *Hachiko's Story,* which is based on the real life dog, Hachiko, who has a statue erected in his honour in Japan. Hachiko was an Akita dog that belonged to a professor at the University of Tokyo. Every day he would meet his master at Shibuya Station, until one day in 1925 when the professor didn't return. Unbeknownst to Hachiko, his master had suffered a fatal brain haemorrhage and would never come home again. But there Hachiko sat, day after day, waiting in vain for the return of his beloved master. Every single day, for the next ten years, till he died, Hachiko would come to the station, wait and go back disappointed. Hachiko was the embodiment of selfless love, extreme loyalty and a reminder of the lengths that one can go to stay devoted to a friend.

Another amazing movie that captures the fact of staying together through difficult times and never giving up is *Marley and Me,* which is based on the book by the same name, written by journalist John Grogan. It is a chronicle of actual adventures with his dog.

I have grown up around dogs, and my own dog now has enriched my life in so many ways. As have countless dogs, all over the world, enriched the lives of those who have had them.

Some years ago I came across a news item about several dogs that were poisoned at a shelter. I felt helpless and couldn't comprehend why someone would want to hurt innocent animals. When I come across incidents of people who abandon their pet dogs and many who ill-treat them, it pains me deeply. I can't imagine the cruelty that some humans are capable of.

My book highlights all of the above, even though the book is not primarily about dogs.

Dogs do make the world a better place. Whatever you give a dog, you get back exponentially, multiplied to the power of infinity. Dogs have that much love to give.

If only the same could be said of humans.

Preeti Shenoy
September 2014

Acknowledgements

Writing this section of the book is always a joy. This is the equivalent of a speech that an actor makes at the Oscars after winning an award. I know many readers who read the acknowledgments pages first.

A big thanks to all of you, my readers, who write me beautiful emails, leave me notes and messages, bring me gifts, shower so much love on me and most importantly love to read what I write.

A big thank you:

To my dad K.V.J. Kamath, who used to love dogs, and who managed to instil the same in me.

To my mom Priya Kamath, with whom I discussed the story first.

To my partner Satish Shenoy, who believes that I am a super woman, for standing by me during the hard times and never giving up.

To my children Atul and Purvi, who constantly try to bring out the new-and-improved version of me.

To Anukul Shenoy, for the emails and basketball matches.

To Mayank Mittal, who I can call up anytime and who makes me laugh.

To Rathi Priya, who thinks I am super-smart, super-successful and a terrific friend. I think the same of her.

To Shabina, my soul sister, for telling me that I have a home in Norwich—hers.

To Suresh Sanyasi, for the prompt and honest feedback.

To Shinie Antony, for being a big morale booster.

To Niall Young, for being a fabulous friend.

To Durjoy Datta, for all the compliments and making me feel great.

To all my women friends: Priya Selva (with whom I can always pick up where I left off), Dipa Padmakumar, Vinoo John (for the boarding school memories), Jayashree Chinne, Suma Rao, Radhika Ramjee, Ramya Ramjee, Haritha Venkatrangan and Nishu Mathur.

To my lovely friends in Norwich: Grace Watson who is so encouraging and loves to read my books; Steven Burkett, also known as Slightly Offensive Steve, who sent me a lovely gift of appreciation; Larissa for all the efforts made to stay in touch; Mary Syder, for the lovely memories of having my children over so many times; and Sam, whose lovely paintings of the greyhounds hang above my desk.

To my friends from the writing world: Nikita Singh, Kiran Manral, Sachin Garg, Madhuri Banerjee, Meghna Pant, Vani Mahesh and Milan Vohra.

To J.K. Bose and Arup Bose for being such great publishers and for recognising my potential.

To the really fabulous team at HarperCollins India.

An extra large dose of thanks to Deepthi Talwar who is easily the smartest and sharpest editor I have ever worked with. Your inputs and incisiveness made the book even better.

Thanks to Pranav Shah for an awesome website and for all help technical.

A big thank you to Nilotpal Baruah, who clicked brilliant photos of me.

And finally my beloved Lostris, who teaches me the meaning of love.

Someone had once snidely remarked that I mention my dog in the acknowledgments page of every book of mine. Here's the thing—she totally deserves it!

About the Author

Preeti Shenoy, among the highest-selling authors in India, is on the *Forbes* longlist of the most influential celebrities in India. Her books include *When Love Came Calling, Wake Up Life, Is Calling, Life Is What You Make It, The Rule Breakers, A Hundred Little Flames, It's All in the Planets, Why We Love the Way We Do, The Secret Wish List, The One You Cannot Have* and many others. Her work has been translated into many Indian languages. Preeti is also a motivational speaker, and has given talks at many premier educational institutions and corporate organizations like KPMG, ISRO, Infosys and Accenture, among others. An avid fitness enthusiast, she is also an artist specializing in portraiture and illustrated journalling.